Captured

Book One in the Chronicles of Bren Trilogy

By Dennis Jernigan

Published by
Innovo Publishing, LLC
www.innovopublishing.com
1-888-546-2111

Providing Full-Service Publishing Services for
Christian Authors, Artists & Organizations: Hardbacks, Paperbacks,
eBooks, Audiobooks, Music & Film

**THE CHRONICLES OF BREN: CAPTURED
BOOK ONE**

Library of Congress Control Number: 2016936800
ISBN: 978-1-61314-310-0

Cover Design & Interior Layout: Innovo Publishing, LLC

Printed in the United States of America
U.S. Printing History
First Edition: May 2016

DEDICATION

This book is dedicated to my children and their children for generations to come . . . and to all those who have ever felt lost or betrayed or in need of rescue . . . and to those who see life as an adventure rather than a burden—regardless of their circumstances.

ACKNOWLEDGMENTS

To all those who have journeyed to and through Bren with me already . . . and to the generations to come who will make that journey.

Enjoy the quest!

Robert and Peggy Jernigan—my parents—for raising me in the country with lots of land and animals and realms to explore. You helped inspire so much more than I can ever express to you.

To my grandmother Jernigan who passed away when I was thirteen. I have never forgotten you. Thanks for inspiring the end of Book Two— *Sacrifice*.

D. Barkley Briggs for believing and inspiring and for allowing me to go into other realms with you. You are a big part of this story . . . and iron sharpens iron.

My wife, Melinda, who believes in me and celebrates the quests of life I feel called to. The story of Bren is OUR story . . . especially this installment!

My children (and grandchildren to come) for bringing so much joy and wonderful adventure to my life. You, also, are part of the adventure.

My favorite fantasy/allegory writers, C. S. Lewis, Jack London, Marguerite Henry, Hannah Hurnard, Gene Edwards, Wm. Paul Young, Michael Crichton, and J. R. R. Tolkien for paving the way . . . for the gift of creative artistry and healing imagination through the written word.

Joanna Dunlap, my friend and fellow writer, for believing in the power of fantasy.

Danny Dunlap, my friend and fellow dad, for just being there.

Captain James Tiberius Kirk, for being my dad in my dreams as a boy and for transporting me to worlds where no man has gone before!

The High King for commissioning the quest I now pursue . . .

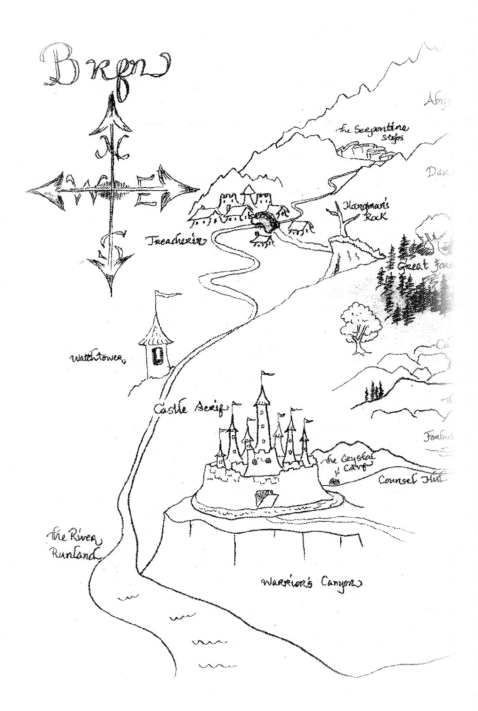

Chapter One

LEE PICKS A FIGHT

L ee picked himself up from the ground, as the boys who had just delivered his latest humiliation—yet another pummeling—walked away mocking him. At least this time he would come away reasonably unscathed. Last time he had walked home with a black eye and a bloodied nose. The embarrassment and shame he had had to endure for almost two weeks of school had taught him to be quick to block the punches to his face. This time he would have the weekend to at least ice the swollen lip he now wore and bring it back to its normal size and shape before school began again on Monday.

Leon Jennings was about to turn thirteen, but for all he had already endured in life he felt much older. Born into a farming family and expected to work the farm, Lee (as his folks called him) found the work easy enough. Every morning at 6:00 a.m. his dad would call up the stairs, "Lee! It's time to get up! The cows won't milk themselves!" Dragging himself from his slumber, he'd somehow manage to dress himself in the dark so as to not wake his three little brothers who shared the attic bedroom with him. Traipsing out into the predawn morning, he would go out into the pasture and find the two old Guernsey cows and herd them to the barn. Once there, he would put some feed in the stall and guide the first cow in. Once he had gotten all the milk he needed, he turned her out to the holding pen where the cow's calf was kept so the baby could have her turn. Then he would drive in the next cow and go through the process once again.

Lee's dad was a good man. Hardworking and silent most of the time (and stern in his discipline), he kept Lee busy. "Idle hands are the devil's workshop," he always said. Lee loved his father and, being a sensitive boy, often hoped he would hear his dad say something to him besides just giving him his next chore list. He really looked up to his dad.

But Lee and his dad couldn't have been more different than night and day.

The boy was quite adept at drawing and spent hours (when he could squeeze time in on weekends between chores and schoolwork) drawing images conjured by his dreams. When he wasn't drawing you could find him playing the old upright piano that had belonged to his grandmother Jennings. Lee's mom had recognized his musical abilities quite early on. It was she who had traded some of her handmade quilts to purchase back the old piano from the elderly neighbor lady who had bought it years before. On his twelfth birthday, she had surprised him with that old piano and he had spent hours losing himself in its vast array of magical tones, improvising and making up tunes that went hand in hand with the adventures he had envisioned for himself from the time he could remember. Although at first glance Lee seemed to be different than the other country boys he was raised with, at heart he was every bit as passionate and every bit as strong as they were . . . just in a different way, a way they could not seem to see.

When Lee had gone to school, he lapped up every art lesson and ached when he had to go on to spelling or math. By the time he was in fifth grade, the other boys began to take a somewhat less than well-intentioned interest in Lee's artwork. The day the other boys discovered he played the piano was one of the worst days of the boy's life. (Incidentally, it also didn't help matters that he was skinny as a rail and had big ears). Innocently, Lee had assumed others would appreciate his talent and be as encouraging as his folks had been. But he was wrong.

One day during the morning recess break, Mr. Tillman, the music instructor, had heard that Lee could play the piano. Asking him to please meet him in the auditorium, the teacher asked the boy to play something for him. As Lee began to play one of the tunes he had made up, one of his classmates was at the door listening. Having heard Mr. Tillman ask Lee to meet him in the auditorium, the boy had assumed Lee was in some kind of trouble and wanted to check it out for himself, hoping to find yet another reason to tease Lee. This discovery would prove to be a goldmine for the boys.

After being dismissed by Mr. Tillman, there were still five minutes left before recess ended and, of course, Lee ran right out the door, where he was met by the group of boys who seemed to have made it their life's calling to make Lee's life at school miserable.

"Hey, Lee!" said Ryan the ringleader, mockingly. "Play us a tune!"

"Yeah!" chimed in the others. "Play us a tune!"

Trying to ignore them always seemed to make things worse, yet he would attempt to walk away this time. Ryan stepped in front of him and gave him a slight shove. "You make a great girl, Lee! Maybe we should call you 'Lee-uh'!"

That was all the other boys needed to hear. Marching around the frightened boy, the bullies began to taunt him saying, "Lee-uh! Lee-uh! We wouldn't wanna be ya! Lee-uh! Lee-uh! You're a girl, it's plain to see-uh!"

Now beginning to tear up, Lee determined he would not cry. Maybe his cousin Dewey, who was in the same grade, would come to his rescue. Looking around the crowd of children that had now gathered around him, Lee was stunned and horrified. His own cousin! His own cousin? There, now joining the other boys in the taunting rhythm was his closest friend, his cousin Dewey! Making matters worse, one of the girls who had come to check out the commotion stepped up to his defense.

"Leave him alone, Ryan!" shouted Debby Jones at the top of her lungs.

Of course, this made the boys even more intent on utter humiliation of the helpless boy. From that day on, Lee suffered the merciless taunting of Ryan and his cronies. He learned to keep to himself as much as possible. He had also determined that he would never give the other boys a reason to mock him again, forsaking his drawings and his piano. This self-imposed moratorium lasted a mere day. The talents and interests that had brought him so much grief were now the only places of refuge the boy seemed to have anymore. He could not wait to get home from school. Once the chores were done, he went to the piano. It was there he could get lost for hours in his reverie—and no one could touch him. Once his dad sent him to bed each night, Lee's adventures would continue. Hiding with a flashlight under the covers with him, he would draw great adventures and outdoor scenes, getting lost in those dreamed-of places as well.

As much solace as the drawings and piano brought to the boy, he still found himself on the edge of despair every time he came home after an encounter with the bullies. In reality, the only place he ever really found peace from it all was when he finally fell to sleep. It was there that he dreamed of great excursions into the unknown. In his dreams he would do great battle with fantastic creatures. Wielding sword and all manner of crafty man-to-man combat moves, he faced witches, giants, cyclopes, and demons. Regardless of the riff-raff he faced in those dreams, there was always one recurring theme. In his dreams he was always captured at some point. And in his dreams, someone always came to rescue him. It seemed that right at the last second when the demonic hordes would put an end to him, Lee's dad would swoop in and save the day.

Lee's dad was his hero, but his dad was not at school where most of the bullying took place. And when Lee had tried to explain to his dad what was going on, his dad had told him, "Defend yourself, Son! Pop 'em in the nose once and they'll leave you alone!" Lee had never quite gotten up the nerve to do that though. It had seemed easier to receive the torture than to fight his way out. Lee's respect for his dad was such that he only wanted to please him. On the rare occasion when his dad would express displeasure in some task the boy performed in a less than obedient manner, Lee would be crushed for days. Whenever his dad would ask him how the bullies were treating him at school, Lee would simply lie and tell him, "They don't really bother me much anymore." At least he wouldn't have to face his father's disappointment due to his cowardly responses to the bullies.

Lee looked forward to the summer with great anticipation. Number one on his list of reasons for enjoying the summer was the reprieve from having to look around every corner as he did at school to make sure Ryan and his gang were not around to make his life miserable. Reason number two—the main reason that actually nullified all other reasons— were his weekly rides to the old shale pit. Having to work the garden and do the normal farm chores gave him plenty of time to look forward to every single Saturday in the summer. On that day, he was given a day off from normal farm work and allowed to ride his horse the three miles to the old abandoned shale quarry the country folk had dubbed Shale Pit.

Usually joining him was his cousin Dewey and his little brother Will. Dewey was a different person when it was just he and Lee. It was when Ryan and the others were around that Dewey became someone else. From Lee's perspective, he understood why. Dewey probably simply did not want the same beating he saw his cousin receive. In a weird sort of way, he felt sorry for Dewey. Still, Lee wished Dewey would come to his aid, but he understood. He had grown comfortable with being betrayed.

Once at Shale Pit, it was off with their clothes and on with hours of a skinny-dipping adventure. After they had taken their fill of jumping from the thirty-foot cliffs and performing great feats of daring from the tall cottonwood's rope swing, they would spend time fishing the clear cool waters and exploring the many gullies and ravines that formed the wonderland called Shale Pit. There had been many legends about strange happenings at the old quarry. Years ago, it was said a young boy had disappeared. Kidnapped by swamp ogres and never heard from again. It was said that at every full moon one could hear his cries for help at midnight. It had been Lee's hope to one day find the courage to camp out at Shale Pit and hear those cries for himself.

On this particular Saturday, Lee was so exhausted from his farm work the evening before that he overslept. Dewey and Will had gone on without him. Saddling up his trusty horse, Sugarfoot, Lee grabbed his fishing pole and barreled toward Shale Pit. As he got closer, he could see where his brother and cousin had tethered their horses. Tying Sugarfoot with plenty of rein to graze, he raced up the hillside, through the trees, and headed for the far end of the quarry. Assuming the other boys were already swimming, he would get to the undisturbed fishing hole first and beat them to the "big one." As he made his way down to the water's edge, he laughed to himself. He could hear the laughter of the other boys at the far end of the pit, so he knew he would have a better-than-usual chance to land a whopper.

Pulling a Mason jar from its burlap wrapping, Lee quickly caught a jar full of fat, green and brown grasshoppers. Placing the jar—its lid poked full of air holes—carefully behind him, Lee grabbed his cane pole and unwound the line, careful to avoid the hook. Putting a freshly caught grasshopper onto the hook, he swung the bobber and baited hook as far out into the water as his pole would reach. He then sat down and began his intent vigil, hopeful that a big bass would latch onto the hook and suddenly cause the bobber to disappear. What a glorious day! What a wonderful life he had finally achieved! No chores. No schoolwork. And best of all, no bullies! Sitting back against a large crumbling shale deposit, Lee began to daydream about how he would be able to get all the fish home, of how great a double flip he would be able to perform on the rope swing, of how awesome the plunge from the cliff they called Big Daddy would be as he felt the warm upper layer of water give way to the cool, refreshing, darkness of the deep waters.

His pleasant reverie was not to last long, though. Just as his bobber was being jerked under and he made that hook-setting pull, he heard an all-too-familiar voice from behind.

"Hey! Elephant ears! Can't you hear me?"

Trying to wrestle in the bass but wanting to drop the pole and run, Lee simply held on and turned just in time to see Ryan picking up the jar of grasshoppers he had worked so hard to catch and casting it against the embankment, shattering the glass and sending the hoppers flying.

"Shouldn't you be home practicing your piano, girly-boy?" mocked Ryan. As the other boys made their way down to where Ryan now faced Lee, Lee pulled the two-pounder ashore as he tried to ignore his tormentor. This was the first time Lee had ever faced the boys without having the hope of a school bell or playground monitor to step in. On this day, even the betraying Dewey and Lee's little brother Will would offer no hope, being at the opposite end of Shale Pit. Lee was all alone. And there, as usual, would be no one to fight for him.

As Ryan closed in for the usual pounding, Lee was suddenly faced with this reality: here, in his own private adventure paradise, his tormentors had intruded. He had worked too hard this week. He had anticipated a day without chores or schoolwork. He had found great joy in not having to face the ridicule of the bullies or the shame of having to face all those who watched him take his daily torture in silence during the school year. But today was about to be the final day of Lee's torment. Before he even comprehended what he was doing, Lee watched his own fist reach back far behind his shoulder. He then felt a rush of rage brought on by the endless persecution at the hand of Ryan and his cronies. And then he felt the deepest sense of satisfaction he had ever felt in his life as his clenched fist met the upturned nose of Ryan the bully. He then saw the glory of a well-executed battle plan as a mixture of snot and blood gushed forth from the stunned Ryan.

He then felt utter panic as he realized what he had done!

Without wasting a second, Lee shoved Ryan into the water and began running for his life! Shocked at the sudden turn of events, the other boys lost sight of Lee in their own rush to pull their crying friend from the water. Lee's only problem now was that he had run the opposite direction around the large quarry and was now caught between Sugarfoot and the bullies! He would have to try and beat them around the pit. Running into the first ravine he came to, Lee quickly made his way up the crumbling slopes. Turning back to look for his pursuers once he reached the top, the boy was horrified at what he saw. Only a few yards behind him were Ryan and two other boys, and running along the ridge going the opposite direction around the quarry were the other two boys. They had him surrounded!

Lee had no choice; he would head back down into the next ravine and duck into one of the crevices he had discovered on his many excursions into Shale Pit. Ducking behind a canopy of willow branches, Lee concealed himself from the other boys. Thinking he had eluded them, he crouched down as silently as possible trying to catch his breath. After a few moments, his breath was once again taken away when he heard the boys sliding down the banks of the very ravine where he was now hiding! Keeping his eyes focused ahead for the rustling of willow branches, Lee began to scoot as quietly backward as he could. Feeling his way with his hands behind him, the ravine wall gave way to an opening. A cave! He had never found this cave before! Yet, here it was. Slinking his way in, he found himself completely out of the sunlight. If he hadn't seen the cave, maybe Ryan wouldn't see the cave!

For several minutes Lee did not hear another sound. Poking his head slightly out to see if he might catch a glimpse of his pursuers heading for home, he saw a figure making its way through the willow branches. "I think he went this way!" yelled Ryan to the other boys.

Turning back into the darkness, Lee began to feel his way along the cave wall. Expecting to find the end of the small cavern, he soon came to realize that he could no longer see any light coming from the tunnel's entrance. Surely he would be safe now! But just as he sat back to catch his breath and prepare to wait out his tormentors, he heard voices coming from the cave opening. Feeling his way deeper into the blackness, Lee began to panic. Barefoot and wearing only his cut-off shorts, the air began to grow very cold. Now shivering from both fright and the chilly air, Lee moved deeper into the cave. In his rush to get away from Ryan, it took him several seconds for his mind to recognize the sensation of falling. Lee had fallen headlong into an unseen hole and was now plummeting down, down, down, into who knows where!

As the seconds became minutes and the fear gave way to numbness, Lee began to think about his life. Flashing before him were images of Ryan hitting him and the other boys teasing him. He saw the piano and he saw the drawings. He remembered his mother and his father and his brothers and strangely wondered if he would ever see them again. He saw Shale Pit and he saw the school. He saw the town's people and he saw the country folk. He felt all the pain of the years of teasing and yet he felt the most peace he had ever imagined possible. He saw Dewey betray him, and he saw no one there to fight for him, as usual, but for some reason he felt safe and secure and unscathed. He felt there was hope now, that somehow, some way, someone was here to fight for him. And then he felt himself slip into a deep, deep sleep.

He never remembered hitting the bottom at all. All he could hear now was an unfamiliar yet very friendly voice calling to him. "Wake up, Leonolis! Today's the big day!"

Struggling to rouse himself from the oddness of a very strange sleep, Lee sat straight up in bed. Groggily, he asked the strangely dressed man, "Who are you?"

Laughingly, the man responded, "Stayed up too late again with your drawings last night, did we? Leonolis, it is not good for the future king of Bren to be too tired to learn how to rule his people! Up and dressed, now, sire! The Field of Testing is calling your name!"

As Lee (or Leonolis!) groggily obeyed, the man helped him into the oddest set of clothes Lee had ever seen. They appeared to have come right out of one of his many drawings of the medieval knights and dragons he had spent so much time meticulously creating on paper.

As quickly as Lee had fallen out of his world and into this strange new one, he had also fallen away from the many memories he had witnessed during his plunge into the darkness and into a whole new reality, complete with new memories and abilities only dreamt of before. And best of all? Ryan and any memory of him were completely erased. As the old pain gave way to the new peace, Lee heard the man calling from the hallway outside his bedroom. "To the royal stables, my lord! This day we ride!"

This would be a good day!

Chapter Two

A BOY'S WORLD

What a day! As Prince Leonolis made his way to the royal stables, his spirits were lifted by the sheer beauty and majesty of the kingdom called Brenolin. The southern boundary of the kingdom was the crystal clear Sea of Arabon, named after one of the earliest Brenolinian explorers, the brave knight Arabon. Its twinkling waves were quite visible from the prince's room, which was located in the southern turret of the great Castle Aerie (named for its eagle-like perch atop a small hill overlooking the mighty river Runland that meanders from the Mountains of Endoria all the way to the Sea of Arabon). The Sea of Arabon—this sparkling beacon of endless expanse—was often the first thing Prince Leonolis saw each morning. And like most mornings, the eastern sun was creating quite the show for the prince as the waves appeared like twinkling lights in the early morning sunrise.

As he made his way through the many twists and turns of the massive fortress he called home, he passed through the Hall of Defenders that was lined with the sculpted likenesses of every king who had ever ruled over Brenolin. In addition, the statues of great war heroes and those who had brought great invention or innovation to the realm were housed as well. Most of these great men were directly related to Prince Leonolis. He never really gave it much thought—that the blood that flowed through his veins had been passed down to him through such valiant heroes of the realm. All he could think of today were the many manly tests of battle he would be taken through as a part of his preparation for his Testolamorphia—the ceremony every Brenolinian boy looked forward to when they would be welcomed into the fellowship of manhood at the turn of their thirteenth birthday.

As he passed out of this great hall, he came to the northern region of the castle from which the vast dark Mountains of Endoria were easily visible, their mysterious snow-covered peaks this morning shrouded in dense clouds of grey. This was the realm of the dark lord, Lucian (one-time second in command of the realm and would-be usurper of the throne held by Leonolis' father, High King Troyolin). This mountainous province of Brenolin was strictly off-limits to young Prince Leonolis. It was no secret that Lucian had vowed to gain his revenge upon the High King Troyolin after the Seven Year War fought over control of the entire kingdom. To all who had been present on that day when revenge was declared, there was no doubt what Lord Lucian had meant when he said, "For this most egregious of insults against a throne that is rightfully mine, you, Troyolin will one day pay! You will pay the highest price. I will exact my revenge from that which you hold most dear." He, of course, had been referring to the newly born infant son of Troyolin, Prince Leonolis. With those words, Lord Lucian had vanished into the mist and mystery of the Mountains of Endoria along with ten thousand Brenolinians loyal to him. Since that day, he had been referred to as the "Dark Lord," and few had been foolish enough to venture into those shadowy, foreboding regions.

Brenolin derived its name from the first great king to rule over the land, Bren of Narthlin. Many were the stories told of brave King Bren who spent many years battling the rebellious, vagabond tribes that formerly ran rampant throughout the land for control of the domain. Their battles were epic and the stuff of lore. Every Brenolinian boy dreamed of battling the barbarian hordes themselves just as good King Bren had done so long ago. On this day, even though the mountains were covered and their majesty enveloped, Prince Leonolis himself imagined riding into battle against the Dark Lord, sword drawn, atop his faithful steed, Arolis, crashing into the front line of the dark forces. Just as his thoughts were about to take him on some new adventure, his faithful bodyguard, Danwyn, stepped from the stable doorway and into the morning light with a joyful yet firm greeting.

"Good morning, my prince! Have you readied your mind for battle this day?"

Startled back into reality, the prince responded. "Indeed I have, my good Danwyn!" He pulled a make-believe sword from its sheath and leapt into an offensive position. "My heart and my soul indeed are ready for battle. May the strength of Bren be mine today!" This was a common saying among all Brenolinian men. In their hearts and minds, the strength of Bren was the strength of the greatest champion their land had ever known. This strength embodied not simply physical strength but strength of mind, will, and emotion—strength of character. This was considered the heart of a true warrior. In fact, the greatest compliment a Brenolinian man could receive was to have it said of him "He has the strength of Bren," for this meant he was a man of highest character, respected by all.

"Your mount is ready, sire. Arolis seems to sense the importance of today. He strains at the bit to be off into battle. I would keep a tight rein until he remembers who is prince."

Laughing at the excitement he sensed in the normally reserved Danwyn, Leonolis mounted the horse and declared the well-known and very revered Brenolinian battlecry, "This day we conquer! This day we overcome the Dark Lord! This day we live or die for the king!"

At that, he gave Arolis a slight kick and they were off. Both Arolis and Leonolis had grown up together. To ride on the back of this shiny, black giant of a stallion was like becoming one with the wind for the prince. Strength and invincibility were balanced with wisdom and sensitivity to each one's slightest movement or physical nuance, making the team of Arolis and Leonolis a most formidable foe on the testing grounds.

Arriving at the grounds a full five hundred feet ahead of Danwyn and his mount, they were greeted by twenty-four other young men, their equine companions, and their military trainers, called Seconds. These Seconds were each appointed by King Troyolin himself to train the coming generation of military leadership–those who would serve to defend and protect the entire land of Brenolin.

Each of these young men had already been in training from the age of eleven. Each was nearing his thirteenth birthday. All would soon be tested in the fundamentals of military skills each Brenolinian male was expected to master. The Brenolinian cavalry, which these boys were all in training for, was considered the most elite branch of the military. The cavalry were the first responders in crisis. To be chosen for training in the corps of horsemen was indeed a great honor—and each position was fought for. Just because one was a prince did not mean he was automatically given the position of cavalry member. Today was the day when each candidate was tested regardless of social class or wealth—the day when the future military leaders of Brenolin would be set aside for the most grueling years of training that would follow—the HommeDressage, which consisted of four additional years of constant training in the arts of military strategy and warfare, alongside even greater and more strenuous bonding exercises between a man and his equine counterpart.

The boys and their steeds were called to divide into two groups and go to opposite sides of the testing ground for the first of many tests. The first test, called the Test of Will, was just that, a trial that on the surface seemed pure adrenalin and brawn—a test to determine if a boy's will to master the many requirements of horsemanship, swordsmanship, and battle strategy would hold sway when face-to-face with the reality of intense confrontation with the enemy. At the command of the field marshal, one boy from each side was to race toward the other at full speed, practice swords drawn. As the boys approached one another, they were to display proper horsemanship and battle posture in addition to demonstrating proper sword position at all times. The goal? To properly unseat their foe while maintaining the position of power and control.

As fate would have it, the field commander called out the name of Leonolis' best friend, Dreyden. Dreyden and Leonolis had grown up in the same kingdom yet were from very different worlds. The prince was, of course, raised in the royal household while Dreyden had been raised by one of the king's servants, the royal gardener, Heath. While Dreyden was responsible for helping his father raise the food that was needed by the royal family, he had been befriended by the prince when they were very young. They met when Leonolis had accompanied his father, King Troyolin, on one of the inspections of the royal farms. While Troyolin talked with Heath, the boys had conjured up a wonderful pretend adventure as they ran through the rows of corn, defeating the make-believe giants and goblins that threatened their kingdom.

While the thrill of the Day of Testing filled the hearts of each and every boy as they awaited the name of Dreyden's foe, the heart of the prince sank as his own name was called. He had only battled his friend on one other occasion . . . and it had gone in the prince's favor. He had pinned his good friend within seconds of the start of their wrestling match. And Dreyden, while always very encouraging of the prince, had seemed a little sad for days afterward. And now the boys were about to enter into what everyone knew was the prince's strongest event. What made this particular test of manhood such a favorite of Leonolis' was something that even the prince did not understand. He had a very unique gift, a power if you will. This power was the ability to communicate with animals. Not in a verbal sense but with his thoughts. As he awaited the word of the field commander to attend his battle station, Leonolis' thoughts were stirred to the noble history of his own great gift.

Though no one had ever come right out and said it, everyone assumed Prince Leonolis would be endowed with some special ability. No one really knew what Leonolis himself already knew. He had just never been given occasion for the public demonstration of his gift. After all, it was to only be used for the good of the kingdom and never for personal gain.

Every single member of the royal line had been given a special gift. Legend said that the first high king, Bren, had been given the gift of telepathy—the ability to communicate with others through his thoughts—by the Almighty King of Creation, the Founder. Each successive generation in the royal line had been given a gift that was to be used only for good in the service of the people of Brenolin. Not all were given the gift of telepathy. The first high queen, Oriana, had been given the gift of healing power. Whenever a warrior had been wounded in battle, Queen Oriana would go to the field hospital (many times very near the front line) and simply touch the wounded area, and within minutes, health would be restored.

King Teslin, another of Leonolis' royal relatives, had received the ability to see certain events before they happened. No one ever really knew what manifestation the gifts would take in each member of the royal line. The Founder had established this gifting in the royal line as a means of serving the people of Brenolin—a sort of seal of the Creator's approval upon the royal line of Brenolin. The gifts would be passed from generation to generation as long as they were used as means of good in service to the people of the realm.

What most in the kingdom knew but few ever publicly spoke of was the fact that the dark lord, Lucian, was actually in the royal lineage and had been given the same gift as that of King Bren—telepathy. When Lucian's rebellion first began, he had tried to sway the masses to join him in his rebellion. His ability to persuade the minds of the people of Brenolin in large numbers had been demonstrated even during the rule of the first high king. You see, Lucian had been doubly endowed with both a good gift and a curse. Sure enough, he could he send his thoughts to others and read the thoughts of others. But when he had rebelled against the high king, he had been banned from the kingdom and had received the curse the Founder had decreed in the ancient writings:

> He who would stand against the high king will be cursed to rule the darkness. He who would lay his hand against the realm of the kingdom will bring upon himself the curse of never holding what he most desires. He who seeks to harm the kingdom will be cursed to walk the dark realm and live though he would rather die. He will be living death.

No one knew for sure how old Lucian really was. The prophecies said his desire to rule would never fully be realized, but there had been periodic seasons where he did seem to wield power over certain regions. Each successor to the throne had been forced to deal with Lucian in one fashion or another. Lucian's desire to rule Brenolin had long ago been replaced with demonic obsession. His curse had now become the curse of Brenolin in many ways. It seemed that each royal era would have to deal with some manifestation of Lucian's rage. With that thought, Leonolis was startled back to reality.

"Leonolis! Get to your mark! Dreyden! To your mark!" The boys readied themselves for battle. Leonolis wanted the best for Dreyden, but royal expectations and the added benefit of his ability to communicate with Arolis meant almost certain victory for the prince. Nearing their marks, the field commander shouted, "To battle!" and they were off.

As Leonolis and Arolis bolted toward the center of the testing grounds, the mental communication had already begun between them. Dreyden and his steed, Graymon, had leapt into action simultaneously, almost throwing the young man to the ground from sheer exhilaration before they had even gotten a good start. As the two mounted, young warriors sped toward the center of the testing ground, Arolis and Leonolis quickly determined they would put into action a new battle move they had come up with in their times of practice during their daily rides through the forests surrounding Castle Aerie.

At the proper time, just before the foes would meet, Arolis would leap high into the air and Leonolis would reach down with his own sword, striking the weapon from the hand of his opponent. The sheer surprise at a mighty stallion leaping full speed into the air above was sure to frighten the opponent into a frozen state of fear and awe. To display this tactic in front of the other boys would surely propel the young prince to hero status in one fell swoop.

Seconds from one another, the boys stared straight ahead with focused intensity that is common in Brenolinian horsemen. Racing like lightning toward one another, both boys raised their swords to battle position, letting go of the reins (each horse and boy had long ago established trust in one another) so as to grasp their weapons with both hands. Just as they drew near Arolis prepared to make the leap, speaking to Leonolis in thought, *Prepare to fly, my prince!*

Arolis leapt into the air and the prince looked down into the awestruck eyes of his friend. Lowering his sword and leaning down he easily knocked the sword from the hands of his bewildered foe. Instantly the boys on the sidelines erupted with loud cheers. At the same time, Arolis and Leonolis turned back to make their way to the exuberant crowd. Just as the prince was about to dismount before the field marshal, Arolis bounded from the circle of young warriors taking the confounded prince with him with only the thought words, *Hang on, my liege!*

What are you doing, Arolis! the boy shouted at the top of his thoughts.

Did you not see, my prince? shouted Arolis.

See what, horse? said the prince.

The Dark Lord . . . watching from the stand of trees!

I saw no Dark Lord, said Leonolis.

Trust me, sire. He was there.

"Back to the Field of Testing at once, Arolis! I saw no one! Take me back this instant! I command you. Take me back!"

As if he were not even listening, the stallion ignored his boy. And with that, the steed made his way back to the royal stables with the protesting prince on his back. The guards, having seen the horse barreling in a frenzy toward the royal barns, had barely gotten the doors swung open when the horse came careening through, narrowly missing the door posts in the process. Sliding to a halt, the prince was thrown head over heels, not hearing his horse's plea to, *Hold on, sire! Hold on!* As the guards tended to the boy, the royal stableman angrily jerked the reins of Arolis, not understanding the brave horse had just saved the life of the future king.

Chapter Three

THE DAY EVERYTHING CHANGED

B y the time Danwyn made his way to the stable, the king and his royal guard had already been summoned. Making his way through the crowd, Danwyn's thoughts were squarely focused on the safety of his royal charge. At the same time, he began to worry that King Troyolin would be none too happy that the prince's personal guard had been derelict in his duty. He greatly feared public reprimand by the high king. Approaching the circle gathered around the boy, Danwyn noticed the stable master leading Arolis angrily away. It had been so uncharacteristic for the stallion to be spooked. Many were the times on his rides with the prince that a rabbit or snake had jumped in fear at the feet of the mighty horse Arolis and never had Danwyn seen him even give the creature notice. But on the testing grounds something had made the stallion bolt.

As Danwyn made his way to the boy, the Royal Guards surrounding him gave way to the high king. King Troyolin was a very large man, muscular and commanding in physical strength, he was even more commanding when he spoke. A stallion of a man, his brute strength was always evident in the way the king carried himself, full of grace and confidence. Yet, his great personal strength was held in check by the reins of his selfless nature. It was evident to all who knew him that High King Troyolin saw himself as servant of the people first and foremost. Protector of the people of Bren, his great power was made endearing by the fact that every subject of the king knew he would gladly put himself in harm's way for any one of them.

Knowing this about the king did not make Danwyn's heart any more at ease. In his heart, he had not fulfilled his royal mandate—to protect the prince at all costs. As Danwyn made it to Leonolis' side, he knelt before the boy in a gesture of humility. At that very moment, King Troyolin commanded the fretting bodyguard to rise. Gazing first at his son, the king placed his hands on the shoulders of the boy as if he were holding the most valuable of treasures. He said, "My son, are you hurt? Did Arolis hurt you when you lost control?"

The boy did not say a word. He simply nodded—halfway in shock yet halfway not wanting to divulge the fact that he could communicate with animals. He was almost embarrassed at the realization, probably due to the fact that he quite enjoyed being considered a normal boy in the realm. Once his secret was out, he knew from his own family's history that he would never be seen in the same "normal" light again. He stood silently as the king turned his attention to Danwyn.

Looking at Danwyn, he said, "Brave Danwyn, what was the cause of Arolis' flight?"

"Your Highness, I saw nothing that would have caused the horse to run in such fear," said the anxious bodyguard.

"Danwyn, I trust you with the welfare of my son when he is in your care. I trust you in the training of my son in the ways of horsemanship. My fear is that you have not only forsaken his safety but that you have not prepared him properly in the ways of a son of Brenolin. Perhaps your assessment that he and Arolis were meant for one another was premature. I cannot allow such a wild and unpredictable horse to carry the heir to the throne. Until there has been a thorough investigation of today's events consider yourself relieved of duty." As Danwyn bowed in utter humiliation, the boy could no longer hold his tongue.

"Father, stop! It was not Danwyn's fault. It was Arolis!"

Surprised by his son's boldness, the king said, "Explain yourself."

"Father, as we completed our first battle run and were returning to our station at the testing grounds, Arolis told me to 'hang on' and suddenly exploded back toward the castle."

"Arolis 'told you'?"

"Yes, Father. I can hear his thoughts . . . and he can hear mine."

Smiling on the inside yet not wanting to diminish the gravity of the situation, Troyolin continued in a serious tone, "By the Founder's good wisdom, your gift has been made known this day. Why did you not say anything before?"

"I was not confident in my gift at first, and I did not want to reveal it until I was sure. But as my confidence grew, I also had a great desire to not be known by my gift but rather by the nature of who I am," said the boy, not sure of how his father would respond.

As if measuring his words, the king spoke in a very reverent tone. "Son, your gift was bestowed on you by the Founder. This solemn endowment was granted to you for a very specific purpose. It has been given as a sign of the Founder's continued blessing on the people of Brenolin, and as the bearer of that gift, it is your duty to never withhold its use if it means the safety and blessing of the good people of this land. What did Arolis see, Son?"

Grateful at his father's unexpected and gracious response, the boy's heart and thoughts were settled enough to answer his father's question. "As we completed our run, he commanded me to 'hang on' and then he shouted these words when I asked him what he had seen: 'The Dark Lord . . . watching from the stand of trees!'"

The high king needed to hear no more. He knew from the history of Brenolin's great kings who had shared in the gift that was bestowed upon Leonolis that the animals of the land could be trusted—especially the horses. The horses of the land had come to symbolize not only strength and dignity but also good and loyal hearts, deep in character. Troyolin knew Arolis would never lie. Calling for the stable master, the high king commanded that Arolis be returned to the care of Leonolis at once. Looking to Danwyn next, the king took him by the hand and said, "My good and faithful servant, watch over my son now. Keep him behind the great fortified walls of Castle Aerie. Take him to the Protected Place . . . now!"

The king then commanded the Royal Guards, "To arms, mighty men of Brenolin. To the testing ground. Away!" The king and his guards were off as the stable master led the good horse Arolis back to the prince, bowing and seeking forgiveness for the way in which he had handled the mighty steed when he thought he had run wildly away with the prince. As Danwyn prepared to usher the boy to the safety of the inner place of the castle, Leonolis said to the stable master, "Arolis wants you to know he was not offended at your actions. He would have done the same in my protection." Danwyn then hurriedly took the prince to the hidden Protected Place deep in the recesses of Castle Aerie as they heard the hoof beats of the king's men head back to the testing grounds in search of the Dark Lord.

As the king's men approached the stand of trees where Arolis had seen Lucian and his men, the testing grounds were empty and eerily silent. What had been a raucous cacophony of teenage boys preparing for battle was now an expanse of very strange stillness (some would later describe this silence as the feeling of dark magic in the air). Circling above the trees were several buzzards, which caused the heart of the king to sink. Surrounding the sylvan cluster, the king's men slowly and methodically closed into a tight circle as they made their way to the center of the forested cluster . . . making a grisly discovery. Tied to a tree, his body riddled with arrows, it was all too obvious that the man had been tortured. Dismounting, Troyolin approached the dead man and quickly recognized him as Merrywell, the Second of Dreyden!

Immediately, the king summoned his royal tracker. "Tracker, how many horsemen were with the Dark Lord?"

Bending down and closely examining the many hoof prints and deciphering the many footprints, the tracker quickly surmised that there had only been fifteen horsemen and riders—a small raiding party designed for stealth. As he gave his report to the king, one of the king's royal messengers approached with the report that Dreyden had not returned with the rest of the boys when the command had been given to make haste to Castle Aerie. Somewhere in the confusion, Dreyden had gone missing!

What had happened was quite understandable, actually. Upon his defeat at the hand of his best friend (even though it was only mock battle), Dreyden had mistaken the sudden charge back to the castle as arrogant gloating. Feeling this was a public display of mockery at his expense, Dreyden had headed the opposite direction from Leonolis in humiliation. Heading for the stand of trees abutting the testing field, Dreyden had been followed by his Second . . . and had quickly fallen into the clutches of Lucian and his men.

Lucian had only been conducting reconnaissance, seeking out possible points of attack against King Troyolin, when he was handed a most unexpected yet most opportune gift. Recognizing Dreyden as the close friend of Leonolis, Lucian had decided to preserve the young man's life for use as a bargaining point should it be required later. As for the Second, the Dark Lord had personally committed unspeakable acts of torture in an effort to elicit information about troop placement and any kingdom business he might find helpful in his schemes. The Second, as brave and loyal as any of the great kings of Bren, had stalwartly defied the Dark Lord and gave up absolutely no secrets of the kingdom. Filled with rage, Lucian had dispatched him in disgust. Taking Dreyden, he and his men headed back for their lair in the Mountains of Endoria.

"To arms!" said the king. "Commander Corellian, take five hundred Royal Guardsmen and pursue this band of rebels. By now they are most assuredly headed for the refuge of the Dark Lands (another name for the regions of Endoria). Young lord Dreyden has fallen into the hands of the Dark Lord. We cannot waste another minute!"

"As you command, sire!" and with that, the five hundred mighty horsemen thundered off in pursuit of Lucian and his band of scoundrels, led by Corellian, Royal Commander of the King's Guard.

As the Royal Guard began its pursuit, the king and the rest of his company headed for Castle Aerie where they convened a royal war council, gathering of all the twenty-four chieftains of the twenty-four royal provinces of the land of Bren. For war to be declared there must be sufficient evidence of enemy activity in Brenolin proper, and a majority of chieftains must be in favor of military action. King Troyolin had no problem receiving a unanimous vote as war was once again declared on Lucian and his mongrel, rebellious hordes.

As the king and his royal cabinet began to devise a plan, it was understood by all that not only would this military action be for the purpose of rescuing Lord Dreyden, but it would also be for the purpose of once and for all eradicating the land of the Dark Lord. While the plans were being drawn and strategies devised, Danwyn and Prince Leonolis were summoned to the war room.

The king addressed his son solemnly with the news. "Leonolis, your faithful steed did indeed see the dark lord, Lucian, lurking in the wooded area near the testing grounds . . . and I have worrisome news to bear to you. Your dear friend Dreyden has been taken captive by Lucian and his men and has been taken toward the Dark Lands. His Second was found dead in the woods."

"It's all my fault! What have I done?" shouted Leonolis as he fell into his father's arms in deep sorrow at the terrible news. "I should have believed Arolis and gone to the field commander immediately . . . but I could not even control my own horse!"

"Son, Arolis did what was necessary to preserve your life. He acted as any loyal steed of the realm would have done. The truth is that once the field commander saw your furious race for the castle, he immediately commanded the entire company back to the safety of Aerie . . . and Dreyden, for some reason, did not follow. There was nothing you could have done. And, Son, we will find Dreyden."

"Justinian, my dear friend of friends, by the Founder's might, I leave you in command of Castle Aerie. I will personally oversee the safe return of young Lord Dreyden. Watch over the good people of Bren with charity and wisdom. I will send word once I have ascertained the next step of action." Justinian and Troyolin had become forged together at the heart from the time of their own Testolamorphia (another story for another day!). Suffice it to say, Justinian and Troyolin trusted each other with their lives, and this trust extended to their families and, by royal decree, to the entire kingdom. The people of Bren trusted Justinian because Troyolin trusted him.

"Father, I will go with you!" said Leonolis.

"You will do no such thing!" shouted the king.

Shocked at a side of his father he had rarely seen, Leonolis fell back into the ready arms of Danwyn who caught the young prince from behind.

"We cannot risk your life. Son. It is not Dreyden Lucian is truly after. It is you! It is my fear that he will somehow attempt to use your friend to get to you. I truly understand your loyalty to Dreyden . . . but the fate of the entire kingdom rests upon the preservation of the royal line. Since the day you were born, the kingdom has lived with the knowledge that Lucian's tormented mind was spent in devising ways to end your life. It is time you understood the gravity of your place in the kingdom. You are the heir to the throne. You represent the heart of the Founder to our people. You represent the very continued existence of the Founder's blessing upon the great land of Bren. We will not put you in unnecessary peril this day. Back to the Cleft of the Rock with you until further notice. Danwyn, take him now."

With that, the good king shouted to his mighty chieftains, "This day we conquer! This day we overcome the Dark Lord!" to which the chieftains replied, "This day we live or die for the king!" And so the king and his men, along with their legions of soldiers, headed for the Dark Lands.

The secret chamber where the prince had been spirited away to was actually the lowest place within the vast labyrinth of underground chambers in Castle Aerie. Known as the Cleft of the Rock, or the Protected Place, the tiny alcove had originally been used as a storage cellar for dried fruits and vegetables harvested from the royal gardens, but since the early days of the reign of King Bren, the little nook in the wall, which opened up into the storage cellar, had proven to be an almost impregnable refuge where many a royal heir had been hidden away when Castle Aerie had been attacked throughout the history of Brenolin. What most did not know was that since the earliest days when Princess Bria had almost been captured during one particularly bloody siege is that the decision had been made to excavate further into the earth a secret escape tunnel. This tunnel was rumored to exist in the gossip of the kingdom, but no one really knew for sure. But it *did* exist . . . and it was ingeniously connected to the magical Crystal Cave.

Chapter Four

THE CRYSTAL CAVE

As his father and the other chieftains readied themselves for battle, Leonolis was still reeling from his father's harsh response to his desire to join the royal forces in their quest to free Dreyden. His father was very firm and sure in his decision-making process. One always knew where the king stood on any given matter, being very wise and very strong. The prince also knew the king to be very caring and sensitive and aware of the feelings and needs of those around him, especially his family. It was this truth that helped the young boy quickly return to the truth—that his father desired only what was best for him and that the king's response was necessary for his son to be able to grasp the severity of the situation.

At the same time, it must be said that the bond between Dreyden and Leonolis was very strong, stronger than two brothers could ever be. Running through the grain fields from the time they were toddlers, the boys had experienced so much of life together. When Dreyden needed anything, Leonolis was there. Whenever Leonolis needed encouragement, Dreyden was there. In addition, they spent much time together because Leonolis had begged his father to allow Dreyden to be taught alongside him (they were both under the tutelage of Maison the Wise—the tutor assigned to teach the prince). It was quite common (and sometimes comical) for the boys to finish one another's statements. When it had come time to begin their formal training as future horsemen of the kingdom, Leonolis had given Dreyden one of his own horses from the royal stable, Graymon.

If one could not find Leonolis, he need only look for Dreyden. And if Dreyden could not be found completing his chores in the royal garden, he need only look for Leonolis. The boys were always together. Even though Leonolis had three younger brothers and Dreyden had three younger sisters, these two seemed closer than even siblings (Dreyden's oldest sister, Marianna, had taken a special interest in Leonolis herself, but again, that's another story for another day!). Dreyden was great at all things mechanical and mathematical while Leonolis was a master of all things creative and artistic. Both were full of passion and very quickly defended their beliefs while at the same time having a deep respect for one another should their opinions not line up. As all men of the kingdom were encouraged to do, the boys, from an early age, had vowed to always fight shoulder to shoulder and to be on guard at one another's backs. The boys were practically inseparable. For the prince to not be able to come to his dear friend's defense was most unbearable. Engulfed in deep sorrow and still feeling somewhat responsible for Dreyden's predicament, the young prince began to grow numb and helpless, his mind overwhelmed with the emotional weight placed on his shoulders this day.

As Danwyn led Leonolis out of the war room and headed for the Protected Place, the prince was drawn to a whisper coming from somewhere overhead—not a vocal whisper but a thought whisper. Looking up as they crossed one of the bridges that connect the many turrets of Castle Aerie to the main inner courtyard, Leonolis caught glimpse of a shadowy figure floating high in the air above the great fortress. The buzzard was whispering his thoughts in such a way that Leonolis knew he was speaking directly to him.

Who are you? the prince asked the buzzard.

I am Beezlebird . . . and I have a message for you.

A message? Who is it from? asked Leonolis.

A friend . . . a friend more dear than a brother, said the bird.

Dreyden! From my friend Dreyden? shouted the prince in thought. He had to quickly catch himself from expressing any emotion due to his conversation with the buzzard so as to not alarm Danwyn.

He is the one, said Beezlebird.

What is it? asked the prince.

He is safe . . . but he needs your help. He says to tell you that Lord Lucian will release him if you can ensure safe passage back to the Dark Lands. Dreyden says you and you alone are the only one who knows the Crooked Way.

Leonolis knew this had to be from his friend. He and Dreyden had been playing hide-and-seek on their horses one day in the Canyons of Callay when the prince ducked between two large pillars of stone that seemed to be a dead end, only to discover that what appeared to be a dead end was actually a very well-concealed passage that led directly to the dark edges of the forests of Endoria. He had not dared to venture any further that day, but in the days since had won many a game of hide-and-seek with the other boys. Never divulging the exact location of the passage, Leonolis had chosen to keep his hidey-hole a secret. Dreyden knew of its existence but did not know the location. Only Dreyden could have known what the bird was now telling him.

You must come at once, said the buzzard.

I am being watched. I cannot come, said Leonolis.

If you cannot come, I am afraid your friend is in great peril. His life will be preserved until I return with your message. I cannot guarantee he will live beyond the night. His fate is truly in your hands, Beezlebird gravely replied as he veered back toward the Dark Lands.

Wait! thought-shouted Leonolis. *I will be there. I will need some time to plan my escape, but I will be there. Where shall I find him?*

Come to the Sleeping Giant. Dreyden will be waiting for you there. And with that, the dark figure faded into the evening sky.

The Sleeping Giant was simply a hill that rose up just before the Canyons of Callay whose outline looked like a giant, sleeping man from a distance. It was a well-known landmark in the kingdom. Leonolis knew he could reach it in one day's time by foot . . . but could get there within a few hours on the back of Arolis.

Just then, Danwyn startled Leonolis from his skyward gaze. "What is it, my lord?" said the guard.

"Nothing. Just thinking about Dreyden."

The entire exchange between Beezlebird and Leonolis had taken only a few seconds, but the prince knew he must conceal his emotions even in the midst of his thought conversations.

"To the cleft," said Danwyn, and they headed to the secret place.

As they passed near the royal stables, Leonolis sent his thoughts to Arolis. *My friend. Can you hear me?*

What is it, sire? Are you all right? I have been very worried about you. There is talk among the beasts that your life is in danger, said the mighty horse.

I am fine, said the prince. *It is Dreyden who is in danger. I need your help. What is it, sire?*

I need you to meet me at the entrance of the Crystal Cave in one hour, replied Leonolis.

Why? asked the horse.

Just trust me and obey, said the boy. *I have found a way to rescue Dreyden.* With that, the boy and his Second headed into the deep recesses of Castle Aerie, well beyond the prince's ability to project his thoughts. Arolis had no other choice but to obey his prince. At least he could protect him if they were together. Unlocking his stable and walking the grounds was not considered out of the ordinary for the great horse Arolis. It was actually quite common for the steed to walk around the castle yards in the evening. The only difference about tonight's walk was that the horse quietly made his way through the Messenger's Gate (a special passageway through the fortress wall where royal messengers could come and go during all hours of the day or night) and into the grounds surrounding the castle. From there he headed to the other side of the great citadel and sauntered the five miles to the other side of Council Hill where the opening of Crystal Cave lay hidden just above the mighty waters of Runland.

Crystal Cave was really a series of old mine shafts where Phrygian Crystals were once excavated. Phrygian Crystals emitted a low-grade light and were thought to contain healing powers. They were also used as light sources in the homes of most families of the realm. Gaining added strength for their inherent, light-giving power from extended exposure to sunlight, the crystals were placed outside during the day then brought in each evening, full of light and even a bit of warmth. When the family was ready to retire for the evening, a blanket or some other covering was used to dim the powerful crystal. It was not uncommon for a sick child to be put to bed with a Phrygian Crystal and wake the next morning as good as new.

This particular mine had long ago been abandoned due to rich deposits of high-quality Phrygian Crystal being discovered in the Canyons of Callay region. Over time, the mine began to fill with water that slowly began seeping in from the underground springs that fed the great River Runland. This took place during the reign of King Miraculin (fifth to ascend to the throne of Brenolin; his reign was known as the Reign of Miracles). Miraculin had created a series of secret indentions in the ceiling every fifteen feet in the main shaft. Once the caves completely flooded, the only way to make one's way through the vast cave system was to swim from indention to indention, going up for air every fifteen feet. The indentions were perpetually filled with air due to the seepage of air from the cave floor that made its way upward from even deeper cave systems. Occasionally, the cave entrance would "belch" forth a great blast of air if the cave became too full of air.

King Miraculin used the caves for secret meetings of his royal cabinet. The cave was also used by the princes of Brenolin to play hide-and-seek. The cavern also came in handy as a royal escape route during times of war. The main shaft floor was still lined with Phrygian Crystal so that once the eyes adjusted to the dark, even the low light was enough to navigate the series of indentions (without sunlight, Phrygian Crystals still emitted light, though somewhat dimmed compared to those charged with sunlight). If the king was ever followed, the one who trailed him could not possibly have known that the series of indentions led to a dead end.

You see, the king in his wisdom had designed the secret passage to veer through a succession of indentions down a passageway not lit by crystals once the fourth indention had been reached. The unlit passage was not even visible due to the placement of stones in the secret cavern entrance. Those who followed would find themselves reaching the tenth well-lit indention before they would realize they had reached a dead end. In the unlit portion of tunnel, the cave floor was lit again at the third indention, meaning that to get to the tunnel exit one must swim thirty feet in complete darkness to the remaining indentions. Once the third indention was reached, crystals once again lit the way. From there, only four more indentions led one to an open cavern above the water line where a cache of rations, clothing, and arms were stored. From there, the cave system led out of the mountain known as Council Hill.

During the days of Princess Bria, the Crystal Cave system had been wisely and secretly connected with the system of tunnels beneath the

Castle Aerie. The main connection was a direct access to the Protected Place. Leonolis had decided to utilize his vast knowledge of the escape route and meet his horse once he exited the Crystal Cave.

From the moment he first learned to swim, Leonolis was taught by his own father the routes of escape. Even though it was not until his eleventh birthday that the prince had actually traversed the cave's indentions, he knew the route in and out since it had been indelibly forced into his mind at the hand of his father's daily insistence to master the map mentally.

When the escape system was first devised, each royal heir was required to learn its many twists and turns as well as how to evade anyone who might follow them in or out. Even Leonolis and his brothers, along with his male cousins, would take their daily summer skinny-dipping treks through the cave, playing underwater tag. What they mastered in fun could one day mean the difference between life and death—the difference between victory and defeat. What was not widely known in the kingdom was that King Troyolin himself still often enjoyed secret swims through the tunnels, just to sort of re-live his own boyhood—and to keep his mind sharp as he remembered the royal escape strategies.

His dilemma now was how to divert the watchful eye of good Danwyn long enough to make his escape into the depths of Crystal Cave. Knowing his guard would be extra vigilant in his duties, the prince would have to be very careful to not give away his intentions. Settling into the sparse furnishings in the alcove, Leonolis knew he would not be able to fool Danwyn very easily, but the life of his friend was at stake. Thinking wildly without betraying his intense desire to run to Dreyden's side, the prince began to devise a plan. He knew that Danwyn would not leave for any reason, and he knew he could not risk waiting for him to fall to sleep. There were plenty of rations and plenty of blankets. Danwyn was under strict orders to protect the prince at all costs, and the boy knew his bodyguard would gladly give his own life to defend him.

The plan he devised was quite simple and actually quite uncomplicated to put into action. Leonolis would simply ask to be excused to relieve himself!

"Danwyn, I need to go."

"Go where, my prince?"

"You know . . . I've got to go."

"Leonolis, you know I cannot let you out of my sight. You'll just have to go there in the chamber pot. I'll turn my back while you tend to your business."

"My good Danwyn, I do not think I can go with you right here with me. Let me just step into the darkness of the outer tunnel. You can check first to see that no one is there."

Feeling somewhat understanding of the prince's fragile emotional state, the faithful guardian hesitantly took a lamp and went into the escape corridor of the secret tunnel. After he was assured that no one could possibly be lurking there, he reluctantly carried the chamber pot into the tunnel and placed it where it could still be seen from the door of the Cleft of the Rock.

Making his way out into the tunnel, carrying his own lantern, Leonolis said, "Danwyn, I am not going to be able to do this with you watching. It's just not going to happen. I'll be fine."

Unenthusiastically, Danwyn closed the door, admonishing the prince, "Let me know as soon as you are done."

As the door closed, Leonolis quickly went to work and lodged a torch he found in a wall sconce under the door's latch in such a way that even the strength of Danwyn would not be able to budge for several minutes.

As quietly as he could, he took his lantern and headed for the waters of the Crystal Cave. Nearing the water's edge, he heard the splintering crash as Danwyn was finally able to burst through the door. He knew his guardian would not be able to follow him through the maze of tunnels. Only members of the royal line knew the exact route. Stripping off his clothes, the boy dove into the water and made it through the dimly lit tunnel to the first indention in no time. Now exhilarated by the sheer adventure he now found himself upon, all the prince could think of was in getting to his friend. After only a few minutes, Leonolis made his way to the darkened portion of his escape. Knowing the cave route so well, he easily maneuvered the darkness and made his way into the cavernous mine opening where he was greeted by Arolis.

Wasting no time, the prince quickly threw on clothes from the cache and saddled his equine friend with an ill-fitting saddle meant for a farmer's horse. It would have to do. Grabbing a sword, a dagger, bow, and quiver of arrows, the two runaways were now fugitives in their own kingdom. Leonolis knew Danwyn had already made his way to the royal stables by now and that an entourage of Royal Guardsmen would be on their way to Crystal Cave. They had no time to waste.

Where to, my prince? asked the fiery stallion.

To the Sleeping Giant!

And into the night flew the horse and his boy.

Chapter Five

THROUGH THE SWAMP

It had taken no time for Troyolin to assemble the finest of Bren's mighty cavalry. Ten thousand snorting steeds with ten thousand passionate horsemen awaited the word of their king. Brenolin's armed forces were easily summoned by a series of low-pitched bells that were perpetually manned by specially trained infantrymen. The bells were placed in fortified watchtowers that were strategically placed in two-mile intervals (like a pseudo-wagon wheel) around the borders of Brenolin. From these watchtowers a series of towers went inward throughout the kingdom like the spokes of that wagon wheel. The bells were placed at the tops of the towers and were sounded only in times of extreme peril to the kingdom, whether that peril be an approaching enemy or a coming flood somewhere upstream from Castle Aerie (Castle Aerie was actually the capitol city of the land since it was the seat of royalty). The low tones of the bell carried further than a high-pitched tone and could even pierce the howling winds of a storm or the cacophony of a flock of twenty thousand migrating mountain geese. These bells had been used to summon the most elite cavalrymen from every regiment stationed throughout the land. A very precise system of tones and patterns communicated the king's message through all of the land in a matter of a few short hours.

Gathering in the great Warrior's Canyon (a sort of natural amphitheater below Castle Aerie, which had become a place of meeting for the coronations of the realm), the king stood at the bottom of the canyon as the troops assembled in regiments above him. Due to the curvature of the canyon walls and coupled with the granite of which they were comprised, the voice of a well-spoken orator could carry easily to the highest level of those assembled.

"My countrymen, my brothers, my faithful servants, my warriors, this day, one of our own has been taken from our midst by the forces of the dark lord, Lucian. It is believed that the Dark Lord himself may have led the raid that seized young Lord Dreyden from the very grounds of testing . . . not before torturing, mutilating, and murdering his Second, the good man, Merrywell. Merrywell was a great man—a husband, and the father of four sons and three daughters of the realm. It is well known that the Dark Lord has vowed to take the life of my own son, Leonolis, and has surely planned this abduction as a part of some sort of plan to carry out his threats. Regardless, one of *our* son's *has* been taken . . . and we must not let this deed go unpunished if we are to remain a free and prosperous people. Will you follow me into battle this day?"

As if rehearsed a thousand times before, the mighty throng erupted into agreement with a mighty shout and one voice saying, "This day we conquer! This day we overcome the Dark Lord! This day we live or die for the king!"

At that, the king responded with, "May the strength of Bren be mine today!" and, again without hesitation, the host of mighty men shouted so as to shake all of Warrior's Canyon and echo throughout Castle Aerie and its confines above, "May the strength of Bren be mine today! May the strength of Bren be mine today! May the strength of Bren be mine today!" As crowds watched from the canyon rim and from the majestic walls of Castle Aerie, a mighty cheer went up from the people, lasting until the last of the regiments had followed their king along the road running beside the great waters of Runland heading to the Mountains of Endoria.

By the time Danwyn had discovered Leonolis had escaped and made his way to the halls of upper Castle Aerie, the king and his men were already several miles down the road (the entire sequence of events had taken several hours to unfold). Running to the royal stables, his suspicions were confirmed. Arolis had escaped as well and was surely already carrying the prince toward the Dark Lands in search of his dear friend, Dreyden. He must tell King Troyolin, but Danwyn knew he would have no chance of catching up to the king due to the miles of cavalrymen taking up the entire width of the road north along the river. He knew what he must do. He would send messengers with the news to the king. It would take some time, but the royal trumpeter would go before the messenger and sound the trumpet fanfare, "Make Way for the King," which was always blasted in great crowds that the king needed to pass through. In the meantime, Danwyn would head out with six of the Royal Guards and try to track Leonolis from Council Hill beginning from the entrance of Crystal Cave.

Danwyn called for the king's messengers and gave them this message for the king: "My king, Prince Leonolis has managed to escape and is headed north to the Dark Lands from the mouth of Crystal Cave in search of Lord Dreyden. Danwyn and his men are in pursuit." As the trumpets blared, the messengers followed. In the meantime, Danwyn and the Royal Guardsmen flew like the wind around Council Hill and to the opening of the great cave. All they found were a set of hoof prints headed toward the northlands. Following the tracks became increasingly difficult as the night began to fall. Danwyn secretly feared the worst—that the prince was headed directly for Maudlin's Marsh, also known as the Forbidden Swamp.

Maudlin's Marsh or Forbidden Swamp at one time had been a great source of peat moss, a common fuel for the households of Bren. Overseen by the man who first discovered the vast deposits of peat, the old man Maudlin, the swampy area had long ago become too flooded to allow the safe recovery of the fuel. Many a lost soul had become hopelessly bogged down in the murky waters unable to dislodge themselves from miry suction of the unforeseen quagmire. There were certain periods during the year when the waters dropped enough in depth that the areas of danger would become settled enough to allow safe passage to the Great Forest, and from the Great Forest to the Canyons of Callay, and from the Canyons of Callay right to the edge of the Dark Lands. It was Danwyn's fear that Leonolis was going to risk the shortcut. To go around the marsh would mean hours of lost time.

"Good men of the Guard, the prince seems to have headed for the Forbidden Swamp," said Danwyn.

"My lord," began one of the Royal Guards, "This is not a time of safe passage through the bogs. Even young Leonolis knows this. You yourself have drilled it into his head for years now."

"Yes, I know . . . but we must remember, loyalty and sorrow can cause even the most sensible and reasonable of men to do senseless and unreasonable things. I have no doubt that our young lord is not being very reasonable at this moment. We cannot waste another breath here. We ride!" And with that, the seven mighty men of Bren began the pursuit of the prince.

Leonolis had been pushing Arolis to the extreme knowing Danwyn would be in hot pursuit by now. Going was not quite so easy. The two runaways had left the familiarity of the wagon-rutted roads several miles ago and soon the sound of sloshing water replaced the sound of clopping of hooves on hard ground.

"My lord," began Arolis. "I must insist we abandon your plan for heading through the marsh. We will make better time traversing the outlying edges of the swamp and simply going around rather than feeling our way through."

"No!" countered the prince (seldom were the times when Leonolis had ever responded so firmly or angrily to his horse). "Danwyn and the Royal Guards will catch us in no time. All they have to do is follow the muddy tracks we leave. Even with the scarcity of moonlight the trail would be easily followed. I must get to Dreyden. His captivity was meant for me. The words of the messenger he sent were very adamant. Dreyden's life is at stake. He is in great peril, Arolis. I must go to him. Don't worry. I think I know how to make it through."

By this time the mighty steed was steadily slowing to a crawl as the waters were now up to his belly.

"Stop here, Arolis." And the two stood silent for a few seconds.

"What is it, sire?"

Then Arolis heard what the boy had stopped to listen for. A conversation was going on very near their feet!

A small raspy voice said, *Something large this way comes, Snuffim. We must remain very still until it passes! Shhhh!*

Another small but less raspy voice nervously responded, *But Sniffum, what will we do if the thing is a turtle eater?*

If a turtle eater it be, we won't be eaten without a turtle of a fight!" said Sniffum. "Quiet, Brother. The movement has stopped. We must be silent as well.

After a brief moment, Leonolis joined in the thought-conversation of the turtle brothers. *Sniffum and Snuffim. A friend your way comes.*

Startled at the sound of their names from a voice in the darkness, the brothers quickly ducked their heads into their shells and submerged themselves somewhere in the reedy shadows.

My dear turtle friends, it is I, Prince Leonolis, Lord of the land of Bren, son of Troyolin, High King of the Realm, and my friend, the great horse, Arolis. I have need of your service this night.

Silence.

Arolis broke the awkward stillness saying, *My lord, perhaps they fear the voice of a human. Let me speak to them. Friends and brothers, I am Arolis, horse and friend of good prince Leonolis. We mean you no harm. We have need of passage through your treacherous land, as we have need to rescue a young lad of Bren from the clutches of the dark lord, Lucian.*

Lucian! thought-shouted Sniffum. *Lucian of the north? The bane of creatures great and small? The turtle-eating fiend of the Dark Lands? What can we do to help?*

My goodness, said the prince. *I think you touched a nerve, Arolis!*

My young human, it has been rumored for scores of years that the Dark Lord considers me and my brethren a particular delicacy. We dare not venture into the daylight lest we be snatched from our watery territories by one of his bat-winged minions! said Sniffum. *We gladly offer our services if it means we might avenge even one of our tribe that has been lost to his evil belly! What do you need from us, sire?*

Dear little brothers, we cannot possibly pass through your land even in the daylight, and much less in this deep darkness. We will surely become ensnared to the grip of this miry kingdom of yours if someone does not lead us through. Can you help us? said the prince.

Help you we will! said the turtle brothers in singsong unison, absolutely giddy at the possibility of helping someone get the better of the Dark Lord. *Good horse, Arolis. We will swim at your side and guide you through the region. We are most familiar with this southern area since it is the lake of our birth. We can take you as far as the Center Isle. There we will entrust your journey to the Keeper of the Swamp,* assured the now-exuberant Sniffum.

Through the night went the unlikely band of brothers. As Arolis came upon miry areas beneath him, the turtles gently assured the huge beast that the soft ground beneath him would hold. *Good Arolis, we know these bogs well. Since we were small hatchlings we have explored and traversed the vast expanse of the southern marsh. If we say you can stand, you need not hesitate to plant your feet.* With that, Arolis no longer hesitated when moving forward through the muck and mire. Soon the foursome began to encounter ever-increasing shallows with each step until the feet of Arolis were firmly planted on solid ground.

We're there! exclaimed the horse.

Not quite, brother horse, said Snuffim. *We have journeyed quite some distance, but we have only gone as far as the Center Isle. We will leave you here in the hands of the keeper.*

Crawling as speedily as turtles can, Sniffum and Snuffim made their way toward a small mound rising from the middle of the small marsh island. From the mound rose a very small wisp of smoke from the tiniest of chimneys. "Jidgel! Jidgel! Are you home?" shouted the terrapins in tandem. "Jidgel! Jidgel! Quickly this way come!"

From a small opening in the mound came a small dwarflike creature. At first, Arolis and Leonolis thought it was some sort of badger or large rodent, but as the creature cautiously peered up at the two, they could make out human-like features.

"What do you want now?" grumbled this thing named Jidgel.

"We have urgent business regarding the occasion we have been afforded this night to bring a bit of retribution upon the Dark Lord, eater of turtles!" shouted Sniffum.

"How is this possible, my silly turtle friend?" laughed the now amused creature.

"We bring Lord Prince Leonolis and his horse friend, Arolis, on urgent business for the Kingdom of Bren," said Snuffim.

Glaring up into the night, Jidgel was somewhat startled at the size of the two travelers in comparison to himself and the turtles. "What business have you in my swamp?"

"This day, the Dark Lord has taken captive one of my brothers, good dwarf," said Leonolis as humbly as possible.

"Good dwarf!" exclaimed the creature. "I am no more dwarf than you are! I am from the clan of swamp ogre. My mother was of the forest ogre and my father of the swamp. Fate has given me the body of the forest ogre, but my heart is of the swamp . . . and you do not want to discover the fierceness of a swamp ogre's wrath!"

"My good swamp ogre, please forgive my human stupidity," pleaded the prince as he jumped from the back of Arolis and bowed his knee to the ogre. He had been already trained in the art of diplomacy, having had to attend numerous royal functions from the time he was born. Proper protocol when making such a public blunder requires that the prince beg for forgiveness on bended knee—an act of royal humility, which served the royal line well to remember.

"My, my!" exclaimed the plump little swamp ogre. "You truly are of the royal line. Why, I one time encountered the great high king Troyolin on one of his forays into the outback of the realm. He made the same mistake . . . and he, too, fell to the knee in rueful sorrow."

"Psst," whispered the now giggling Snuffim. "High King Troyolin is the boy's father!"

With that news, the ogre fell to *his* knee in obvious respect of the royal line. "Troyolin, the friend of ogres," we call him in these parts. Had it not been for his royal decree, ogres would have long ago been banished from the realm . . . that is, if Lucian had gotten his way!"

"Rise, ogre friend. We have need of passage through your swamp this night if I am to preserve the life of my friend," said the prince.

"Not before you've had a short rest and a meal," said the now-not-so-gruff little ogre. "I have plenty of marsh figs, fresh catfish, and flour from the marsh reeds from which I will stir up a batch of reed cakes."

Leonolis had stumbled upon a real treasure of the realm when he met Jidgel. Having served the king in his younger days when the swamp was still accessible as a passageway between the southern realms into the great forest, it had been Jidgel who had craftily come up with an ingenious way of putting an end to the practice of the raiding parties of the Dark Lord using the swamp as a shortcut to the southern regions of Bren. Using his vast knowledge of Maudlin's Marsh, Jidgel had devised a plan involving the beasts of the marsh. Jidgel's service was rendered for the most part during the reign of King Lairdon—Leonolis' grandfather, the father of Troyolin.

Once a week, the beavers were directed to divert the water's flow creating dry (yet still boggy) land where there had been none before. He also devised a plan using the small in stature but mighty in number turtle army to nip at the feet of the raider's horses causing mass confusion. Utilizing the skies, the keeper had constant reconnaissance from the bird population, always receiving news of impending invasions long before the raiding party ever set one foot in the swamp. The birds also came up with their own clever idea of amassing their numbers in the thousands and following the raiders wherever they turned, constantly bombarding them with their acrid droppings. Out of sheer frustration, the Dark Lord had abandoned the use of the swamp even before the peat moss fields were abandoned. Jidgel had been considered a hero, but as time has a way of causing the mind to forget, Jidgel's heroism had fallen into that place of forgetfulness in the kingdom, partly because many still feared the ogre race and partly because Jidgel had a way of deflecting praise to those around him. For the past twenty-five years, he had contented himself to watching over the swamp and crafting the finest (if not smallest) canoes in the kingdom in his spare time.

"We don't wish to inconvenience you," said the prince. "And we really must be on our way."

"I insist. You will eat and then I will lead you out," declared Jidgel.

By this time, Arolis sent a thought to the prince saying, *Perhaps it would be wise to take just a few moments to gather our strength, sire. We are certainly many miles ahead of the search party by now.* Secretly, Arolis was hoping his young master would give up this very hasty put-together trek . . . or at the least, that the search party would catch up to them and help Leonolis go about a more well-thought-out plan of action.

Twenty minutes then, said the prince as he dismounted his marsh-weary friend.

In a short time, Jidgel had prepared what seemed a feast for himself and the prince while Arolis enjoyed a nice meal of tender, well-watered swamp grass. The turtles, having already partaken of quite a feast of tadpoles and tender reed shoots earlier in the evening, merely enjoyed hearing the conversation between the keeper and the prince.

"Young prince, why are you alone in your quest? Where is your guardian? Why are you so insistent upon going through the swamp?" asked Jidgel.

Leonolis quickly ran through the events of the day, even honestly admitting that his father had confined him to the royal safe haven in the depths of Castle Aerie, concluding his story with, "Even as we sit here, my father and ten thousand of Bren's finest cavalrymen are on their way to try and intercept the Dark Lord. But earlier in the day, I received a communication from my friend's captors telling me I must come to the Sleeping Giant or my friend's life was in peril. What else was I to do?"

"What else were you to do? Perhaps that question would have been best asked of your father," replied the little ogre. "You have barely done enough living to be qualified to make such weighty decisions on behalf of the kingdom. Perhaps a good night's rest would be the wiser step in seeking your friend's safe return."

"The buzzard told me if I did not come to the Sleeping Giant that he could not guarantee that Dreyden's life would be spared. I must go! There is no other way, good Jidgel!" declared the prince. "Your wisdom is duly noted, Keeper, but I will continue the journey with or without your continued help."

"Sire, I must agree with the keeper. The greater wisdom would be to wait and consult with your father . . . or at least to wait for the help of those who seek your safe return. As your friend, I must not allow you to take another step until daylight has come," said Arolis.

In the rashness of his youth, Leonolis stood up from his unfinished meal and promptly slogged right into the swamp. "Come, Sniffum and Snuffim. You will lead me on to the northern boundaries of the marsh."

"Sire, as we told you. We are not familiar with those regions. We would be of no help in your quest. We are afraid we must also insist that you go no further," said Sniffum.

Now anger, combined with his grieving heart, caused a great determination to rise up in the prince. Blinded with his need to get to his friend, he disappeared into the darkness. Leonolis had no trouble finding his bearings. Maison had filled his young mind with a vast knowledge of navigation by teaching him the ways of the stars. North was where he headed. But after only a few minutes, the prince became ensnared in a bog. Had it not been for a small patch of mature reeds within arm's reach, the boy would have surely met his demise before he was able to complete his self-designed mission. His pride kept him from calling out for help while his grasp of the reeds kept him from sinking further.

Something about being a boy—or perhaps something about the feeling of being utterly alone and unable to get oneself out of a perilous predicament—soon caused the prince to swallow his pride. "Arolis! Jidgel! Can you hear me?" Leonolis called into the night air. "Help me! I have become mired in the bog . . . and I need you! Help!"

Before he had even finished his languishing plea for help, a tiny dugout canoe with a tiny little torch blazed into the darkness as if from nowhere. It was Jidgel, and slogging along in his wake was Arolis. "What you lack in wisdom you certainly make up for in heart, my prince," said the ogre. "I will guide you through. Better to be scolded for aiding your escape than for leading the search party to find your drowned body."

Arolis gently and nimbly bit into the upturned collar of the prince's shirt, lifting him easily from his miry confinement. Climbing onto the horse's back, Leonolis simply said, "Thank you," to his rescuers. Jidgel then led them with great agility through the northern reaches of the swamp and by morning had brought them safely to the edge of the Great Forest.

"My friend, Jidgel. My friend, Arolis. I humbly beg your forgiveness for the impetuous attitude I demonstrated last night. Had it not been for your sacrificial service to me in spite of my somewhat passionate point of view, I would certainly not have survived. I cannot repay you at this moment, but I will honor your sacrifice one day. And know this: I will take utter and full responsibility for my actions, completely absolving you both of any wrongdoing. You simply obeyed my commands."

And with that, the boy and his horse bid the little ogre goodbye as they ran headlong into the darkness of the Great Forest.

Chapter Six

THE MATTER OF DREYDEN

F rom the time it was discovered that Leonolis had gone missing and the messengers of the king had been dispatched to bring the news to him, a full hour had elapsed. By the time the trumpeter had cleared the way through ten thousand speeding cavalrymen, evening had begun to fall on the massive military procession. Reaching the front of the equine convoy, the royal messenger finally reached the flanks of the king's personal bodyguards.

Signaling for the troops to halt their forward motion took another ten minutes of valuable time. Finally coming to a complete stop, the king dismounted and rushed to the messenger's side before he could step down from his own mount. "What is it, Lord Stirling? What news do you bring that warrants such a standstill of our mission?" asked the king.

"Sire, I bring news of dire urgency from your loyal servant, the good Danwyn, who says, 'My king, Prince Leonolis has managed to escape and is headed north to the Dark Lands from the mouth of Crystal Cave in search of Lord Dreyden.' Danwyn and his men are in pursuit."

At the moment the news reached his mind, King Troyolin's heart began to race, he became lightheaded, and he stumbled backward slightly, causing one of the royal bodyguards to reach out to steady the king. "Your Majesty! We will take the route east from Eagle Falls and intercept the prince before he can attain the Great Forest," said Corellian. "I can assign Commander Destrin to continue in search of Lord Dreyden"

Before Corellian could get the commands out of his mouth, he was interrupted by King Troyolin. "No, Commander. Our mission is to retrieve Lord Dreyden. Danwyn will find Leonolis. Our mission is clear: the Dark Lord must be stopped. Whether it be Dreyden or Leonolis or *any* son of Bren, our cause is just. By the Founder's mercy, Leonolis will be tended to. Dreyden's life and the peace of Bren are at stake. Again, I say, our mission is clear. We continue."

As quickly as the troop's forward motion had ceased, the military march was set back in motion. Corellian knew the heart of the king was set and there was no point in arguing. They quickly passed the serene majesty of Eagle Falls and soon had the foothills of the Canyons of Callay within their sights as the last vestiges of daylight faded into a dark and foreboding Brenolinian night. As darkness fell, the command for a brief rest and feeding for the horses and their men was sounded. While the men tended to their horses, Troyolin assembled his regimental leaders for a briefing on the recent turn of events.

"Sire," said Corellian, "Our trackers have detected the trail of the Dark Lord's raiding party. They have taken a turn for the Sleeping Giant. If they gain passage through the canyons it will be nearly impossible to catch them. Our best chance for cutting them off from entering into the Dark Lands is to continue on our present course and attempt to beat them to the Dark Lands by going around the canyon land and lying in wait for them, placing regiments at each of the possible points of entry into the Dark Lands."

"Then make it so, Lord Corellian. As soon as the horses have taken their foodstuff and the men their victuals, we will again ride north at full pace until we have cut off the Dark Lord's forces from entering Endoria," commanded the king. And they were off. Even though the night had fallen around them, the main trade route across the land paralleled Runland for a great distance, finally veering into a northeast tact cutting diagonally through the Great Forest and rimming the northern boundaries of the Canyons of Callay. They would journey through the night in order to make the canyon area by daybreak.

Around midnight they entered into the even deeper darkness of the Great Forest, not realizing they were already ahead of the pace of Leonolis and Arolis. The fugitive prince and horse were headed due north while the cavalry had already made its way through the central reaches of the wooded lands. Arolis, being trained in the arts of stealth and warfare alongside Leonolis, had encouraged Leonolis to allow him to not take the main routes through the forest, knowing full well that what they lost in time would be made up by the difficulty their pursuers would find in trailing them.

As the pair prepared to cross the trade road, they had no way of knowing that only a few minutes prior to their arrival at this point the last of the royal regiments had passed by. Bolting across the road, Leonolis began to cough. "Why is all this dust in the air tonight, Arolis?" asked the choking prince.

Using his keen sense of smell, Arolis quickly recognized the scent of legions of men and horses having just passed this way. "Sire. Thousands of horses and their men have this way passed. The smell of war is in the air," declared the stallion.

"My father has already rallied the cavalry! They are surely fixing their arrows on the Dark Lord!" exclaimed the prince.

"Then we follow them, sire?" asked the horse.

"No. We must get to Dreyden before they do. Once the Dark Lord hears the sound of those mighty hooves of Bren, I am afraid he will waste no time in dispatching Dreyden. The buzzard made it very clear. I am to come alone! Arolis, we must go at once!" And into the night the two charged once again, their strength renewed with a new urgency.

Indeed, the Dark Lord had received news of the approaching forces of Bren but had already put his evil scheme into action. It was not Dreyden he was truly after. All along he had planned to use Dreyden to get to the prince, knowing that any hope of catching the prince without the cover of his Royal Guards would have been next to impossible. He had been plotting Dreyden's capture for weeks and had surmised that the greatest surprise and chance for his plan to succeed would begin with snatching the boy right from the midst of the mighty men of Bren in broad daylight. And the plan had worked perfectly. For several weeks he and his men had waited patiently for the right moment, and on that morning they had not expected Leonolis to make a mad dash for the castle . . . and had certainly not expected Dreyden to ride right into their midst! His plans were all working—all too well.

Soon the king's forces were within five miles of the Canyons of Callay and the trail that led to the Sleeping Giant. As they rounded the bend of the road known as Oaken Fork (named for the hundred-year-old oak tree that stood in the crotch of the forking road, one cutting back to the northwest and the other cutting toward the northeast), the king signaled his royal trumpeter and his royal signal man (an expert who signals commands by night using patterns he draws in the night sky by a torch held in each hand and by day with a series of patterns by flags) to give the signal for immediate halt. "Sound the 'halt'" was also shouted from the front of each regiment and passed back down the line behind by verbal shouts making for quite an impressive display of how an army works together as one unit.

"What is it, sire?" shouted Corellian to the king.

"Someone or something is tied there to the tree in Oaken Fork," shouted Troyolin above all the shouts of the "halt" going back down the line and over the sound of thousands of horses snorting their displeasure at being so suddenly stopped in the forward charge.

"Shine a light, Soldier," commanded the king to one of the torchbearers.

Even these mighty men of Bren were taken aback at what they saw. There, stripped of his clothing and bloodied from head to foot, was the mangled body of the boy, Dreyden. Tied with his arms pulled around the tree in a grotesque hug, the boy had been whipped and beaten beyond recognition. The king leapt from the back of his mount and rushed to the boy's body. Carefully yet firmly the king reached for the boy's slumped head and placed his hand on his neck, feeling for a pulse. Nothing. Leaning in with his ear to the boy's nose, he listened for the slightest hint of breath. Nothing.

The king slumped to the ground, falling to his knees in tears. "This was meant for my son! This could have been Leonolis!" moaned the king. "Why little Dreyden? Why the son of the good man, Heath?" The first few rows of cavalrymen as well as the officers surrounding the king were quite taken aback at the king's sudden outpouring of sorrow and passion. Sensing the gravity of what this meant, each man within earshot dismounted and fell to their knees as an unspoken means of identifying with their sovereign's sorrow. One by one, row by row, the reverent whispered news of what had just been discovered made its way all the way back to the very last row of men in the very last regiment. Each knew that soon enough their time of avenging the evil deed would be rendered without mercy.

"Send for the physician's wagon," Corellian directed one of his men. "Let it be known that special care be taken of the boy's remains. Clean him. Clothe him. Prepare him as much as possible to lessen the blow to his parents. They need not see him as he now appears."

Several men gently held the bloodied body while another cut the ropes that had bound him to the oak. Wrapping him in a sheet, they gently lay his body respectfully into the physician's wagon that had been brought to transport those wounded in battle. As the physician began to gently wipe the blood from the boy's face, a faint murmur came from the boy's throat. The murmur grew into a gasp for air and then into a series of throat-clearing coughs. Dreyden was alive!

"By the Founder's mercy, the boy lives!" shouted the physician. "Sire! He lives!"

"Quickly! Bind the boy's wounds!" commanded the king as he bounded into the back of the wagon. "Dreyden! Dreyden! You are going to be fine!"

Slowly opening his eyes, the boy ever-so-gently and oh-so-slowly turned his head from side to side. "You came for me . . . so many came for me . . ." and he drifted in and out of consciousness for the next few minutes. It seemed that the presence of so many familiar faces somehow breathed new life into the badly wounded boy. Able to take a drink of water, and then another, the boy began to speak.

"Where is Leonolis?" asked the boy.

"Don't worry about the prince right now, Son," answered the king. "He will be fine."

"Where is Leonolis?" insisted Dreyden in a whispered yet determined tone.

"Dreyden. Leonolis will be fine. You need to preserve your strength. Your body is in need of rest. We will get you back to Castle Aerie and commence with your healing, Son," said the king firmly.

"Where is Dreyden? They have lured him into a trap . . ." said the boy as he once again lost consciousness.

The king then lifted Dreyden's head gently and began to wipe his fevered face with a cool, wet cloth the physician placed in his hand. The boy began to revive. "Dreyden . . . what kind of trap? Where?" asked the king.

The boy somehow managed to open his eyes and, though weak and in great pain from the ordeal he had just gone through, began to recount the day's events.

"My lord, after Leonolis and Arolis took off for the castle, I in my shame, ran to the trees to avoid facing the ridicule of the other boys. Merrywell dutifully followed me . . . and before we knew what had happened, the Dark Lord and his men had surrounded us. They sorely wanted to know where Leonolis had gone so quickly. They began to beat Lord Merrywell, demanding that he disclose the whereabouts of the Secret Place. Of course, Merrywell knew nothing . . ."

At this point, Dreyden's eyes began to fill with tears. By the quiver in his voice, it was obvious the boy had witnessed something terrible. "They began to . . . they beat him . . . they made small cuts into his flesh . . . they burned him with hot irons . . . they pierced him again and again and again . . ." And the boy became so choked up he could not continue for a few moments.

"We know, Son," said the king solemnly. "We found his body. You need say no more."

But the boy once again summoned the strength to continue. "They bore down upon him like demons . . . like monsters . . . but sire, he would not say a word. He just kept saying, 'May the strength of Bren be mine today. May the strength of Bren be mine today.' They finally became so frustrated with what they called his 'foolish obedience to a fool of a king.' But he was not foolish, sire. He was so loyal and so brave . . . and they just filled his body with arrows."

"We know, Son. We know. But what about a trap? Tell us about the trap," said the king.

"They took me with them to the Sleeping Giant. It was there that I overheard them talking about how to get Leonolis to come to them. All I know is that they sent some sort of messenger named Beezlebird to deliver a message they were sure would stir the heart of the prince to come to them. At that point, they began to perform some of the same terrible deeds upon me as they had done to poor Merrywell. They kept asking me about the habits of my friend, Leonolis. They had heard he knew of a secret passage through the Canyons of Callay . . . and kept trying to beat the knowledge of that secret out of me . . . but I knew nothing. About to endure the same fate as my Second, good Merrywell, I determined I would die as he had—faithfully loyal to Bren and to my king . . . and to my friend, Leonolis."

"The trap, Dreyden. What about the trap?" pressed the king.

"They soon began talking about what to do with me, sire. Said that I was not the one they were after . . . that I would be more useful in slowing the forces of the king. They delivered me into the hands of two flying creatures. More bat than human, yet speaking as a human would speak, they flew through the night to the place you now stand, sire, and tied me to this tree, knowing you would soon pass this way and stop to render aid. They lie in wait at the Sleeping Giant. The last thing I remember before waking up here was that the Dark Lord was laughing saying, 'He's coming. The fool is coming right to us' and then I heard your voice and awoke, sire."

At that moment, Troyolin knew what had happened. Lucian had perfectly manipulated the loyalty Leonolis felt toward his friend, Dreyden. Sending this Beezlebird, whoever that was, to deliver a message of Dreyden's dire need, of course Leonolis had escaped and headed to his friend straightway, without a moment's hesitation. Secretly, Troyolin felt a swelling of pride in his heart over his son's virtuous response. He, the king, would have done the same thing!

By now, the king realized, Leonolis was in grave danger. They must act now. "Physician, take the boy back to Castle Aerie. Summon his parents. Make them a place in the royal residence. They are my personal guests until the boy fully recovers. Corellian, dispatch a division to pursue Lucian from the southern approach to Callay. I will take another division and head to the north. Commander Destrin, disperse regiments along every route in and out of Endoria. We must become the wind and fly!" pronounced the king.

The trumpets began to sound, the torches signaled as the shouts to mount and ride simultaneously readied the troops to their mission. Echoes of "May the strength of Bren be mine today!" could be heard for miles as the king and his army headed into the darkness.

Chapter Seven

THROUGH THE GREAT FOREST

A rolis and Leonolis had no way of knowing what had just taken place at Oaken Fork. Still riding through the dark of night, their only concern was for the rescue of Dreyden. While Arolis still had reservations about the sanity of their current adventure, he could not deny the loyalty and devotion he sensed from the heart of his young charge. This passion alone was enough to drive the mighty horse through the blackness. Before they knew it, they had ridden long enough to see the sun begin to rise. As the darkness they had charged through all night long gave way to the first rays of light, hope began to rise in the hearts of the two travelers. Unfolding before them was a most magnificent display of grandeur. Standing as if a great army of giants, the great pines stood to attention as far as eyes could see. Rising and falling with the many slopes that form the forest floor, the great horde of trees appeared to be in constant motion. Sensing there was more to this tree motion than merely a Brenolinian wind, Leonolis brought Arolis to a stop.

"Arolis. Do you see what I am seeing?" asked the now tense prince.

"Yes, sire. I have been observing a strange movement among the treetops . . . and it is not the wind as I had first assumed. Someone is there. Many someones," said Arolis.

"Who goes there?" shouted the prince, who by now had begun growing in his princely confidence since the encounter with Jidgel at Maudlin's Marsh.

"Sire! Should you be so bold?" said the horse in a hushed yet apprehensive tone.

"Arolis, we do not have the luxury of taking the time to practice proper diplomacy. My friend's life lies in the balance!" the prince stated firmly. "Again I say, 'Who goes there?'"

What happened next can only be described as surreal and otherworldly. For a few brief seconds, it appeared to the duo that the trees themselves were melting. Beginning near the mid-trunk sections of at least two hundred trees surrounding the pair, the trees began to melt all the way to the top. Not quite believing their eyes, Arolis and Leonolis began backing away from the trees directly in front of them and simultaneously began plotting through thought-speak their getaway strategy, only to find that the entire forest seemed to be melting away. It took a few seconds for them to realize that the tress had not actually melted. What had seemed as "melting" was in point of fact a host of "tree people" who had inexplicably been able to make themselves appear to become part of the trees themselves!

Even adjusting their eyes to the actuality that people were now standing before them, the pair felt as if they were seeing a mirage or some type of optical illusion. Everywhere they turned, the faces and hands and legs (any exposed skin area) seemed to change color—to blend in with the surroundings—to the point one felt they were seeing a floating image of sorts as their eyes had to constantly readjust to make out the ever-changing skin tones of these strange people!

A tall, greenish-skinned man slowly approached the twosome and spoke in a strong yet warbly voice, "Who are you and why do you dare to cross our land? We are peaceful people who seek to harm no one. You surely bring trouble. We sense it in your demeanor, even from our lofty perch. Why do you disrupt our peace? You have no business here."

"I am Prince Leonolis and this is my horse, Arolis," began the boy. "We mean you no harm. The trouble you sense is most certainly my concern for my good friend, Dreyden, who only yesterday was taken captive by the Dark Lord of the northern lands, Lucian."

The entire oddly colored group seemed to gasp at once. "You have brought the scourge of the Dark Lord to our fair lands?" snorted the leader.

"No! No! No! I simply pursue him!" shot back the boy. "My only reason for crossing your lands, and I had no idea you were even here, was to save time in my journey. My dear tree friend, I must go to my friend at once."

As if by some strange unseen signal, the tree people began to close ranks on the horse and the boy. "I am Sylvan, king of the Treesants. We have lived in these treetops for many generations," said the tree man. Going on, as if giving instruction to a would-be student, he said, "We are a race of creatures—though not fully human—who have the ability to change the color of our skin to adapt to any setting. When we are in the trees, we are green with the needles and grey with the bark. At ground level we become blue as the sky or black as a cave. In the snow we are white and in the water we are clear. We live in the treetops and prefer the higher elevations of the Great Forest. This gives us a greater vantage point, as we do not care for unnecessary contact with those who would be enemies. We also feed mainly on the sweet juicy fruit of the juji vines that grow in the treetops. So, there. All your questions have now been answered," snorted Sylvan.

"Good sir, I mean you no disrespect, but I did not ask you any questions," said the prince as humbly as possible.

"But you *were* thinking about asking those questions. You all do!" harrumphed the tree man.

"Lord Sylvan, you seem to be a good and most virtuous people. We honestly mean you no harm. We simply must be about the rescue of my friend," pled the prince.

"Your very presence here threatens our existence. How do we know he has not already followed you here? Do you not know that for centuries the dark forces have sought out our kind for all manner of so-called scientific experimentation? Our ability to blend in with any surrounding has been both a blessing and a curse. For certain, their dark interests in our abilities are for nothing but evil purposes. Imagine if the Dark Lord could conceal himself as we do," said Sylvan.

"Lord Sylvan, surely you must realize that I represent the good of the realm. I am Leonolis, son of the high king, Troyolin. He is a good king and I bear his honor this day. The good people of Bren desire your safe and unhindered existence within the entire realm. I beg you, kind sir. I only desire to be on my way to my friend's aid," implored the boy.

As Leonolis and Arolis awaited Sylvan's response, the tree throng crowded in ever more closely until there was absolutely no room for, or ability to, escape. Suddenly, Leonolis felt something strange, like a rope, begin to enclose his wrists, bringing them together and binding them to the horn of his saddle. Looking down, the boy realized the "rope" he felt tightening around his wrists was no rope at all. A vine proceeding, as if by magic, from the hand of Sylvan had bound him to his horse. Simultaneously, the feet of Arolis were bound on all four sides with hobbles from the vines of the tree men surrounding them.

Commanding the Treesants, Sylvan said, "To the treetops. We will end any further intrusions into our peace by making an example of these who would dare bring discord into our very midst. To the trees with them. We will drop them from the precipice of Hangman's Rock onto the jagged edges below. All who pass will see and fear entering our lands!"

"Wait! Wait! It's never too late! Never too late to make things straight!" came a fluty voice from somewhere above.

"Who dares interrupt the proceedings of a Treesant gathering?" shouted Sylvan into the morning air.

"It is I, Lord Sylvan! Friend Ollieman," shouted back the voice.

"Ollieman, you have no business sticking your beak into our business!" trumpeted the leader of the Treesants.

Landing authoritatively upon the overhanging branch of a nearby tree, a large greying old barn owl took center stage. "I have every intention of making it my business," Ollieman replied. "I know you know me as a simple friend of the Great Forest, but what you need to know (and I had hoped to avoid divulging) is that I am working as a sort of regional watchman for High King Troyolin."

"You what?" snapped Sylvan.

"It is true. Though born in these very trees, I, along with the entire owl clan, have been employed by his Royal Highness for the purpose of being the eyes and ears of the kingdom. We owls watch over these lands for any sign of the Dark Lord's intrusion. This very night we observed a band of the Dark Lord's horsemen patrolling the outer edges of the Great Forest, eventually making their way to the Canyons of Callay," replied Ollieman. "We have nothing but the highest regard for King

Troyolin and his care for all citizens of the kingdom, be they man, beast, or Treesant. And furthermore, all the boy says is true. Because I know the honor of his father, I trust his honor and that of his beast as well. I urge you, friend, to release them to be about their responsibility."

Again, as if by some unseen signal, the Treesants all began to converse with their leader in an unknown tree language. After a few tense moments, Sylvan began to speak. "Friend Ollieman, you have kept this from us all of these years. Why should we trust you now? My people feel you have violated their trust of not only you, but of all owldom!"

"My dear Sylvan, put yourself in my place. If it had been you the king had asked to guard over me, would it have been in my best interest that everyone know . . . or would prudence tell you that sometimes protection is better carried out when the children are left within their boundaries to play?" the owl stated wisely. Continuing (and thinking it wise to appeal to Sylvan's Treesant pride), Ollieman avowed, "This day, should you release the boy, I will implore—nay—I will *demand* that good King Troyolin immediately instate you, good Sylvan, king of the Treesants, as watcher over the high realms of the Great Forest lands. We owls would be most honored to serve under your wise gaze. And as an added bonus, the owl clan, though not fanciers of your treasured juji fruit, would be glad to divulge the location of several as yet undiscovered treetop fields of your delicacy should you elect to do the right thing."

Again, the Treesants began talking one to another, obviously asking Sylvan all that had taken place. After a few minutes of back and forth tree dialogue, Sylvan once again addressed Ollieman. "Wise Ollieman, you are indeed wise to seek out our aid in watching over the Great Forest lands in service to the realm. We despise and loathe the dark workings of Lucian and his evil ilk. We have lost enough of our own to his darkness, that is to be sure. Of course we Treesants have great care and concern for all that takes place within our lofty domain, and, dare I say, for all the good people and creatures of the entire land of Bren. We will grant safe passage between here and the Canyons of Callay, accompanying the boy and the horse as far as the Sleeping Giant. All we ask is that we be given advance notice should any further business be conducted in our realms." And with that, the Treesants began to melt their way up into the recesses of the treetops. From somewhere high above, Sylvan shouted down to the boy and his horse, "We will lead you! Follow my people and we will take you by a less treacherous way than the course you are currently taking!"

"Arolis, fly!" shouted the boy to his steed. And they were off, finding it quite easy to follow the flow of the melting treetops as these hardy Treesants leapt with great speed, agility, and deftness through the treetops, almost as fluidly as a mighty river coursing its way between its banks.

"This day! This day! A friend to save! This day! This day! We're on our way!" hooted Ollieman.

"How can I repay you, my feathery friend?" shouted Leonolis up to his newfound friend as he glided through the trees just above the head of Arolis.

"No need, my young lord! I simply do what was once done for me!" shouted Ollieman.

"What do you mean?" answered the prince.

"I was once a captive of the young lord Lucian before he became one with the darkness. Captive from the time I was a nestling and teased and treated as no bird should be treated. It was your father who stood up to Lucian and demanded I be set free, and it was your father who personally returned me to these very woods long before you were even a twinkle in his eye! We have often spoken in the years since concerning how best the owls can serve the kingdom and vice versa!" shouted the owl. Having no response but even greater respect for his father, the boy simply fixed his eyes on the treetops and rode as one with Arolis toward the Sleeping Giant, pondering the sudden realization that he and his father shared one the of the same gifts given from the Founder.

Meanwhile, King Troyolin had dispatched his many regiments to cut off the Dark Lord, keeping to the northern reaches of the Great Forest, taking the well-traveled roads of the lower areas. It was the lower regions of which the Treesants rarely ventured. Their much-documented love of the juji fruit, which grew only at the highest levels of the trees from the upper regions of the Great Forest, kept the Treesants an unseen race, only a rumor. At the same time, Leonolis and the Treesant waves moved through the higher elevations unbeknownst to King Troyolin, though only a few miles apart.

As the king and his troops rounded the next bend, they caught a glimpse of a boy on a large black stallion. "Your Highness, Leonolis and Arolis!" shouted one of the cavalrymen.

"I see!" shouted the king. "To the chase!" And they were off in hot pursuit of the boy. Troyolin knew catching up to the speedy Arolis would be no small feat. Arolis had been bred for not only strength and speed but for endurance as well. Mile after mile the chase went on. It seemed that with every flying reach of the stallion's hooves the gap only widened between the pair and their pursuers. Even though all involved had been running all night long, there was a difference between a lone horse running away and a legion of horses trained to keep pace with one another. The lone horse will always win the day.

Finally in frustration at his own son's flight away from him, the king ordered the main cavalry to slow their pace and ordered the two fastest horses to the front of the charge. Within thirty minutes, the gap had been closed enough for the soldiers to call out for the boy to halt. Realizing there was now no escape, the boy brought his horse to a stop. As the soldiers kept a confused eye on the pair, the king and his troops finally made their way to where the pair had been stopped.

Dismounting and running to his son's side, the boy had turned his head away in shame, looking down at the opposite ground. Something wasn't right. "Leonolis, this is not Arolis! What have you done with your horse?" the king demanded to know.

Turning his head to face the king, the blond-headed boy was someone other than Leonolis. "Who are you? Where is Leonolis? What is going on here?" the confused and horrified king demanded to know.

"It is I, Belimond, of the northern town of Brestling."

"What are you doing here in these woods?" asked the king.

"I was approached by one of your own men last night and instructed to engage you in the royal military games you would be conducting this day. Did I succeed, sire? Did I do well?" the boy asked sincerely.

"There are no military games . . . and I told none of my men to employ your service on my behalf. What did this soldier look like?" asked the king.

"He looked like a man of Bren . . . a beard and the uniform of a Bren cavalryman . . . the only thing that seemed odd—but I know what it was even though I've only heard it a couple of times in my life—was that he spoke in the dialect of one who dwells in the Mountains of Endoria," replied the boy.

By this time it had become painfully clear to the king, to Corellian, and indeed to all those within earshot of the Leonolis double. This had been part of an elaborate trick to pull the king's men away from the actual location of the prince. In fact, the terrible truth would be known soon enough. The ploy had been executed with such stealth that by the time the doppelgangers were discovered, several hours had passed, and it was becoming more apparent that wherever Leonolis and Arolis were right now, that was not a good place to be.

Chapter Eight

WHAT HAPPENED AT THE SLEEPING GIANT

B y midmorning the real Leonolis and the real Arolis, accompanied by the Treesants and Ollieman, arrived at the outer boundaries of the Canyons of Callay. These canyons extended ever downward from the northern edge of the Great Forest and for another twenty miles further north until the deep chasms once again rose to the beginning edges of the Dark Forest of Endoria. These canyons, comprised of hundreds of walled chasms, were carved thousands of years before and, through time and weathering, had become a very intricate series of twists and turns, tunnels and hidden nooks—a maze of sorts. Only the most experienced guides could make it through without becoming lost for days. Even though there was a road that ran north and south and a road that ran east and west (the two intersected in the center of the canyon system), they were frequently washed out by the latest rainfall. The only thing that made one's whereabouts distinguishable if one strayed from a main route was the large hill formation in the northeast sector of the canyons called the Sleeping Giant. But the rise was only visible from the canyon rim. And the form of the Sleeping Giant was only distinguishable as a sleeping man from the southwest rim or the northeast rim of the canyon.

Leonolis knew he could not use the main roads. From his many times of playing hide-and-seek with the other boys, he would be able to chart a path through the maze. "Leonolis, it is here I must leave you, my friend," hooted Ollieman, breaking the long silence of their journey through the morning (they could not afford for their conversation to give away their whereabouts).

"Goodbye, new friend. I hope we meet again," said the prince.

"I'm sure we will," said the owl as he floated back into the forest canopy.

"Good Sylvan and good friend Treesants, thank you for your silent guidance through the forest. I also hope we meet again as well," shouted the prince upward toward the well-hidden tree people.

"We will be ever-watchful. And we call you 'friend' as well. Any enemy of the Dark Lord is a friend of ours!" shouted a voice from somewhere in the treetops. "May the Founder be with you!" said the voice, now recognizable as that of Sylvan. And with that, the treetops began melting away into the deepness of the forest, and Arolis and Leonolis were once again alone in their quest to rescue Dreyden.

Heading down into the canyon from the southern rim, Leonolis spoke to Arolis saying, "Do you remember the way, Arolis?"

"Of course I do, sire. Why don't you try to get some rest. I will awaken you when we are near the Sleeping Giant."

No sooner had the horse offered respite than the young man was soon sound asleep atop the horse. Since they had practically grown up together, they had become quite accustomed to moments such as this. Arolis was so familiar with the many nuances of Leonolis' bodily habits he had grown quite adept at shifting his own weight as needed if he felt the sleeping prince was slouching out of balance. With a slight hop from his right haunch, Arolis could gently lift the weary boy back into a balanced position. This was actually quite an amazing feat and quite uncommon in the annals of horse and rider-dom!

Soon Arolis was making his way off of the main northern route and began heading through one of the many gorges that comprised the system of canyons. The walls were now rising hundreds of feet on all sides, many appearing to be like silent statues of ancient sentries set to guard over this territory. Though the area was often besieged by flash floods from sudden downpours, the area was generally devoid of water. Once again, only the most well-traveled explorers of the canyons knew precisely where the hidden springs of cool fresh water lay waiting to quench a weary traveler's thirst. It was at one of these innermost hidden fountains that Arolis decided to wake the prince. By the time they made it to the spring they had traveled for several miles and had taken a couple of hours to do so.

Nudging the prince's leg with his nose, Arolis said, "Leonolis. Sire. It is time to drink and stretch your legs."

With a yawn and a long stretch, the prince wakened. "Humph . . . what? Oh . . . Where are we, friend?"

"We have come to the inner spring. We are only an hour's ride from the Sleeping Giant. I thought you should take some time to refresh yourself. Take the reed cakes from my saddlebag and take eat, sire. You need to be as strong and alert as possible, for we know not what truly awaits us," the horse wisely admonished.

"Of course. You are right, Arolis," said the prince as he clumsily dismounted. Taking the reed cakes, wrapped in oilskins by good old Jidgel, Leonolis found a place to sit right next to the spring and began to eat voraciously. After a few moments, he looked up to see that Arolis was not eating.

"Arolis. You are not eating?" asked the boy, sincerely concerned.

"Sire. There is no grass here . . . and in our haste to leave Crystal Cave we forgot to pack any victuals. Do not worry, though. I had my fill on the small meadow surrounding Jidgel's little burrow. I also took an occasional bite from the tall grass in the several small glens we came through in the Great Forest. I am fine. Besides, should we need to make a hasty departure from the Sleeping Giant it would be better for me to not have a full belly," said the sensible steed. At that, Leonolis went back to his meal. After taking their fill of the cool, clear spring water, the two once again were back on their journey.

After about an hour they came into the area of the Sleeping Giant. Arolis stopped about five hundred yards from the main pathway up to the top of the giant's belly (the giant slept on his back!). "Leonolis, if I sense even the slightest hint of trouble I will make no hesitation in carrying you to safety," declared the horse.

"Arolis, you are a good friend. I had no doubt that this would be your heart in a moment such as this. I expected nothing less," affirmed the prince.

Just as they began the final few steps toward the pathway to begin their upward trek, Arolis noticed a small, dark figure gliding down as if floating from above.

"Prince Leonolis," whispered the buzzard Beezlebird. "Follow me."

"I thought we were to meet at the Sleeping Giant," said the prince in a hushed tone.

"We are. We are . . . but I can take you to where Dreyden is held captive. Perhaps, by stealth, you may engineer a nimble escape, undetected by the dark forces," countered the bird. "Lucian waits in the giant's neck hoping to conceal himself from your vision, but the one you seek is being held in the old grotto near the giant's feet. Turn around and I will take you there. But we must hurry because I do not know how much longer the Dark Lord will tarry before he tires of waiting for you. If we are to save the boy's life we must go at once."

Their senses heightened and muscles tensed as the sudden urgency and fear for Dreyden's life caused the two would-be rescuers to follow Beezlebird.

"Leonolis, I do not trust the bird," said the horse. "How do we know he is not leading us right into a trap?"

"Horse! Why would I mislead you? I have risked my very life to bring about the boy's safety. We buzzards are widely despised yet we continue to serve the kingdom in great faithfulness. If nothing else, we are loyal to the throne. We must go now," insisted the bird.

"Arolis, what else can we do? At this point I have risked the wrath and the much-deserved harshness of my father by disobeying his direct orders to stay hidden in Castle Aerie. Is Dreyden's life not worth such risk? We must go with him," implored the prince.

The tension of the next few minutes grew so heavy one could almost feel it in the air. Dripping now with sweat and glancing apprehensively around every corner, the unlikely trio came to a stop. Just a few feet ahead was the entrance to the grotto. The cave seemed to be dark, yet as they ever-so-cautiously drew near they could see a dim glow coming from deep within the back of the little cave.

Alighting on Arolis' neck, Beezlebird whispered to the pair, "Let me go in. I can fly to the entrance and walk in silently. I will come back and let you know where the guards are stationed and exactly where the boy is being held." And before either Leonolis or Arolis could respond, the bird was gliding low to the ground, making a soundless landing just before the cave entrance. It seemed like an eternity before the buzzard returned.

Flapping excitedly and speaking loudly in a flurry of words, the bird said, "He is alone! They have left him alone! There are no guards! The boy has been hurt and is in need of your assistance. We must do this at once! Come, horse! Come, boy! To the cave! I will keep watch while you enter and will sound the alarm should anyone approach."

Caught up in the bird's hurried excitement and filled with adrenaline-infused passion, the horse and the boy launched into action. Galloping straight into the cave, Arolis stopped long enough for Leonolis to dismount and rush to the side of his friend. Slumped over and leaning against the cave wall next to a small fire was the boy. As Leonolis lifted the boy's head he called out, "Dreyden! I'm here! Dreyden! It's me! Arolis and I have come to take you home!"

Suddenly, Leonolis fell back in horror, narrowly missing the fire, as he realized this was not his friend at all. "Who are you? Where is my friend? What have you done with him?" shouted the prince, now suddenly numb with shock.

"Leonolis, we must go at once!" whinnied Arolis. "Now, boy! On my back!" Staggering in distress to the side of his horse, Leonolis somehow managed to climb atop. Racing toward the exit and making it safely outside, Arolis and the boy barreled down the path they had followed away from the grotto. As they rounded the last curve in the trail, Arolis suddenly pulled up and began to rear back and up onto his haunches, narrowly avoiding throwing the prince onto the ground. There, directly in front and blocking their escape was the dark lord, Lucian, himself, accompanied by at least twenty armed men. Spinning around wildly to head back the way they had come, Arolis once again planted his feet and reared high into the air. Facing them from the direction of the cave were more of the Dark Forces barring their escape. There was nowhere to run—and their hearts sank.

Arolis and Leonolis were seized by the malevolent mob. Leonolis was snatched from his mount and Arolis was immobilized as they placed hobbles on his hind feet. He could no longer utilize his speed nor the power of a well-placed kick to gain their freedom.

"Well, well, well. Look what we have here," sneered Lucian. "The most favored son of the king, Prince Leonolis"

"Where is Dreyden!" shouted the prince. "What have you done with him?"

"Hush, boy!" screamed the Dark Lord. The sheer hatred with which the Dark One responded would have been enough to make even the most wicked woodland ogres shiver in their lairs. "You will speak when given permission to speak."

Feeling a quiver coming to his lip and trying to squelch a tear from coming to his eye, the boy turned his head away in terror.

"Look at me, boy! How dare you look away from me! Look at me!" yelled the crazed Lucian.

Slapping the boy's face, Leonolis began to cry as he screamed back, "My father will find me, and he will deal with you as he should have long ago!" At that moment, good Arolis could stand no more. Lunging at the Dark Lord, he was suddenly pulled to the ground as the rabble pulled tightly on the hobbles, causing the horse to cry out in great pain. The next thing Leonolis saw was his horse being whipped mercilessly into submission as the boy was dragged moaning back to the cave.

Throwing him against the wall, the boy was bound with his hands above his head, hanging just far enough above the cave floor to keep his feet from touching the ground. Laughing so hard it seemed he would lose his breath, Lucian began to ponder the best way to make a public spectacle of the boy's death, the better to humiliate the king with. "Shall we hang him upside down from the mast of a ship, pierce his body with a thousand arrows, then send the vessel down the Runland to Castle Aerie? Not only would the city folk have the good fortune of seeing my handiwork, but also a great deal of the country folk would benefit from the display as well. Or shall I cut off a different body part each day for the next week and send that body part by special messenger to the king?" mused Lucian, now crazed with obvious hatred for the king.

Every once in a while during his diatribe, Lucian would give a slight, malicious pinch to the boy's midsection, eliciting a most pitiful cry from the poor boy each time. "My, my, my! What a prize I have given myself this day! The son of the king, here in our very midst! The son of a *so-called* king," said the Dark Lord mockingly. "I told him this day would come! Did he believe me? No! In his arrogance he did not believe!" Pausing as if a small child about to open a much longed-for gift, he became as giddy as a young lad of Bren at his promotion into the ranks of men. And he went on. "I've got it! We will draw and quarter the boy and send a piece of him to the four corners of this fair land! I'll keep his head on display from the highest turret of Castle Aerie once I have taken my place on the throne! What a day! What a day! By the Founder, what a day!"

The boy could take no more. "By the Founder! What do you know of the Founder?" Leonolis shouted at Lucian.

Drawing back to slap the insolent boy into submission, the Dark Lord stopped in midstroke, as if abruptly deciding to conduct himself with great diplomacy and constraint. Scoffing at the boy, he said, "Oh please, my prince, do go on."

Opening the eyes he had closed in expectation of the Dark Lord's fist, and slowly relaxing his tensed body, the boy confidently said, "The throne cannot be occupied by one who does not honor the Founder. By your own anger and cruelty this day you have demonstrated a lack of a king's heart."

"A king's heart, you say? Do go on!" laughed the Dark One.

"You will see. You may desire the throne and all its privilege, but you lack the heart to rule with the benevolence the Founder intended. And besides, only those through whose bodies flow with the blood of royalty can rule this great kingdom," the boy stated matter-of-factly.

"Royal blood, you say? Royal blood through the veins? Hmmm. So your father has not told you?" asked Lucian.

"Told me what?" asked the prince.

"That I am the son of his uncle, the good prince Regalion. I am your father's cousin . . . and that makes you my cousin . . . and that means royal blood flows through my veins—the same blood that flows through yours," scoffed Lucian.

"You are no cousin of mine!" declared the boy.

"Of course he didn't tell you. I was not born of his wife, but of a maiden of Endoria with whom he had a brief tryst. Of course the royal family did everything they could to keep me hidden, even to the point of making me believe I had been orphaned and graciously taken in and raised by the royal family. They thought they had fooled everyone in the kingdom. They thought they had fooled me! But talk has a way of getting around and eventually it got around to me. When I discovered who my father was I realized I was next in line for the throne, but when I came to make my claim, some little long-forgotten rule (or suddenly and secretly concocted rule is the truer statement) declared that the heir must be born of the royal marriage, effectively denying me my rightful place over the kingdom simply because my mother was not married to my father," said Lucian. "Your own father banished me on the day my father died. He had already claimed the throne since my father, being the elder brother, had born no *so-called* legal heir. You were but an infant when this took place. Of course they would keep it from you. Why fill your head with the truth?"

As his aides prepared the knives for cutting the boy apart, Lucian suddenly had a change of heart. "I have suffered longer than you have even lived," the Dark One vehemently said to the boy. "I think I shall take my time with your death . . . and perhaps give your father a longer period in which to suffer his grief at your captivity. Knowing you are alive and with me will make for much better torment and agony on his part. Cut him down. Tie him to his horse. We ride for the Dark Lands at once!"

Before Leonolis could fathom the depth of the meaning of Lucian's plan for him, he had been placed back upon Arolis and tied to the saddle. Arolis had been whipped, his body covered with foam and sweat and dust and dirt from his anguished writhing when he fell. Now free of the hobbles but closely guarded on all sides, Arolis and Leonolis began the silent march through the Canyons of Callay northward toward the Forest of Endoria and the Dark Lands beyond.

Arolis, are you all right? thought-whispered the boy without any facial expression whatsoever.

Yes. I am fine. A few cuts and scrapes, but I am none the worse for it, said the horse.

We must take any opportunity to escape should an opportunity present itself. They plan to kill me! said the boy.

Are you able to hold on should the moment of flight present itself? asked Arolis.

Yes. My hands are bound but I am holding fast to the saddle horn. I will be right there with you. Think, friend. Think. There must be some way to distract this gang, said Leonolis.

Perhaps distraction and a little confusion might do the trick, said Arolis.

What do you mean? asked the boy with a hint of hope in his thought.

Remember how Jidgel told us how the birds were once used to thwart the raids of the Dark Lord through the marsh? If we could summon a few birds, and they were able to amass a small flock of mercenaries, we might be able to cause a moment of confusion that would allow us to make our escape, said the horse.

From that point on and for the next couple of hours, the human and the horse called out silently to every bird that passed within thought range. Crows, sparrows, finches, and even an eagle agreed to help, promising to go for more of their feathery brethren as time would allow. While the avian force was amassing, Leonolis was able to get word to a nearby eagle to have the flock begin their assault when they reached the northern leg of the crossroads that intersected in the very center of the canyons. By the time the band of kidnappers and their bounty reached the intersection, several thousand would-be bombers were assembled, waiting in the cliffs and crags surrounding the junction.

Just as the group of horsemen began to make the northward turn, Leonolis thought-shouted, *Now, my feathered friends! Now! Bombs away!*

Without warning, the skies were suddenly filled with a dark cloud of every manner of winged creature. Bats, starlings, owls, and herons lifted into the sky. Larks, cardinals, crows, and ravens stirred the air. Jays, eagles, hawks, and kites soared into battle as the skies grew dim. Filling the air with every imaginable tweet, chirp, scream, and hoot, a deafening cacophony frightened the Dark Lord's horses (as well as his horsemen!), sending the entire troop into a stirring mishmash of confusion. Lucian's attempts at calming his forces were drowned out by the roar of a combination of bird wings and birdcalls, the likes of which had never been heard before! As the droppings began to pummel the horrified dark forces, a great cloud of dust began to rise from the ground, stirred by the panicked dance of the frightened mass.

In the ensuing chaos, Arolis made his move. *Hold on, master! We fly!* With those words, Arolis bolted from the midst of the panicked throng and headed through the most obvious opening, heading north onto the main route. Running as Leonolis had never seen him run before, the horse flew like the wind.

Once the birds were satisfied that Arolis and Leonolis were far enough ahead, they ceased from their raucous onslaught. By the time it was discovered that their captives were gone, there was little evidence that could point them in the proper direction. Every track had been sufficiently covered with bird droppings! Arolis and Leonolis were no longer on the main route, having ducked into the secret passage through the canyons Leonolis had discovered during the games of hide-and-seek.

As they continued their hasty departure, a voice suddenly called from above, "My friends! My friends! I your lives defend. It's me! It's me! It's me, my friend. It's me! It's Ollieman!"

"Ollieman! Dear Ollieman!" cried the boy. "Can you help us? Can you guide us once again? We will make it out of the canyons, but not to a land I am much familiar with. Will you help us once we reach the Dark Forest?"

"Of course, my lord! Of Course!" the owl called out.

Without wasting one second, the reunited trio forged ahead toward the darkness of the Forest of Endoria.

Chapter Nine

THROUGH THE FOREST OF ENDORIA

J ust as the three travelers entered the shadows of the Dark Forest, a group of fast-moving horsemen could be heard approaching from the west. Sparing no time, the three instinctively dashed into a gulley. Surrounded by trees the gulley was made even more secure by the fact that there was much overgrowth of brush that helped to conceal their hidey-hole. If only they would have dared to peer out to see whom exactly it was passing by they would have had a very pleasant surprise. Thinking it was the forces of Lucian, they did not risk being seen, so they had not seen one of the regiments dispatched by King Troyolin, passing by in hot pursuit of a black horse and a blond-headed youth. Each regiment had been duped just as King Troyolin himself had been duped. The ensuing confusion left the king's troops in scattered disarray from the banks of the Runland all the way to the eastern reaches of the kingdom.

Soon after it had become apparent to the king just how massively far-reaching the great deception was that had been used to throw him off of his son's trail, he called for a royal messenger to get to the nearest watchtower to sound the alarm throughout the kingdom for the reassembly of the troops. The regathering of forces would take place at the northern route out of the Canyons of Callay—the very place near which Leonolis and his fellow fugitives were now in hiding. By the time the troops would gather, the threesome would be long gone, vanished into the darkness of Endoria.

Once the trio felt it was safe to emerge from their hiding place, they realized it was not safe to go back the way they had come. They also determined that the Dark Lord would never suspect they would cut through the Dark Forest, heading toward the Dark City. At least this would buy them some time before their pursuers were able to find their trail. The plan would be to cut northward for several miles then head back due west to the Runland. Then, they would make their way to one of the watchtowers to at least let Troyolin know they were safe.

Intuitively, the three remained as quiet as possible as they made their way into the forest. Although the trees did shield a great deal of the sun's light from reaching the forest floor, Leonolis was quite amazed at the beauty of his surroundings. Daring only to speak in thought, he mused, *Are we sure this is the Dark Forest? I thought it would be more much more menacing than this.*

Oh, my lord, do not underestimate the beauty of the dark lands. Treachery comes in many shapes and sizes and is often quite beautiful. Do not be deceived. There are things lurking in this land that would terrify the bravest of brave should they ever be encountered, some of them exquisitely beautiful. By the Founder, let us hope we pass through undetected, thought-hooted Ollieman.

I agree, my prince. I sense great evil in this ominous land. We best be on our way, chimed in Arolis.

Once again, they quietly made their way onward. Still, Leonolis was amazed at the amount of color in the flora that carpeted the forest floor. Deep red lilies scattered around the decaying trunks of massive trees. Splendid orange-yellow primroses rimmed the lips of crevices lining the many ravines. Luxuriant greens even more intense than the emeralds adorning the crown jewels of the kingdom seemed to be everywhere he set his eyes. The moss covering the trees and rocks was like the jade his mother collected for the royal museum. Though dark, the land held a different kind of beauty and was quite peaceful to the young boy. The lack of wind only added to the utter quiet, the only sound coming from the flutter of owl wings and the clip clop of horse hooves. As they journeyed on to the north, the earth began to slope gently upward. Arolis and Ollieman were ever vigilant in their forward surveillance of the land.

Around each outcropping of rock, Ollieman would fly to check for would-be attackers. Arolis' keen sense of sight and smell were on high alert as they passed through rocky ravines and the occasional cave opening they came across. The air was beautiful but the atmosphere was tense. Though the horse and the owl had the immediate surroundings under intense scrutiny, it was Leonolis who saw the movement first.

Arolis! Ollieman! thought-shouted the boy. *Did you see that?*

See what? asked the animals simultaneously.

Something is floating there high above us. It has been keeping pace with us for several minutes, said the boy.

Spying a cave, the horse and the boy darted inside so as to elude whatever evil this floating thing was. The owl flew high into the trees to investigate. Dismounting, the boy crept as near to the cave entrance as he dared, to try and catch a glimpse of what the thing might be. After several minutes of anxious waiting, Leonolis stepped out of the cave, followed by the curious horse. Just as they stepped into the greenish light of the forest, they heard a girlish voice exclaim, "There you are!"

As they looked upward to where the voice had come from, all they saw was a large red-tailed hawk floating down toward them. As the creature majestically extended her wings to glide in for a landing, the hawk began to transform into a beautiful red-haired maiden covered in a wispy, flowing white gown. Leonolis had never seen anything quite like this! One moment a hawk was there and the next the hawk had become a most stunning red-haired girl, her arms appearing to fall from above her where her wings had once been.

"Greetings, weary travelers. Do not fear. I am Galennia, maiden of the Hawken, watchers of the Dark Forest, preservers of all that is good," began the hawk girl. "I have watched you for some time now," she hesitated for a moment. "I have watched you and I have perceived that you are good. In you, boy, also have I sensed a royal quality. You are of the royal line, yet you are full of fear. Who do you fear? From whom do you run?"

Still in awe at what his still unbelieving eyes had just witnessed, the boy blurted out, "You're a hawk! But you're a girl! How . . . what . . . I . . ."

"Peace, my royal friend. What you have seen is true and real. Yes, I appear to you as human in this moment but my true essence is Hawken. To the horse I appear as a horse, and to the owl I appear as an owl," said Galennia.

And it was true. While Leonolis had perceived Galennia to transform into a girl, Arolis saw a beautiful red-coated filly appear, while Ollieman gazed upon a red-tinted owl maiden.

"How is this possible?" asked the puzzled trio all at once.

"It is our way. Given as a gift from the Founder in days of old, we are the peacemakers. Our way of life, bestowed upon us by the Founder, is to bring peace where there is darkness. Much evil in these lands do lurk, but we find our purpose in lending peace where chaos does abound. Our Hawken nature allows us freedom to move about the Dark Lands while our ability to be seen in the likeness of those we seek to bring peace to only enhances our ability to administer said peace," said the humbly spoken maiden. "While we are not always successful in bringing about peace in every situation (you see, we cannot make those in turmoil or conflict choose to accept peace), our very presence tends to help maintain a general sense of tranquility, even in this dark land. The dwellers of this land know us and respect our purpose . . . for the most part."

In that moment, Leonolis was startled out of his stupor by a flitting light that shot through the forest then zipped by him fast as lightning, grazing his right ear and vanishing into the cave. At that very moment, Galennia began to laugh uncontrollably.

"What was that?" said the startled boy. "And what's so funny?"

"Rania! Rania! You're frightening our friends!" laughed Galennia. "Reveal yourself, my silly friend."

Darting back and forth across the front of the cave's darkened entrance, the light went back and forth in amazing patterns that gave the impression of a hawk changing into a girl. Whatever this thing was, it seemed to be mocking Galennia.

"Rania, you impudent fairy! Stop at once!" shouted the Hawken, still giggling to herself.

Just at that moment, the tiny girl froze in midair, hanging from a vine that draped down from the cave ceiling, revealing a brown-haired, blue-eyed girl in a flowing white gown similar to that of Galennia. Her wings were shaped much as a butterfly's, yet almost clear, like a pane of opaque glass, milky white, allowing light to pass through. This tiny person could have been no more than six inches tall. Around her waist were several tiny bags (they seemed to be made of the most miniature burlap the boy had ever seen).

Laughing to herself, the little fairy flitted toward Leonolis. Coming close to his astounded face, mouth agape in wonder, the little creature reached into one of her bags, blew the contents into the boy's face, and then sped back to her perch upon the vine. Before the boy had even had time to gain his composure, his amazement gave way to terror as he slowly began to rise from the ground! He finally stopped rising about ten feet into the air, levitating there with a look of "someone please do something" upon his face!

"What are you doing, Rania?" shouted Galennia. "Bring him down at once!"

Instantly, the fairy rose to the boy's level, pulled out the most miniscule of magic wands, and gently touched it to the frightened boy's nose. Slowly and steadily the boy floated gently back to earth. As he touched the ground, he began to laugh uncontrollably saying, "Do it again, fairy! Do it again!"

Just as the fairy reached back into her little bag of fairy dust, Galennia held up her hand to the fairy saying, "Enough, dear Rania. Our friends here are in great fear. We must help them find their peace."

Hovering near the shoulder of the Hawken maiden, the little fairy began to speak. In the tiniest, yet amazingly clear, voice, the pixie said, "I am Rania, princess of the Forest of Endoria. I serve the great king of the fairies, Kelsin, lord of the underworld of the Dark Forest. We serve and protect all the creatures who live beneath the earth. We make our home within the burrows and subterranean passageways. It is our duty to bring jocularity and laughter to these dark places."

Rania was as humorous and amusing as Galennia was serious and wise, yet they both seemed to bring out the best in one another. Rania helped Galennia find the comical in noncomical situations, while Galennia had the ability to help rein in Rania's sometimes out-of-control antics.

"What are your names, dear friends?" asked the Hawken girl.

"I am Leonolis, prince of Bren, son of Troyolin. This is my faithful steed, Arolis, and this fine owl is my good friend, Ollieman," said the prince.

"Leonolis? We have just this day received word through the gossip of the forest creatures that you were in trouble—that you had been taken captive by the Dark Lord himself."

"Yes, we had been taken captive, but through the efforts of my avian friends we were able to escape from his grip and evade him through secret passageway through the Canyons of Callay. We are now headed back toward the river Runland so we might get word to my father that we are well and safe," replied the boy. After taking the time to tell Galennia and the fairy all the events of the past two days, the Hawken girl pondered the news for a few moments before responding.

"It all makes sense, the recent activities we have observed here in these parts. We have seen the comings and goings of the Dark Lord and his forces of late. We always assume he is up to no good . . . but because he seems to mean no harm to the inhabitants of our dark land we allow him safe passage. We can really do no more than divert his attention should we sense danger. His magic is much greater than ours. Should we sense his dark forces in our midst, we will create a diversion and hopefully send him on a wild goose chase. This should give you time to make good your continued escape," said Galennia.

As the boy leapt onto the back of his horse, Galennia continued. "As you follow this trail to the top of this rise, you will begin to hear the faint murmur of a small stream. Follow that stream all the way to the bottom of the pass. This will lead you to one of the roads used by trappers and hunters. From there you must follow its northward progression until you come to the Dancing Meadow—a large, secluded opening in the forest where the local denizens meet for their moonlight festivals and dance the night away in graceful abandon on the first night of every full moon. From the Dancing Meadow you must turn due west and remain in that heading until you arrive at the river Runland."

"Dear Galennia and dear little Rania, thank you for your assistance," said the boy. "I will remember your kindness. This day you have honored the throne. Your friendship is truly a treasure of the realm."

As Galennia transformed herself back into her true hawk shape, she called to the threesome as she flew into the trees, "Beware the swine rats!" And as she rose out of sight, the little fairy Rania flitted away into the distance going the opposite direction, eventually vanishing into thin air.

"Beware the swine rats? What did she mean by that?" queried the horse.

"Oh, that can't be good," countered Ollieman.

"I guess we'll know them when we see them," said the boy.

As the boy and his associates made their way to the top of the rise, sure enough, they began to hear the babblings of a small brook that flowed down from some unseen height. As they followed the stream down, Arolis thought it a good idea to walk in the stream so as to hide any trace of their tracks. Once they made it to the bottom of the pass, they found themselves on the old hunter's road. Following this northward, they soon came to a vast open field, enclosed by trees on all sides, which could only be Dancing Meadow. It was here they decided to take a break and take advantage of the sunlight to warm their skin and refresh their spirits.

"My lord, may I suggest you take time to eat something from the victuals remaining from our time with good Jidgel? I will also take my fill of this wonderful feast of grass," suggested Arolis. As the boy fetched the remaining reed cakes and fish from the bag, Ollieman flew in circles above the meadow keeping watch as the two friends regained their strength.

Wandering off lazily through the meadow, Arolis lost himself in the feast that was before him. He had not eaten much since the escape from the Dark Lord. At the same time, Leonolis gorged himself on the remaining foodstuffs. Finishing off the last of his meal, he fell back into the grass and dozed off quickly into a peaceful slumber. Ollieman continued his watchful circling around the meadow. All were thinking at the same time what an adventure this had been. Just as the boy began to dream of jumping from the cliffs near Castle Aerie with his good friend Dreyden, he was startled into consciousness by the loud whinnying of Arolis.

Jumping to his feet just in time to hear Arolis scream, "On my back! Now, boy!" Leonolis' dream suddenly became a nightmare. Bounding toward the boy and the horse was a herd of the strangest creatures Leonolis had ever seen.

"What are they!" shouted the boy as he mounted the horse.

"I would assume that perhaps these are the swine rats good Galennia warned us about!" surmised the horse.

Running wildly across the field to the north, the horse and the boy by this time had gained the attention of Ollieman who flew down to join them and to shout encouragement and direction as they tried to elude the beasts. Looking back, Leonolis saw them. Standing about four feet tall at the shoulders, these hunchbacked animals were covered in coarse, grey hair. Their ears resembled those of a rat while their elongated faces tapered down into a snarling mouth full of razor-sharp teeth. The snout was as long as a rat's would be but ended in a pig-like snout. Galloping nearly as fast as Arolis, these crazed creatures ran on front feet that were clawed as a rat's would be, but they were propelled powerfully from cloven hind feet that were those of a pig. Their tails were long and wiry, like a rat's, and their screaming squeals were an evil sounding mixture of rat squeak and pig squeal. There were five wild swine rats, crazed with hunger, closing in on the horse and the boy.

"To the road!" hooted Ollieman.

Without questioning their feathery friend, the horse and the boy made their way to the smoothed road where they began to put some distance between themselves and the demented beasts. Following the road, they left the openness of the meadow and found themselves suddenly with but one way to run. Although their instructions were to go east from the Dancing Meadow, their current circumstances called for a detour to the north. Looking back, the boy could see that the animals were still in hot pursuit.

"Arolis! Where did they come from?" shouted the boy.

"I don't know! I was grazing near the edge of the trees when I began to hear those squeaks and grunts. You know as much as I do, sire! Perhaps they were drawn to the smells emanating from your fish and reed cakes!" whinnied the horse.

This gave the boy an idea. Reaching back into his saddlebag, he took out one of the empty bags that had once held his provisions. Tossing the bag to the ground, he turned and urged the horse on. After a few moments he looked back to see the pigs had suddenly stopped to rummage through the small bag. "It worked, Arolis! It worked!" shouted the boy.

"What worked, my lord?" asked Arolis.

"I threw my lunch pouch onto the road and they have stopped to have a sniff! They've stopped chasing us!" replied the boy gleefully as they pulled to a stop. As the horse turned around to investigate for himself, Ollieman flew down from somewhere above in a flurry.

"Stopped, they have not! Stopped, they have not! Off with you, horsey, before you are caught," sang the owl in his most frenzied hoot.

Sure enough, the swine rats were once again bearing down upon the duo. As they ran over the next rise in the road, Arolis veered hard to the rapidly soaring owl as he blazed a new trail through the forest. "Where are you taking us?!" shouted the now frantic horse.

"I am taking us nowhere! It is the Fairy, Rania! She leads me as I lead you!" shouted the owl.

There in front of the owl was a tiny light blazing through the dark forest air, leaving a slight trail of sparkling residue that quickly vanished after a few seconds. Following this trail of fairy dust, the owl led the horse and the boy up and over an embankment and then down into a gulley that was not a gulley at all. The fairy had led them to a huge opening beneath a giant oak. Running inside the enclosure, the horse, the boy, and the owl stilled themselves as much as possible while Rania flitted like lightning back out into the forest. In a few moments, the air was filled with the squeals and grunts of the hungry swine rats. Just below their hiding place, the trio glanced through the maze of exposed roots behind which they now found themselves just in time to see Rania come to a hovering stance just out of the reach of the sweaty, foaming-at-the-mouth creatures. Floating down into their midst came Galennia, who suddenly transformed herself into the appearance of a swine rat. Rania had gotten their attention, and Galennia was now leading them away from the hidden escapees!

Flitting back into the hiding place through the roots of the mighty oak, Rania spoke to the boy. "We cannot guarantee they will not find your scent again, but we can buy you a few minutes of time. Do not go back from whence you came. These beasts are merely the scouting party for the entire herd. There are surely more whom you would encounter should you go back," said the articulate little fairy.

"Where shall we go, then?" asked the boy.

"From this tree, follow the ravine upward until you come to the ridge. Follow the ridge. It follows the road, but do not take the road until you have passed by the city of Treacherin," said Rania matter-of-factly as she abruptly flitted away.

"Shouldn't we take our chances and head back the way we came?!" asked the boy.

"No. She is the keeper of these woods and knows its denizens and their habits well. We will fare better by heeding her advice," declared the owl, and once again, they were taken further into the dark world of Endoria. At this point, Leonolis felt a slight tinge of despair come over his heart. Sensing the boy's loss of hope, the good horse Arolis comforted his friend.

"My boy, Leonolis. I know you must be discouraged and disheartened at the turn of events our journey has become. But we cannot afford to lose heart. What would your father say in a moment such as this? He would find a better way of looking at our circumstances than we can now see with our physical eyes. Envision this, my prince. Somehow we made it through the swamp. Somehow we made it through the canyons to the Sleeping Giant. Somehow we managed to escape from the Dark Lord's strong grip. Somehow we eluded the dark forces. Somehow we managed to evade those snarling swine rats. What I am trying to say is this: perhaps you have been ordained for this very special task? Perhaps the Founder Himself has assigned this mission to you? Could it be that someone has been watching out for you? It appears to me that every time it seems hope has been lost, a way of escape has come forth. I know what your father would say—" said the horse in all sincerity.

"I know. I know," interrupted the boy. "He would say, 'Son. There are no roadblocks to those who see opportunity.' And he would say, 'Why waste our time in sorrow when life is waiting to be lived.' And I know that he would be right . . . but right now, my good Arolis, I fear not only that has Dreyden met a most unsavory fate, but we find ourselves in the midst of the Dark Lands—a place my own father forbade me from venturing into under any circumstance. Now I understand all too well why he warned me so firmly and forcefully. This is an enchanted land, and we know not what lurks here around us now. And as Ollieman has already said, even the beauty is deceptive. I find myself trusting no one, and mostly not trusting myself or my abilities. I mean, look at where I've gotten us," declared the boy in dismay.

The horse retorted, "We do not have time for sorrow, Son. There is too much life waiting to be lived. And might I add that if you will but open your royal eyes you will see that what lies within you is the ability to see not a roadblock, but an opportunity here. I suggest we not worry about the 'what ifs,' sire, but rather about how to go about the king's business of rescuing your friend, Dreyden. To do otherwise is to give in to the darkness that creeps all around us even now."

As they headed up the ridge, Arolis almost would have believed his own words had it not been for the eyes he sensed watching them from many hidden nooks and crannies.

Chapter Ten

THE JOURNEY TO TREACHERIN

From the top of the ridge, the boy, the horse, and the owl began to make their way further north. Even though this was taking them further away from their planned escape route, they knew this was their only course of action until they were out of the range of those lovely swine rats. Almost immediately they were all laden with a sense of foreboding—like someone was watching them—and it wasn't the good kind of watching over they had felt from Galennia and Rania . . . or even Jidgel for that matter. This was more sinister.

Making their way onward, they began to catch glimpses of the road to Treacherin just as Galennia had told them. Following the road the travelers tried to remain out of sight as much as possible. Every so often they saw the occasional tradesman guiding his horse and wagon full of goods headed for some market. When they heard someone on the road, they simply ducked down behind the western side of the ridge they traversed and were able to continue their journey unseen. Ollieman kept a moving vigil above, which proved to be a most helpful tool in their desire to remain undetected.

As evening began to fall, the threesome began to grow weary and hungry and thirsty. Even though they had taken time to eat and rest back at the meadow, their hurried flight from the ravaging teeth of the swine rats had taken quite a physical toll on them.

"My lord," said Arolis, "I believe we need to find a place to rest for the night. And more importantly, I must have water . . . and if possible, find something to eat."

"I know, Arolis," said the boy. "Perhaps if we head down to the bottom of the ridge we will find a suitable place to camp for the night.

Ollieman, would you mind flying down ahead of us to see if such a place might be near?"

"Not at all, sire. I will call for you should I find a fitting place for the night," said the owl in a voice that expressed his own gratitude at the possibility of being able to cease his endless flight.

After a few moments the owl began to hoot softly, "This way! This way! I've found a place our heads to lay."

Following the voice downward, the horse and the boy eventually came to a small stream. Next to that stream was a secluded grotto of sorts. While not actually a cave, they would be sheltered from the elements should it begin to rain. The shelter was actually a large outcropping of rock that hung over the stream slightly, providing a roof and a place they could all lie down in peace.

"Arolis, why don't you find yourself a grassy place for a meal. I will gather some dried wood for a fire. I'm sure these woods will be getting quite cold this night," suggested the boy.

"Sire, I will find myself a few mice in these woods. May I suggest that you will find a tree full of sweet apples just a few feet downstream. You will find them quite filling I am sure," said the owl.

Taking their time to quench their thirst in the clear little stream, the three then set out in separate directions after Leonolis dutifully unsaddled Arolis. Ollieman headed further upstream in his quest for mice while Arolis found a small clearing just across the stream and a few hundred feet from the campsite where there was plenty of grass to feed his hunger. Meanwhile, Leonolis walked downstream and quickly found the apple tree. Eating two of the bright red fruits without taking many breaths between his bites, the boy's sense of dread began to ease. After he had finished off the last bite, he began to fill his pockets with the fruit. Using his shirt to cradle as a basket for the excess fruit, he made his way back to camp. Laying his sweet treasure in an indention in a rock underneath the overhang, Leonolis went back out to begin gathering wood.

Walking along the streambed he quickly found enough driftwood to make a fire. After several trips, he had collected what he thought should be enough for the night. Since the grotto was not fully enclosed, he surmised it would be safe (and warmer) to build the fire in the center of the "floor" underneath the hanging rock. Placing the kindling first, he methodically laid the wood for his fire in such a way as to ensure a good draft of air and an easy start. Taking his trusty flint fr. "Don't take another step or I will have my horse trample you without avail! He is well trained in just such maneuvers."

"Whoa! Hold it right there, my dear brave man-child!" said the voice. "I mean you no harm!"

"Approach slowly with your hands where we—*I*, can see them," said the boy, realizing that the man must not know of his ability to speak with his animal friends.

Walking slowly into the dim light still emanating from the campfire's embers, an older man, unshaven and unkempt, very grizzled in appearance, came into view.

"My name is Moonrysin," said the man. "Who are you?"

Thought-speaking to the boy, Arolis warned, *Do not give too much information, sire. There is something I do not trust about this one.*

I agree! I agree! Do not trust the enemy! chimed in Ollieman.

Moving further into the light, the scruffy man held both hands stretched above his head in an act of submission. Armed with a small sword at his side and a bow and a quiver full of arrows, the man's apparel was that of a hunter or trapper. Wearing garments made of deerskin, the man had many skins, obviously collected from his snares, tied in a bundle and hanging from his back. He also carried a small provision bag made of rough leather slung over one shoulder.

"So you can talk to the creatures, can you?" he asked the startled boy.

"W-w-what do you mean? T-t-talk to the animals? Who c-c-can do that?" stuttered Leonolis, giving away any hope of concealing his gift.

"It's all right, boy. Your secret is safe with me. I'm nothing but a poor trapper. It's no business of mine. This forest is full of all kinds of magical enchantments. No surprise here," said Moonrysin.

"How could you tell?" asked the now puzzled boy.

"It wasn't so much that you gave anything away in your mannerisms, boy. It's just that the beasts themselves seemed to be hanging on your every word . . . like they could understand you," continued the man. "And by the way, I mean you and your friends no harm. Just noticed your fire and wondered who could be stopping here, seeing as this spot was empty when I passed through only six or seven hours ago. Thought you might be someone I know. Doesn't matter. Any friend of the animals is a friend of mine."

And with that, Moonrysin proceeded to loose the bundle of freshly harvested skins from his back. Setting them aside, he then took his sword and handed it, along with his bow and arrows, to the boy, saying, "I trust you, son. And you can trust me. Let me warm myself here by your fire for a bit and then I'll be back on my way. You keep my weapons until I'm ready to go . . . just a gesture of my good will toward you and your friends." And he sat down.

Bewildered at the man's casual manner and at the way he so readily handed over his arms, the boy didn't know whether to command him to leave or ask him for advice on how to find their way back to the river Runland. He decided the latter would be the more prudent and mannerly course of action.

"Sir Moonrysin, are you alone this night or are there others with you?" the boy asked.

"Snaring animals—no offense to your horse and your owl—is one of those occupations that is better suited to us loners. I do not have much use for people—no offense, young man. The element of surprise and the level of profit are both better served when alone. I prefer being by myself. But to answer your question, I am alone. There is no one with me," said Moonrysin.

"Arolis, my stallion, and Ollieman the owl will be watching just in case. Just earlier this past day we have escaped the grasp of the Dark Lord and do not intend on allowing ourselves to become ensnared in that grasp again. So, please forgive us if we seem less than hospitable," said the boy, impressing his equine and avian friends.

"For a young man you certainly speak with a lot of wisdom. Where did you learn to be so bold?" queried the grizzled man.

"That is not important right now. What is important is that my friends and I find our way back to the river Runland and to the nearest watchtower that we might send word to the king that we are fine . . . and to alert him as to the whereabouts of said Dark Lord," stated Leonolis firmly. In his weariness and his sudden startled awakening, the boy had found no use for being any less than matter-of-factly honest with the man.

"I see. I see. Well, you'll get no trouble from me. Any time the dark forces are in the land the entire animal kingdom seems to go into hiding. It took me twice as long to get these few measly pelts as normal. Now it makes sense. The dark forces must be wandering about these parts up to no good, no doubt," responded Moonrysin.

Feeling somewhat less threatened than when Moonrysin had first appeared, Leonolis decided to ask for help. "Kind Moonrysin. I must get to the southern kingdom as soon as possible. Will you help us get to the Runland?"

"If you can wait until tomorrow evening I will be glad to lend my aid. If I do not get these pelts, even as few as they are, to the market in Queensland by morning, I'll have a hard time convincing Mrs. Moonrysin that I really have been working," quipped Moonrysin.

"We cannot possibly wait until tomorrow afternoon. Can you not simply tell us how to get out of this dark place?" asked the boy.

"If you're in such a hurry, there is a way out, but it requires you to go through Treacherin . . . or at least round about the city's perimeter. The Runland actually makes its way right through the city. If you can continue to follow the road toward Treacherin, you will come to a slim gorge with high, tapered walls, wide enough for but two horses walking abreast, called the narrows. This pass will lead you directly to the river. Should you not take the narrows, your only other choice is to go into Treacherin itself, and that would not be a safe place for even a boy of your obvious abilities. They call it the City of Thieves for good reason," warned Moonrysin.

"Then to the narrows we will go," said Leonolis.

After an hour of rest and talk of his escapades in the trapping trade of the Dark Lands, Moonrysin tied the bundle of skins to himself, strapped on his sword and bow and arrows, and vanished into the darkness, headed downstream for the pelt market at Queensland.

The three friends did not get much sleep the rest of the night, opting to go ahead and make their way to the narrows. Following closely along the crown of the ridge that ran alongside the main road, the trio became quite adept at dodging any passersby they encountered along the way, which wasn't too many since they were traveling before dawn. As the first tinges of sunlight began to make their way from the east through the dense forest covering, Leonolis and his friends began to see a much rockier landscape. Still covered with dense forest, the land itself took on a rougher characteristic. This was the beginning region of the foothills of the Mountains of Endoria. Soon, the ridge on which they had counted on for concealment began to draw very near to the road, so much so that after another mile, the ridge gave way to a sliver of a road.

Rising on both sides were tall outcroppings of granite that rose like giant needles through the forest as if they were competing with the trees for domination. Every few hundred yards the granite needles would open up into narrow canyons, one of these surely being the narrows.

"What should we do, Arolis? We cannot just set out down one of these trails lest we come to a dead end," said Leonolis.

"I have an idea," offered Ollieman. "Let me fly ahead and see what I can see. Perhaps the narrows will be more apparent from my vantage point." And with that the good owl was gone.

Moving ever so cautiously ahead, they had no choice but to continue on the road toward Treacherin. Luckily (or perhaps by virtue of some unseen Fairy guardian) they met no one else. Making their way to the top of a rise in the road and going around a craggy curve, their eyes began to wince as they came out into the glaring sunlight of a new day. There below them, perhaps a mile away in the little valley, lay the trading city of Treacherin, complete with Runland dividing the little village neatly in two. As their eyes adjusted, they continued. Halfway down the hill they met Ollieman who was just returning from his scouting excursion.

"I have located the narrows, and I am afraid there is more bad news," hooted the owl.

"What is it, good Ollieman?" asked the boy.

"I am afraid that the narrows is more narrow than not. Once I found the entrance, I thought it wise to fly into the gorge to make sure it indeed did lead discreetly to Runland. What I found was a small band of workers methodically toiling to remove tons of fallen boulders that had blocked the passage. There is no way through. And another thing: the workers kept cursing at those it seems intentionally caused the rockslide . . .

some creatures they called the Chiroptera," said the owl with a hint of dread in his voice.

"Chiroptera? What are these Chiroptera?" asked Arolis.

"I am not really sure, but my sense is that from the conversations of these workers, the Chiroptera are not a race we should like to meet," said the owl.

"So what do we do now, friends?" asked Leonolis, once again, downtrodden.

"Sire, it is early. It seems not many in the town are astir as of yet. Rather than turn back and risk meeting the forces of Lucian, or those malevolent swine rats, may I suggest we simply and silently make our way through the city and follow the river from there? I am a good swimmer, sire. All we need is but one brief opportunity and we can be riding the crest of the current as far as the nearest watchtower," suggested Arolis.

Not expecting such a seemingly rash idea from the wise stallion, Leonolis was taken by surprise and leapt at the thought of being on their way home within the next few moments. It seemed the trio was indeed more weary than wise. In their desperation to get home, they were willing to take their chances in the City of Thieves. Alighting on the shoulder of the boy, Ollieman gave his exhausted wings a much-needed reprieve. Soon they were winding their way through the well-kept streets (much more well-kept than the moniker "City of Thieves" might indicate). It was quite difficult for the horse to mute the clip clopping of his hooves. After just a few moments of hesitant plodding, the three decided it might make less of a scene should they simply act as if they knew what they were doing.

Within just a few minutes, they began to hear the babbling of the mighty river as they drew nearer to the city center. Turning onto what appeared to be the main thoroughfare through town, they came into a large opening between the buildings—the town square—already bustling with activity as vendors and shopkeepers were busily readying their wares for sale. Walking into the center of the activity, the boy and his companions became part of the crowd. Making their way toward the bridge, their hope was to find a way (unnoticed, of course) down into the river's mighty flow. Just as they were about to step onto the bridge spanning the Runland, someone cried out to the trio.

"What will you take for your owl, sonny?" asked a boisterous, round old woman.

"He's not for sale, ma'am," Leonolis politely responded.

"Everything's for sale. It just depends on what the right price is, now don't it, sonny?" insisted the woman.

"Ma'am, I don't mean to be rude, but my owl is not for sale, and I am on an errand for my father. He will not take kindly to my lack of punctuality," said the boy in the most convincing tone.

"How do we know it's even his owl?" piped in a tall, slender weasel-voiced man. "They don't call this the City of Thieves for funsy, now do they, boy?"

Now beginning to panic, the boy tried simply tried to ignore the remarks as he simultaneously coaxed Arolis onto the bridge.

"Wait just a minute there, young man!" shouted yet another voice.

Turning slightly in the direction from which the voice came, Leonolis' heart sank as he recognized the symbol of the crescent moon on the left side of the stocky man's shirt. This symbol signified his authority as a member of the peacekeepers. This was the town constable!

What do we do? Think, Arolis! Think, Ollieman! What should we do? thought-shouted the boy frantically.

Before the horse or owl could respond, the constable had taken hold of the reins. "Come down, boy! Now!" ordered the constable. "Show me the owl's papers of identification."

"What do you mean 'papers of identification?'" asked the boy innocently.

"This owl, sacred to the inhabitants of Treacherin, is a much-revered creature. Only the houses of wizards are allowed ownership of these most hallowed of beasts. From which wizardly line do you descend?" the constable demanded to know.

Before the boy could concoct an answer, someone else shouted, "He's from no line of wizards! Look, he's not even from these parts. The markings on his sword . . . the markings on his saddle. This is no son of Treacherin! This is surely a spy sent from the southern realms, sent to keep an eye on us 'thieving' Treacherins! And a boy, no less! They send a boy to do a man's work?"

Just as the boy was about to be dragged to the ground by the now-gathered mob, a familiar voice somehow broke through the din.

"He is mine! Good constable, he is with me!" shouted Moonrysin over the noisy throng. "The boy is my nephew, sent from my brother in the southern regions of Bren to bring me this sacred owl for the Wizard of the Heights, the White Wizard of Endoria, Gothgol."

A hush fell over the crowd at the mention of the name Gothgol. Evidently he was quite revered to people of Treacherin. As Moonrysin shouldered his way through the crowd, he said in a tone loud enough for all to hear, "I have been looking for you, son! Next time I tell you to wait for me before we enter the market, I strongly suggest you obey!"

As meekly (yet secretly overjoyed) as possible, the boy said, "I am sorry, Uncle Moonrysin. I will not disobey you again. I beg you for your kind pardon, dear uncle."

Letting go of the reins, the constable grudgingly allowed Moonrysin and his "nephew" to pass across the bridge. As they made their way across, Moonrysin called back to the constable, "Good sir, thank you for securing my nephew. I will see to it that he behaves. We're off to the high places. Gothgol expects his delivery before noon. We must be off." And waving good-bye to the constable, Moonrysin instructed the trio under his breath.

"When I heard of the landslide at the hands of the Chiroptera, I knew you would need assistance. I will take you as far as the Viamorte and from there must leave you to your own ways once again," said the trapper.

As they climbed to the opposite side of the valley from where they had entered Treacherin, Leonolis could only look down upon the Runland one last time before they headed into the highlands and the treachery that would be the Viamorte.

Chapter Eleven

CAPTURED

Dreyden was taken back to Castle Aerie where he was placed under the care of the king's personal physician. He would live, and he would have many scars to show for his violent experience at the hand of Lucian's thugs. Meanwhile, on the day after Dreyden's rescue, the king had finally assembled a good half of his troops to the northern rim of the Canyons of Callay. He had also sent for his right-hand man, his friend of friends, Justinian, to join him. King Troyolin trusted Justinian like a brother, with his life.

As the troops stood at ease, Troyolin and his regimental leaders gathered to discuss the strategy for rescuing Leonolis and, in the king's mind, putting an end to the Dark Lord's maniacal scheming once and for all.

"Gather around, men. Time is of the essence. We do not know exactly what has happened but we do know that Lucian has lured my son into the wilderness of Endoria. Our scouts have determined that the dark forces did indeed encounter Leonolis," the king said gravely. Beginning to quiver with emotion, his voice took on a more transparent, fatherly tone as he continued.

"As you know, Lucian and his demon hordes have sought to destroy my son as a means of destroying me, and by so doing, he hopes to gain the throne of Bren. As fathers of sons and daughters, my chieftains, you know what you would do in such a moment. It has taken all that is within me by the Founder's strength to keep from storming wildly into Endoria and putting the sword to any man or beast that might stand in my way. As a father of sons and daughters, my lords, my duty is to serve all of Brenolin and not just my own needs. I am but a man in this moment before you. It is your wisdom and your valor that I require in this hour of testing. I submit my desire for revenge to you in the hope that all Brenolin might be spared any more sorrow at the hand of Lucian's wickedness."

"Sire, if I may," Corellian spoke humbly. "We follow *you*, sire. If you sorrow, we sorrow. If you are at war, we are at war. If one of the sons or daughters of Bren is harmed, we are all harmed by Lucian's evil."

"Corellian, you are a good man. You carry a warrior's heart within the heart of a father. I have no doubt you or any of your other mighty men of Bren would offer such a response. All I ask is that you help me rein in my anger if it no longer serves the good for all of Bren. Lucian will pay. He *will* pay, of that I have all assurance . . . but for now, let us first set our attention upon finding my son, Leonolis," said the king.

No sooner had those words come out of the king's mouth than a rider approached from the west. By the very hurried pace of the horse, all could tell news of some kind was at hand.

Sliding to a stop, the horseman dismounted in one smooth motion and was bowing the knee to King Troyolin. "Sire, I have news of Leonolis!" said the messenger.

"What is it, good man? Speak!" exclaimed the king.

"One of the scouting teams assigned to the western regions of the Forest of Endoria came upon this," declared the soldier as he held out what appeared to be tattered cloth of some kind. The king fell to his knees, unable to keep his mind from thinking the worst.

"What is this, sire?" asked Corellian.

It took Troyolin several moments to gain enough composure to answer. "It's his bag. It's one of Leonolis' bags. This is one of the bags I had designed for my son to be kept for use in the supply cache in Crystal Cave. He must have taken it when he made his escape from Castle Aerie."

Turning back to the messenger he asked, "Where was this found?"

With much sorrow the man said, "I am sorry to have to tell you, my lord, but this was found on the northern road to Treacherin. It was surrounded by the tracks of at least five or more swine rats. It was these beasts who tore the bag to tatters. But sire, there was nothing else. No evidence that the beasts had actually injured either Leonolis or Arolis. In fact, there is a bit of good news, sire. Tracks were found leading away to the north. Only one horse made the hasty retreat from the beasts on that road, sire. The scouts followed the tracks as far as a stream where it appeared they had camped for a part of the night. From there, the tracks were lost. It seems young Leonolis has been trained well, sire. It seems he does not want to be found. As I speak, the scouts are seeking to locate his tracks, heading for Treacherin as the most logical destination since that was the direction he and the great horse, Arolis, were headed."

The king thanked the messenger and sent him back to his duties, then turned back to his chieftains. "Let us pursue all avenues of escape the Dark Lord might use. Corellian, make the proper assignments and send the regiments to cover every route into Endoria. We will meet and reassemble en masse on the shores of Menden Lake. Once there, if we have not secured Leonolis, we will determine how best to mount our assault on Dark City."

As the king was about to dismiss the men, a trumpet fanfare was sounded. This was not the royal fanfare but the fanfare of the envoy of the king. Justinian had arrived. Embracing the king, Justinian said, "My lord, my friend of friends, I have come bearing good news. Young Dreyden will survive! He is at rest and lower Bren is secure."

"Why did you not simply send a royal messenger with the news?" wondered the king, "And who is minding the affairs of the realm if you are here with me?"

"My lord, I beg your forgiveness, but I could not bear the thought that I could allow my friend of friends to go into the dark realms alone. Would you not insist on being at my side were it one of my sons in need of rescue? And besides," continued Justinian with a chuckle, "there was no arguing with the high queen, Melania. It was at her insistence that I join you here, and she did not have to twist my arm, sire! I think the realm will survive and, indeed, prosper under her wise scrutiny!"

Laughing and embracing, the two men then rode off with the regiment assigned to insert itself via the road to Treacherin, while the remaining regiments were dispatched to every major route into Endoria.

Meanwhile, back on the northern route out of Treacherin, Leonolis, Arolis, and Ollieman, led by the trapper Moonrysin, continued to climb out of the valley, entering the northern continuation of the Forest of Endoria. Having had their plan of entering the Runland and floating back to the safety of lower Bren inadvertently thwarted by the encounter with the constable, they had no choice but to continue their ruse until they reached a place to cut back through the woods to the river. No such route ever presented itself though. Moonrysin assured them that he knew of and frequently traveled an old mining road that wound its way down to the Runland just a few miles further. So on they went. And with each step, the boy's heart grew heavier and heavier.

Arolis, thought-whispered to Leonolis (as if Moonrysin might somehow hear them).

What is it, sire? asked the horse.

Something is not right here. I can feel it. And I do not like to admit it, but I have a most dreadful feeling about the fate of dear Dreyden. What if he is dead? What if we do not make it to the mining road? What if the citizens we encountered in Treacherin send word to Lucian that we are here? the boy went on and on.

Why do you focus on what you have no way of knowing, my lord? posed the horse.

What do you mean? responded the boy.

You ask questions that are of no use to us right now. They are pure conjecture. These kinds of questions always lead to discouragement and fear and despair, Leonolis. May I remind you that we have somehow made it thus far? And may I remind you that we have more important things to worry about right now? We do not know Dreyden's fate. We do not know if anyone has alerted the Dark Lord to our location. But we do know that our destiny is in our control at this moment. I propose that we prepare our escape. Ollieman, fly ahead and see that no one lies in wait for us. I have no desire for any more surprises. The boy and I will keep our eyes fixed on the trapper. There is something about him I do not quite trust, advised Arolis.

Without saying a word, the owl simply flew on ahead. "Where does he think he's going?" asked Moonrysin.

"He's going to check the road ahead and make sure no one lies in wait for us," said the boy.

"Good idea," responded the trapper. "Better safe than sorry."

The route had been gradually rising for some time, but now the surroundings were becoming much more mountainous and the road much steeper and much narrower. By now it was midday and the trees were thinning at the higher elevations, yet the darkness of the forest never abated. Looking up, the horse and the boy saw nothing but craggy, barren peaks being consumed by one of the almost daily storms that tended to frequent the Mountains of Endoria. They soon came upon a signpost.

Stopping Arolis so he could read, Leonolis read aloud, "Beware. Before you lies the road to Viamorte. Many have slipped and fallen to their deaths while traversing its treacherous ruts. Continue at your own risk and peril. What should we do, Moonrysin? Shouldn't we have reached the old mining road you spoke of by now? Perhaps we should head back down a ways and seek shelter from the incoming storm?"

"Ahh, don't believe everything you read, boy. Besides, we're almost there. The old mining road is just around the next bend and just beyond the downward trail there lies an old abandoned mine where we will find sanctuary from the tempest," assured Moonrysin.

"What about Ollieman?" asked the boy. "He should have come back by now as well."

"Perhaps he encountered the storm already and has taken shelter in one of the nooks and crannies along the Viamorte. I am sure your friend is wise enough to not continue on in the squall," suggested the man.

Hurrying now, they made their way through the increasing winds and the rain that began to pelt them. Rounding the bend, they came upon another group of travelers going in the opposite direction, toward Treacherin. There between the two groups, opening into the mountain was the shaft of an old abandoned gold mine. Both groups headed for the promise of shelter as the lightning began to come perilously close to the road. Arolis, Leonolis, and Moonrysin ran into the mineshaft just a few seconds before the group of hooded horseman. As the boy dismounted, Arolis shook himself violently like a giant dog shaking off the water after a romp in a stream. Moonrysin went to the mine entrance to get a good look at who their fellow travelers might be.

Three cloaked men rushed into the cave just as a huge crash of thunder shook the mountain around them all. "Come in from the weather, strangers!" called out Moonrysin. "Where are you headed?"

"We are emissaries of the kingdom of Larovia, which lies to the north of Brenolin. We have been sent on a mission of peace from our sovereign, the good king Sandovar. We seek to warn the rulers of the surrounding nations concerning the lord of Dark City, the one they call Lucian. Our seers have discerned that a great evil is afoot in the land called Endoria, and if that evil is not managed with great care, the entire region from Brenolin to Larovia and all adjoining lands will fall into a most terrible darkness. Ruled by deceit and manipulation, the multitudes of people will fall into slavery to the darkness, causing much pain and suffering to all the inhabitants. This very moment we are on our way to procure a meeting with the sovereign king of Brenolin, High King Troyolin," spoke the obvious leader of the three men.

Breathing a sigh of relief at their good fortune, Leonolis replied, "My Larovian brothers! King Troyolin is my father! I am Leonolis, son of Troyolin, High King of Bren!"

The emissaries looked at one another as if in shock at the words of the prince.

"Why does this surprise you, my friends?" asked the puzzled boy.

As if seeing an apparition, all three emissaries bowed in reverence to the boy.

"Why do you bow to me? I am but a prince! I am not the king! It is I who should be bowing to you as emissaries of King Sandovar!" said the bewildered boy.

"It has been prophesied since the days of the Founder that 'in the days of darkness there would rise a lion of the light, born to free the world from the grip of the shadows.' We just had not expected that the lion would be a . . . a *boy*!" said the emissary.

"I am no lion!" declared the boy, now more perplexed than before.

"You do not understand," said the ambassador. "It is your name that reveals your nature. The name 'Leonolis' has been foretold to our priests and seers for centuries. 'He will be born of a southern realm, the son of a king,' goes the legend."

All of a sudden, the ambassador became very agitated. "Oh my! Oh my! We must continue our mission at once, my brothers! We must go at once!"

"Wait! You can't go around telling people that they are the 'lion' of prophecy without giving them proper explanation!" exclaimed the boy.

"We cannot tarry! The time is at hand! Your appearance to us means only one thing: the darkness is soon to fall. All friendly nations must be warned. Wherever it is you journey this day, my young lion, it is your destiny. You must go where you must go . . . and we must go where we must go," said the emissary as the three men quickly pulled their cloaks back over their heads and made their way hastily to the mine opening. "It has been ordained, my son. This day shall you deliver the world from darkness! This day begins the rescue of mankind from the forces of darkness." And they were gone.

"They have lost their minds!" cried the boy. "I am no more a deliverer than I am a lion! I am just a boy!"

Walking to the entrance, Arolis calmly looked out to the weather. Turning back to his boy, he said, *My prince, if this is your destiny, there is nothing we can do but watch it unfold. If this is truly the path chosen for you by the Founder, then He will make a way. It is imperative that we return you to the safety of Bren at once. We must go at once. I sense great peril should we remain here any longer.*

At a loss for words, the prince obediently climbed as if devoid of emotion into the saddle. Over the past two days, he had endured a lifetime's worth of trial and adventure, and now it seemed he was completely drained of mental strength. After all, he was but a boy, but a boy on the verge of becoming a man—a lion of a man.

Though the wind battered them and the thunder shook their bodies at its closeness, the trio once again set out upon the treacherous road, north on the Viamorte. Blinded by the rain, the boy held onto the mane of Arolis for dear life. Moonrysin did the same, holding onto the horse's girt strap while using the horse's body as a blockade to the wind. Almost feeling his way, the horse was steady and sure as he gingerly placed one hoof in front of the other, slowly making his way up the narrow ledge of a road. For what seemed like hours, the three silently fought their way through the torrent. Perhaps it was fate. Perhaps it was simply exhaustion, but they completely missed the old mine road that would have led them back down to the river Runland.

Finally, the storm began to subside sometime in the late afternoon. As they looked out from their lofty perch on the mountainside, they looked down upon a blanket of clouds with several peaks jutting their craggy heads through. The relief they felt at finally being out of the storm morphed into complete awe at the majesty of the view. For a brief second, Leonolis had the fleeting thought that all he had been through over the past two days was worth this special moment. But that feeling evaporated quickly. Flying at them from the north, his wings aflutter with panic, was Ollieman.

"Be off! Away! You can't afford to stay! Pure evil flies on lofty wings to carry you away!" hooted the owl in the most dreadful of hoots. "Back down the mountain! Back down the trail! Back to the safety of the storm's misty veil!"

Without waiting to ask what he meant, Arolis and Leonolis simply complied with their trustworthy friend, while Moonrysin shouted, "Run! Just run! I can take care of myself! Run!" Ollieman zoomed past, leading the horse down the mountain, continuing to screech out a now unintelligible warning. He had come through for them so many times already in their short friendship, why would he fail them now? Bounding full bore down the mountain trail, the horse and the boy and the owl flew like the wind they had just gone through minutes before. Fear—palpable fear—gripped all three. The energy produced by this run for their lives was every bit as powerful as what they had experienced in the flight from the swine rats. But this was even more intense because they knew not what they were running from. In moments of terror, the mind can conjure up some very dreadful and horrifying images. But what happened next took their fear to a new level of dread.

Swooping in from seemingly every direction came a flurry of giant, black-winged creatures. Alighting in the road directly in front of Arolis, it felt to Leonolis as if they would not be able to stop in time before they crashed headlong into the mass of giant bat-like creatures cutting off the trail in front of them. The sound of massive wings beating against the air behind them brought the reality that turning back would be as futile as heading over the ledge and taking their chance at plunging thousands of feet to the rocks below, hoping to live to tell about it. In fact, even should they have truly desired to plunge into the abyss from the trail, these strange airborne beings blocked that route as well. Suddenly, the air above them grew dark as if new storm clouds had ominously rolled in. And a storm of sorts had, indeed, rolled in.

Surrounding the three would-be rescuers of Dreyden were giant bats, yet their facial features were those of men (albeit with pointy bat ears and sharp bat teeth) and instead of claws extending from mid-wing they had actual fingers, though with long claw-like fingernails extending in a menacing fashion. Those who had landed on the ground made bird-like hops toward the shaken heroes. Those who hovered in the air above and to the side held large stones in their hands, ready to wield great destruction on any whose head they were dropped upon. Cocking his head to one side and then the other, the apparent leader of these creatures hopped toward Arolis and the boy.

In an eerie screeching voice, the thing began to speak. "What have we here? A boy, a horse, and a tasty morsel of an owl. What is your business here, human?"

Shaking, Leonolis tried to speak, "We . . . I . . . er . . . um . . ."

"Why the fear, boy? We only seek to protect our own. Why trespass here in the high places of the Chiroptera? Speak!" demanded the creature.

Closing his eyes, the boy tried to calm his racing thoughts by reminding himself of the words from the emissaries just a few moments before, that he was the lion-hearted hope that would deliver the world from darkness, but those words did not exactly measure up to his present reality. Forcing himself to finally look at the one who had spoken, Leonolis began. "Sir, I did not know I was trespassing. We were taken by surprise when the storm came through. We sought shelter in the old mine . . . and if the truth be told, I am lost. This was the only road I have been able to find that would lead me to the river Runland," explained the boy.

"Ha! You lie!" screeched the thing. "If you were truly seeking the river Runland, why were you headed in the opposite direction when we encountered your intrusion?"

Not wanting to give away his true mission or identity, he simply said, "Sir. I am but a boy who became separated from his father who, as a result, has become hopelessly lost. My only desire is to find my way home. I mean you no harm and am most regretful that you would think I have willfully encroached upon your territory. I simply want to go back to the land of lower Bren."

"What is a human of lower Bren doing in these dark regions to begin with?" said the creature. "A boy alone in the Land of Endoria? Doesn't make sense. Not at all does it make sense."

"Sir . . . I missed your name, sir," replied the boy.

"My name is Falling Rocks (because of his practice of dropping rocks on the heads of passersby), lord of the Chiroptera," said the bat man.

"My good Falling Rocks, I was sent on an errand by my father but encountered swine rats in the Forest of Endoria. I lost my way in the confusion and now find myself here, still lost and still hoping for some kind soul to show me the way home," lied the boy.

Cocking his head like a curious bird, Falling Rocks asked, "What is *your* name, human?"

"My name? My name . . . is . . . Leonolis."

"Leonolis. Leonolis. This name sounds familiar. This name I do not know. Peculiar yet somehow fitting for one as odd-looking as you humans tend to be. You will go with us until I have decided if you are telling me the truth. Something about your story makes me think you do not speak in a truthful manner. The humans have long shown themselves less than tolerant of our kind. How are we to know you have not been sent here for the sole purpose of searching us out? What better ploy than to send out an 'innocent' boy to catch us off guard. Where is the hunting party who seeks the fine bounty Chiroptera pelts would bring at market?" asked Falling Rocks.

Just as Leonolis was about to respond, a familiar, gruff voice called out, "Falling Rocks! Your wings are all a-tizzy for nothing, my old friend," Moonrysin called out, huffing and puffing. He had finally caught up with the group. "When you came flapping your wings, chasing the poor, helpless owl, you frightened the horse! The boy is not your enemy. I myself was trying to help give him direction when you and your soaring minions burst out of thin air!"

"Moonrysin, the harvester of fur, I see," said the bat. "Why should I trust you who would sell his own mother if it meant a profit?"

"Have I not been the friend of the Chiroptera? Have I ever once taken one of your kind and sold his fine, leathery flesh for gain? Have I not been anything but mindful of your rightful claim to the high lands of Endoria, harvesting only the pelts I need and leaving the bulk of the creatures your kind finds appetizing? I am offended, my friend!" proclaimed Moonrysin (it seemed he had dealt with the Chiroptera before and was proving to be quite adept at manipulating the somewhat easily distracted creature to his own way of thinking).

Suddenly backtracking at the thought Moonrysin might find him offensive, the creature changed his tone. "My friend! My friend, I meant nothing of the sort! Of course you have always shown our kind great kindness. If you say the boy speaks truth, we will let them pass. All I ask is that the owl we were after when we came upon the boy and the horse be returned to us. After all, fresh owl is quite the delicacy."

"The owl is with the boy. He is a pet, trained from a nestling to hunt for rodents and small game. How do you think he provides sustenance for his own family? The boy would be heartbroken and his family would starve should the bird become your meal. Allow the owl to go with the boy and I will, in return, show you the secret nesting place of many owls upon my journey back," bargained the trapper.

"Very well," screeched the bat man. "We will await your return once you have shown the boy his way back home. To the heights!" And as quickly as they appeared, the Chiroptera disappeared into the upper reaches of the crags of the Mountains of Endoria. The horse and the boy and the owl once again breathed a sigh of deep relief.

"Come, boy. We must waste not one more second should the capricious nature of the creatures cause them to change their minds. The storm rages below. There is only one more way I know of which will lead you back to Runland and on to Bren. The journey is not one I would choose had we any other choice, but as it is, it has become our only choice," said the now solemn Moonrysin.

So the frazzled trekkers headed north, into places no mother would ever wish her child—or foal or owlet—would ever go.

Chapter Twelve

JOURNEY TO ABYSSTINE

T he mountain road to the capitol city of the region of Endoria was not the path our heroes would have chosen for their journey had they any other choice in the matter. Moonrysin told them of one more passage to the Runland, but that they would have to pass over the mountains and into the upper reaches of the valley that contained Dark City. The real name of the city, which rested in the eastern end of the valley, was actually called Abysstine because of the depths to which the valley seemed to plunge between the mountains that surrounded it. Like an abyss, the valley was quite deep and long and narrow—a place no one from lower Bren ever wanted to travel on purpose (or by accident!). Since days of old, Abysstine was the seat of the Dark Lord—the place where he ruled, the place from which he conducted his dark business and launched all his maniacal missions. Thus, the nickname "Dark City" had been much easier to say than Abysstine.

The journey over the pass that led through the Mountains of Endoria went without major incident. Even though Arolis had to be very careful not to venture too near the edge of the narrow trail, at least they had not had to deal with any more swine rats . . . or dark forces . . . or Chiroptera. Something about this lack of trouble actually troubled the boy. Perhaps it was the frenzy and the stress of all they had been through or perhaps it was simply his thoughts about his dear friend Dreyden, but whatever it was, Leonolis could not shake the feeling of impending doom and disaster. It seemed he would never get home, never see his father again, never see Dreyden.

Once again, Arolis encouraged Leonolis to rest as much as possible while in the saddle, but the boy had other things that filled his mind. Images of his good friend Dreyden and the many days they had spent in mock battle and imagined adventure paled in comparison to the events of the past two days. He wondered at the fate of his friend, believing the worst. Where had all the days of endless exploits on horseback gone? Would he ever again share with his friend the many escapades and mischief he and Dreyden had shared before everything had fallen apart? Would he ever again partake in such a deep and enduring friendship as he had experienced with his friend of friends? For hours, thoughts like these flooded the mind of the prince while Moonrysin and Arolis and Ollieman watched over him.

Suddenly, Leonolis' ruminations were interrupted when Moonrysin said, "We'll stop here for the night."

Looking around as he dismounted, Leonolis had not realized they had left the high, craggy peaks of the mountains and were now entering into a kinder, gentler terrain. Trees, tall pines, and shimmering alders framed the pathway on both sides now. "Where are we?" asked the boy.

"This is Menden Lake," replied the trapper. "We are approaching the valley of the abyss. This lake is full of bounty, from the fish that make it their home to the many animals that come here to quench their thirst to the pleasant meadows full of grass (for Arolis) and field mice (for Ollieman). I have taken us far around the lake, away from the main trail. We will be well hidden here for the night. Boy, can you make a fire?"

As Moonrysin headed into the darkness of the woods, Leonolis called out to him, "Of course I can make a fire. Where are you going? Are you just going to leave us here?"

"My good prince, of course I am not leaving you here. I am a trapper. I hunt. Aren't you hungry?" came Moonrysin's reply. "You are hungry. I am hungry. The horse and the owl can fend for themselves. I would rather not starve."

"How far are we from the passage to the Runland?" the boy asked as he began to unsaddle Arolis.

"Only a few miles, but it would be best if we waited for the cover of darkness if we care to navigate our way without our presence being found out by any dark forces, which are most assuredly roaming about the main roads this night. We should eat and get some rest, then make our way after midnight, thus securing our secrecy as we pass through." Moonrysin then slipped into the darkened forest.

Leonolis turned to Arolis and to Ollieman who had both witnessed the entire conversation without saying a word. Arolis spoke first.

"My lord," said the stallion in an agitated manner, "something is not right. We passed through the mountain pass without passing one single sentry or sentinel of the Dark Lord? How is that even possible?"

"I must concur with my equine brother, dear prince. Some great evil is at work this night. In my opinion, our dear friend Moonrysin may be up to no good," replied Ollieman as Arolis shook his great black mane in agreement.

"But he has saved us on no less than two occasions in our brief acquaintance. First, from the people of Treacherin and then from the Chiroptera. Why would he save us just to lead us into a trap?" retorted the boy. "I think you've lost it, my friends!"

As the boy began hurriedly collecting small pieces of wood for kindling, the horse and the owl followed him. "Sire, regardless of what you think are his good intentions, I sense that even now our dear friend and two-time rescuer may not be out to trap some witless animal. For all we know, he is leading us right into the clutches of the dark forces. Sire, have I ever led you astray?" asked the horse.

"My prince, ponder this. Did you not notice that in his hurry to go hunting for food that he forgot his traps, and that he lay down his bow and arrows?" said the wise old owl.

At that revelation, the boy's blood ran cold and his breath became short. In denial at this most unfortunate news, the boy said, "But why would he put his life on the line twice for us if he meant us harm?"

"We do not have all the answers as we would like, sire. But we do have irrefutable evidence that he is lying to us now. I must insist that we leave this place at once," said Arolis.

"But . . . I . . . we . . . ," said the boy as he tried to make himself believe the best of Moonrysin, but the more he thought about the hunter not taking the tools of hunting with him, the more his mind caught up with the truth that they must leave—and now!

Throwing the saddle on the horse and quickly tightening the cinch, the trio was once again off in yet another escape attempt. Flying ahead, Ollieman assumed his now familiar position in front, flying ahead to detect any concealed adversary that may lay waiting for them in the darkness. There was no use in trying to head back over the mountain pass. Their only recourse was to head for the opening to Runland that Moonrysin had spoken of as they passed through the Mountains of Endoria. Of course, each of our heroes recognized that no such opening or passageway probably really existed at all. Their hope would be in their ability to avoid detection and to somehow find an actual route out of the Valley of the Abyss and back to the river Runland.

Arolis quickly headed into the forest following Ollieman. They had both wisely determined that they must avoid the main roads at all cost. While trying to maintain a steady pace they could not afford to go at full gallop. Stealth was of the utmost importance. Gingerly placing his feet as quietly as possible, the horse was able to continue steadily in a hurried walk. Where possible, the horse walked with the flow of small streams so as to cover his tracks. Only when the stream plunged over impassable falls or became too narrow would they be forced to walk on the bank. Ollieman kept a watchful flying vigil overhead and Leonolis held his sword at ready while Arolis maneuvered the meanderings of the stream in a near pitch-black night. Only occasionally would the moonlight pierce the upper canopy of forest. And oh how all three wished for an appearance by their friends Galennia and Rania, but no such appearance was forthcoming.

After about an hour of this quiet, yet steady progression downward following the stream (their hope was that it would run its course all the way to the Runland), the stream unexpectedly disappeared.

Where did it go? thought-whispered Leonolis to Arolis.

It would seem that our stream has taken a route that would have proven very useful to us. It has coursed its way underground I am afraid, sire, said the horse. *We have no choice. We will continue downhill and hopefully the stream will make its way back to the surface. At any rate, I think it best we continue our downward course.*

The horse and the boy were very much on edge without the babbling of the stream to hide the sound of their trekking. With every snap of a twig or rustle of a branch the pair felt as if they were being pounced upon by some unseen demon. Whenever a distant sound of the forest made its way to their nervous ears, the two froze in silence for a few uneasy moments until Ollieman would whisper the "all clear." Winding their way through the forest in this manner seemed to take forever, and due to their unfamiliarity to the landscape (even had it been broad daylight) they had absolutely no idea whether they were making any valuable headway or not.

Eventually, they grew weary of this mode of travel and decided perhaps it might be better if they simply stopped right where they were and waited for daylight. At least with the light of dawn they would be able to determine if indeed there was anyone—or anything—dangerous attached to the sounds that were the cause of the constant stopping and starting.

My prince! thought-spoke Ollieman. *Arolis! Quiet! Someone this way comes!*

Frozen in place, Arolis and the boy seemed more like a statue than living, breathing beings. Of course, the boy and the horse felt as if every heartbeat sounded as a pounding kettledrum in the dead quietness of the forest. Every breath seemed to be louder than the next, and the boy and the horse and the owl (even high above!) felt as if their hearts would pound right out of their chests. And then they heard them. Footsteps. One or two at a time at first, as if the maker of said footsteps was stopping to listen every so often. Step. Step. Step. Stop for a few moments. Step. Snapping twig. Stop. Soon the steps began to grow closer and sounded as if they were now directly in front of the downward facing horse and boy. If they did have to run for their lives, at least they would have the advantage of being able to charge full bore downhill at whomever or whatever was stalking them. The boy could tell from the way the horse was tensing and lowering slightly on his haunches that Arolis was about to pounce, so he readied himself, sword in battle position.

From just a few feet in front of them, the silence was suddenly broken. "Leonolis," whispered the voice. "Leonolis, prince of Bren. Are you there? It is I, Moonrysin. I've been searching for you all night."

Still afraid to break the silence, Leonolis spoke to Arolis. *It's Moonrysin! What should we do?*

Calling down from somewhere above, Ollieman joined the silent conversation. *Sire. Arolis. He appears to be alone. I see no one else. It is truly Moonrysin, but I still think we dare not trust him.*

Agreed, said the horse. *Leonolis, speak to him, but let him know in no uncertain terms that we do not and will not trust him.*

"Moonrysin, we have come to an agreement that in these parts we can trust no one," the boy said wisely.

"I am hurt, my lord! Have I not brokered your freedom no less than two times in one single day? Your words cut deeply! How dare you . . . and after I have even this night sought to secure your freedom, traipsing through the darkness, fearing that you had been taken by the dark forces that patrol these parts day and night," said Moonrysin.

Do not let him manipulate you into false guilt, my lord, warned Arolis. *Do not trust him! Do not allow him to sway you!*

"I know you think me incapable of reason and wisdom because of my youth, dear Moonrysin. But due to all I have endured over the course of the past two days, I no longer have patience, nor do I have the luxury of time to wait here and argue with you over the trustworthiness of your character. Here is the truth: you left us by the lake in a frenzied hurry this night. Who were you in such a hurry to meet with?"

"I met with no one!" shouted the trapper. "I went in search of sustenance for *you*, my lord!"

"Then how is it that you had no need of your trapper's tools or for your bow and arrow?" came the boy's reply.

For several seconds, an awkward silence ensued, once again causing the horse and the boy and the owl to prepare for a mad dash to freedom.

Speaking with an obvious sadness in his trembling voice, Moonrysin broke the silence. "My lord, please forgive me. I have brought great evil to you and your friends this day."

"What do you mean?" asked the boy.

"It is true. I did not go to hunt at all. I went to alert the forces of the Dark One that you had entered the region of Abysstine . . . and that you would be easily taken at the encampment. You do not know my joy to find you gone upon my return, yet utter sadness upon my own reality."

"How could you, Moonrysin? We trusted you!" responded Leonolis.

"You do not understand, young sire. I had no choice. Lucian has taken my wife and five children captive. He told me they would be slaughtered without mercy should I fail in bringing you to him. On two occasions now have I seen in the Crystal Orb that adorns his riding staff my own family in the hands of his henchmen. There was nothing I could do. I am sorry . . ." said the grieved trapper. What Moonrysin had no way of knowing was this: Lucian had *not* captured the man's family. Moonrysin had done such a great job of protecting his family by the way he had built his home in a secluded and well-hidden area of the Great Forest that Lucian had been unable to find them despite his great effort. He had conjured up the images in the Crystal Orb, deceiving the poor trapper. Only later would Moonrysin realize he had been duped.

"For your family I am truly sorry, but you must tell us at once how we might escape from this great evil. My father will surely send troops to rescue your family, dear Moonrysin, should you give us aid," pled the boy.

"It is too late, my prince. Even now you are completely surrounded. Should you take flight in any direction, your way will be cut off by his horsemen. Should you be suddenly able to fly, your flight would be cut short by the Chiroptera that patrol above us as I speak. Should you find a cave and try to make good your escape, the underground-dwelling race of earthen ogres—the Terrebithians—lie in wait for you there. There is no escape, sire. The lives of your horse and your friend owl will be spared upon your peaceful surrender. I am sorry. Even now they come," said the trapper, overcome with tears of sorrow.

His worst nightmare being realized, Leonolis responded in such a way that the boy-blood that coursed through his veins began to give way to the man-blood that was his destiny. Doing the honorable and noble and manly thing, he slid down from his perch atop the stallion in the hope of sparing the lives of Arolis and Ollieman. At this brave act, the woods around them began to crawl with unseen activity. The footsteps of dozens of horses and their riders could be heard rustling the leaves and debris of the forest floor. From nearby caves and crevices the footsteps of unseen ogres making their way from their underground lairs could be heard. Above the forest canopy came a flurry of dozens of flapping wings as the Chiroptera began their frenzied descent. And then a light appeared, but not the light in darkness that usually brings relief and a feeling of security. This light came from the many torches that were being lit by the dark forces, revealing a crawling mass of ugliness and evil the likes of which Leonolis had never seen.

As the dark forces made their way to the boy, they closed their ranks, encircling the boy and the horse in an eerie glow. As Ollieman flew down and alit on the back of Arolis, dark figures began to lumber into the light from the dark forest around them. Ugly and grotesque ogres with bulging leathery noses and tiny dark eyes came lumbering toward them with battleaxes at the ready. From above, the Chiroptera hovered, many lighting on the trees just mere inches above the frightened trio. And then the entire group began to part. Slowly, as if to convey some universal importance, Lucian rode in, his bodyguards flanking him on either side. What the Dark Lord meant as a demonstration of regality came across as an arrogant display of pride and false power.

Dismounting, the Dark Lord approached the prince. Without saying a word, he slapped the boy hard across the face, but Leonolis recovered himself and avoided going to the ground, avoided tears, avoided humiliation. He stood there bravely as one who was confident in whom he was and willing to stand for what was right, regardless of the consequences. The man-blood was now coursing heavily through his veins.

"Still defiant, I see," chided the Dark Lord. "We'll remedy that."

Turning to Arolis and Ollieman, Lucian commanded his guards. "Take the horse to my stables. He will make a fine plow horse. And the owl? To the Chiroptera."

At those words, Ollieman took flight and disappeared into the darkness, with four or five salivating Chiroptera in hot pursuit as Leonolis shouted, "Fly! Ollieman! Fly!" His shout silenced by yet another glancing blow at Lucian's hand. This time, Leonolis went to the ground.

"Your insolence will not be tolerated, Prince of Bren. Guards, show the prince what we think of such foolishness," snorted Lucian.

All at once, four guards ruthlessly stripped him of all but the garment covering his loins. As they held him down, another took a sharp blade and cruelly cut away his golden locks, leaving him with a crude and misshapen haircut. Both acts were meant to humble and humiliate the boy into submission, but he remained defiant as they yanked him to a standing position. For the entire journey to this point, Leonolis had only desired to rescue his friend. The thought that now consumed his mind was for the safety of all of Bren.

"Put the leash on him," commanded Lucian. "For all the power of your father, the so-called king of Bren, it seems he has no power to save you. Whether you know it or not, boy, this day has been in the planning since you were conceived in your mother's womb. My plan had been to simply put you to death, but the arrogance of your father in refusing me my place at the table of rule over the land of Bren calls for something more demonstrative of the pain and humiliation I have endured by his betrayal. Something that will cause him to pay for the pain he has caused me. All of Bren will bow before me, and all will understand the wrath of Lord Lucian toward those who defy my rightful place. You have become more valuable to me alive than dead. Something about watching another man's anguish at knowing his son is in service to the one he loathes fills me with a very satisfying joy. To Abysstine. To the Dark City."

With a leash around his neck, Leonolis was forced to walk behind Lucian like some human pet. The boy gazed sadly into the eyes of Arolis as he passed by. As the throng began to disband, the ogres mocked the boy while they spit upon him. The Chiroptera sounded as if they were in a feeding frenzy—like a hundred clucking hens squawking all at once over a morsel of food. The dark forces, led by Lucian, slowly and triumphantly made their way through the forest to the main road. Each time Leonolis lagged behind, a guard yanked on the leash and caused the boy to choke. By the time the entourage made its way to the outskirts of the Dark City, the boy's bare feet had become raw and blistered. The royal treatment he had been accustomed to seemed very distant from his thoughts, and the treatment he was about to receive from the citizenry of Abysstine would bring the boy to the edge of hopelessness. As they entered the city, dawn was breaking, and with the breaking of first light, Leonolis came to realize all too quickly just how dark the light of day could be.

Chapter Thirteen

ABYSSTINE

Abysstine was not at all what Leonolis had expected. Though nestled deeply into the eastern end of the deep, dark valley, the look of the city itself was not so dark. It was the reputation of the one who ruled over its inhabitants that had given it that name. A walled city, Abysstine was much larger than the boy had anticipated. The thirty-foot wall that surrounded the entire city was interspersed with guard towers every fifty feet or so. Leonolis noticed that each of these towers was manned by at least two watchmen, crossbows at the ready. Within each tower hung a bell that was visible from all sides high in the watchtower. The bell was open to the air so as to allow the sounding of alarm to carry over the entire city and, indeed, the entire valley.

The many buildings of the city itself seemed to be made of a lightly colored stone, giving the city a dim glow as one might see from a field of cotton on a moonlit night in the fields of Runland Valley. Tall buildings lined the main street that ran through the city. Looking down from the valley road, even in the dimness of dawn, Leonolis could see that the main road led up to a vast castle that rested against the mountain wall on the eastern end of the valley. The city itself was a buffer between opposing forces that might come against it. The high mountains protected its backside while the vast city and surrounding wall gave protection from all other approaches. Castle Jadon was impenetrable. Within the confines of the city wall, the fortress of Lucian was surrounded by yet another wall within the city wall. Symmetrical in appearance, from each side of the castle grounds rose many turrets. Each turret grew in height the nearer one came to the mighty central turret that commanded the highest vantage point from the castle. From a distance, the castle looked like a many-faceted crown as it rested upon the head of the city.

Marching through the night down the valley road and through the Dark Forest had not been quite as distressing as one might imagine. Though poked and prodded for the smallest lag in pace, the prince had grown accustomed to the tempo of the entourage and, in some odd way, felt secure from the myriad evil sounds that bantered back and forth in the forest all around him. What Leonolis could not have known was that those eerie cries in the night were the news of his capture going from creature to creature, from witch to witch, from ogre to ogre, from manwolf to manwolf, until the news had already made its way into the very heart of Abysstine. In this realm, such news was considered good news. At one time the people of Abysstine were considered good and honest, hard-working people. Under the rule of Lucian they had known only oppression and fear and had come to be a very deceitful lot. The news of the capture of Leonolis meant the oppression they felt daily would be relieved for a season since the entire citizenry knew this was the one thing that seemed to be ever-present on Lucian's mind, and that his frustration through the years had been taken out on them. This was indeed good news for the people.

As dawn broke, the valley was still dark, the sun's rays being kept from the valley floor until almost mid-morning. (This phenomenon also helped perpetuate the nickname "Dark City.") What at first Leonolis thought to be the sound of rushing water—as if a river flowed mightily nearby—was actually the sound of cheering from the walls of Abysstine. Lining every wall and rooftop for as far as the boy could see, were the people of Abysstine who had come out to applaud their ruler upon the completion of what all assumed was merely the first step in Lucian's conquest of the entire realm of Brenolin. Also assumed was that once Bren fell, all surrounding nations would fall without much of a fight. What the poor boy could not have known was that on the minds of the Abysstinians, he was the reason they had to live under such a tyrannical ruler. They reasoned that if Leonolis were out of the picture their burdens would be lightened, and, to an extent, they were correct in this way of thinking. Lucian was absolutely ecstatic!

As the victorious dark forces made their way to the valley floor, the walls of the city, even though still a ways off, took on a very menacing feel to the boy. He no longer had that strange safe feeling he had experienced in the forest. That feeling gave way to utter dread and despair as the realization of just how inescapable his predicament appeared to be sunk in. By the time they were within five hundred yards of the city gate, the noise of the people was deafening. Looking up, Leonolis felt small and helpless. Through the cacophonous din, he tried to communicate with Arolis through thought but either the noise was too great and confusing or the mighty horse was too far back in the troop to make communication possible. Arolis held his head high, proud and defiant, though hobbled and muzzled. He held out hope that the boy was doing the same—and that King Troyolin was surely on his way.

Entering the city gates, Leonolis could see Lucian leading the way, head cocked in triumphant arrogance, hand waving as if he had just won some great military victory. This seemed so incredulous to Leonolis. He had captured a boy and a horse, yet he received a hero's welcome. Only when the boy with the bloodied feet and bruised body began to walk through the multitudes of people who lined the street did it dawn on him that they were also directing a great deal of their spiteful glee upon him.

The first to come near to the boy was a sweet, little old lady from whom Leonolis expected to receive pity and consolation. Instead she cried, "Fie! To the wretched son of the tyrant of Bren! Spawn of Troyolin, where's your papa now?"

"Ha! Ha! Ha!" laughed a group of boys the same age as the prince. "We bow before the mighty Prince of Bren. Oh wait! He doesn't look so mighty now! Where's your crown, dear prince? Here, let us shower you with royal adoration!" Spitting on him, the boys continued to follow as far as they could before they were swallowed up in the crowd, but their mocking words and harsh treatment of the boy continued, taken up by the next group along the way.

Nearly naked, bleeding, and weary, the intensity of emotion and fear that now gripped the prince's heart had brought him to the point of collapse. Anger and bile were cast at him from every place he looked. There was no escape. Covered with spit, the poor boy had also been pinched, kicked, slapped, and tripped—all to the glee of those he was paraded through. Rotten vegetables and every sordid piece of refuse in the city seemed to find its way to the boy's battered head and body.

Beyond humiliation by the time they mercifully reached the Castle Jadon, the boy finally fell under the weight of his exhaustion. As the dark forces beat back the crowd that tried to follow them into the castle grounds, Leonolis was dragged unconscious into the main courtyard.

Dismounting, Lucian walked over to the boy's body. Stirring him with an outstretched foot, the Dark Lord's boot dug into the boy's side eliciting nothing more than a sorrowful moan. "Rouse him but do him no more harm. He is more valuable to me alive. Clean him then bring him to the throne room," commanded Lucian. And with that, he disappeared into the recesses of the massive fortress.

Leonolis was wrenched back into consciousness as the cold water from the guard's pail shocked his body. Pulled to his feet, the boy was stripped and thrown into the watering trough near the castle stable and told to wash himself, although they gave him no soap or cloth with which to do so. Stepping out of the trough, a guard threw him a rough piece of cloth with the words, "Put this on!" Pulling the garment over his head, it was nothing more than a long shirt with no sleeves. The shirt gave the appearance of a dress, its length going to just above his knees. Leonolis thought he had just experienced the most embarrassing moment of his life when he walked through the gauntlet of the entire population of Abysstine, but for a boy of any culture, especially this one, to be made to wear something akin to a girl's smock was both shameful and degrading.

The leash was once again placed around the boy's neck and he was prodded by the guards to move toward the main doorway leading into the central turret area of Castle Jadon. As he walked toward the entry, he heard a shuffling sound from above. Turning to see what was making the commotion, Leonolis saw that the statues of gargoyles that decorated and served as conduits to drain excess water from the rooftops of the castle turrets were not actually gargoyles at all. Stationed on every rooftop of every turret were members of the Chiroptera clan. Evidently, Lucian had secured their services as his personal sentries (no doubt through some means of evil manipulation and deception). Inside, it took several moments for the boy's eyes to adjust. What he saw once he was able to open his eyes was a vast, cavernous hallway, much like the medieval cathedrals of old. Lining each wall were columns of granite and marble and beneath each column was a statue, each appearing to be different poses of the same man. Upon closer inspection, Leonolis realized that each sculpture was a different rendition of Lucian. This was a hall, much as the Hall of Defenders in Castle Aerie. Unlike the Hall of Defenders that portrayed all the great kings and heroes of Bren, this hall was dedicated solely to the arrogance and self-importance of Lucian.

Making their way through the lengthy cavern of a room, the guards led Leonolis to a grand staircase rising from the center of the hallway near the end of the massive corridor. At any other time, the boy would have bounded up the stairs taking two and three steps at a time, but in his weakened condition, it was all he could do to muster the strength to take even one step at a time . . . and his badly blistered feet were not helping matters. After receiving several strokes from the lash of one of the guard's whips, Leonolis finally arrived at the top. From there, an enormous doorway stood before them. Each of the doors looked as if they would accommodate several elephants standing atop of one another! It took three men on each side of the colossal panels to move the turnstiles that caused them to swing open. As they opened, Leonolis could not help but gasp at what the opening revealed. As son of the king, he had experienced what he thought was opulence befitting royalty, but his experience paled when compared with what lay before him now.

Just as one's eyes must adjust when coming out of a dark cave into the brightness of the sunlight, the prince's eyes had to readjust to the massive brightness emanating from this huge hallway. From floor to ceiling, ornate golden sculptures and intricate gilded carvings adorned every place the eye could see. Lit from massive stained-glass windows depicting, once again, images of Lucian in all manner of heroic postures, and a myriad of flaming torches themselves embellished with all manner of exquisite ornamentation, this room had the very feel of a place of worship. And indeed it *was* a place of worship, designed by Lucian *for* Lucian for the worship and adoration of Lucian. Laid out before him on the marble flooring was a magnificent woven carpet that served to mark the pathway up to the massive steps at the end of this hallway. And at the top of these steps was an incredibly large throne with a back that must have risen twenty-five feet into the air, complete with golden carvings adorning its surface. Seated in the throne as if he were the Founder and

Creator of all sat the smugly smiling Lucian, self-proclaimed Lord of Endoria.

Once again, Leonolis was prodded to head down the carpet toward the steps leading up to the throne. Once there, the guards released him from the leash and nudged him to approach the throne alone. Making his way wearily upward, the boy arrived at the feet of Lucian and stood there silently.

"You may bow," said Lucian. Leonolis stood there in defiance, not willing to bow to one who would pretend to be a king. "I said, YOU MAY BOW!" this time shouting. Nodding to one of the guards that stood on either side of the throne, Lucian pointed toward the boy. Stepping curtly behind the boy, Leonolis was struck with the rod of the guard's spear and fell forward very near the feet of Lucian. "That's better!" snarled Lucian. "From now on, you will either bow in my presence or we will help you make the proper adjustments to your posture. I suggest you not put yourself through any unnecessary pain."

Still reeling from the blow, the boy managed to get to his hands and knees, then slowly raised himself up to one knee. Pulling at what little reserve of energy he still managed, the boy stood to his feet. "I have been trained in the ways of court and courtly manners. To bow before one's king is proper decorum for a royal subject, and I am no subject of yours," calmly stated the boy.

Once again, Lucian nodded to the guard and once again Leonolis felt the power of the blow of the spear, and once again he found himself on his face at the feet of the Dark Lord.

"In due time," said Lucian, "In due time you will learn that it is I who truly rule over this land. In due time you will see the throne that is rightfully mine, and you and all those who pathetically bow the knee to your father will rightfully bow the knee to me."

This time, remaining on the ground, the boy responded boldly. "The people of Bren will never allow themselves to be enslaved to your dark tyranny. They would rather die free than to live in slavery to you."

"Then die they will," Lucian sneered. "And as for you, you will serve the purposes of my bidding. Not only will you bow before me when in my presence, but you will also serve the purpose of my realm."

"You may beat my body into bowing, but you will never make me bow my heart. I am son of the true king and I serve the purposes of the true kingdom. And soon, my father will make quick victory from whatever evil forces you may bring against him. Soon enough you will see. Even now I am sure he and the full force of Bren will be making their way to my rescue and your defeat," the boy proclaimed confidently.

"Tsk, tsk, tsk," murmured Lucian. "You are correct about one thing: your father and his forces do approach . . . and we are more than prepared. Do you not think I would engage such an endeavor as your capture had I not a plan in place? Soon enough you will see what reality truly looks like, boy. But the sad, sad truth for you is that your very own father will be willing to sacrifice *you* for the sake of his own power. Mark my word. You are nothing more to him than a trophy on a shelf, meant to be looked at and admired as the bounty of his royal loins but worthless for any other use. Do you not know you are simply his showpiece? You will see! Your father is no different than I or any other one chosen to rule. He will do whatever it takes to remain in power. Whatever it takes . . . ," said the evil lord as his words trailed off in laughter.

"My father is *nothing* like you!" shouted the boy. "He rules because it is his destiny! He rules in grace and compassion for his people, thinking more of them and their needs than even his own! He is nothing like you!"

"Ha! We shall see! We shall see," laughed Lucian. "To the dungeon with him!" Waving off the guards, Lucian turned and walked into a doorway leading away from the throne area as the guards pulled Leonolis to his feet and shoved him down the stairs. Managing somehow to maintain his footing while being pushed down most of the stairway, the boy tripped and fell the last few feet, landing with a thud on his back. The guards then dragged him to a hallway leading from the throne room into an even deeper place in the castle. Coming to a doorway that seemed to be more of a gate than a door, one of the guards rang a bell. Almost instantly, a chain that seemed to hang from beyond the door from the ceiling began to clink and clank as it went into motion. Soon, after much metallic creaking and groaning, a small enclosure rose from the floor. Shoving the boy in, the guards closed the gateway behind them then rang the bell again. This time, the cage began to descend. Leonolis finally made sense of what was happening. An ingenious mode of transport was lowering them into the deep recesses of the belly of the castle. This ancient elevator reminded Leonolis of one of the contraptions used to bring water up in a pail from the well of Castle Aerie.

Descending for several minutes and passing many levels where much activity was taking place (from men working forges and beating swords into shape on several levels to hearing the moans of torture from what must have been prison cells on others), the boy's feelings of helplessness melted into feelings of hopelessness with every creak of the elevation machine. Finally reaching what seemed to be the lowest level, Leonolis was pulled from the cage and shoved toward a dark hallway. Once in the hallway, he was directed for several hundred feet toward to a lone doorway standing at the very end of the hall. Taking a key from a pouch at his side, one of the guards fumbled with the lock and forced open the rusty-hinged door.

"In you go!" said the guard as he threw the boy through the doorway and onto the ground. With a heavy thud, the door closed behind the boy with a finality that caused the boy to nearly faint simply from his utter despair. Lying there in the darkness, his eyes slowly became accustomed to the tiny bit of light that crept in from the small flame lighting the outer hallway. As he lay there quietly crying tears of exhaustion, he thought he heard something . . . or someone. Startled back into sanity, the boy called out, "Who's there?"

Laughing softly, another voice calmly said, "It is just I."

"Who is 'just I'?" asked the boy.

"Just an old man who means you no harm," replied the voice. "And to whom may I say 'thank you' for providing me with much longed-for conversation this day?"

"How do I know you mean me no harm? I may be a boy but I have learned enough of treachery the past few days to put nothing past Lucian. For all I know, you were placed in this cell to gain important information from me," said Leonolis.

"You are wise in your summation of the dear Lord Lucian, but you are safe with me. I have been in this cell for over thirteen years now and do not expect to be going anywhere anytime soon." His voice was quite obvious that of an old man. "What is your name, son?"

Hesitating, the boy thought about his options, and his fear melted at the words the old man spoke next.

"My son, I am an old man. I have known happiness and joy. I have known hardship and pain. I have suffered indescribable humiliations at the hand of dear Lucian. For whatever reason he has to place a young boy in such confines, you may rest assured that I will do nothing but my utmost best to make your stay here as comfortable and as bearable as possible. What is your name, son?" again asked the old man.

"My name," said the boy softly and with a hint of sadness, "My name is Leonolis, son of Troyolin, High King of Bren."

Saying nothing, the two captives sat in the darkness for several minutes. After a while, the silence was broken with the sound of tears, and not the tears of the one you would suspect. The old man was now crying!

"Why do you cry, sir," gently asked the boy.

"My name is Regalion, son of Lairdon, brother of Troyolin, father of . . ." said the old man.

And completing the old man's sentence, Leonolis cried out, "Lucian! You are my father's brother, Lord Regalion, rightful heir to the throne before my own father! But you were killed before I was even born! I have heard the stories of your bravery and of your greatness! But you are supposed to be dead! You went into the Mountains of Endoria where you were ambushed by the forces of Gothgol, Wizard of the Heights, the White Wizard of Endoria!"

"Yes, yes. I know how the story goes," said Regalion.

"But you were never heard from again! In fact, as proof of your death at the dark magic of Gothgol, your finger along with the royal signet were cut from your hand and sent back to the council at Aerie! I myself have seen the ring!" said the unbelieving boy.

"Yes, sure enough they cut off my finger and sent it back," said the old man as he held up his right hand, sans the ring finger. "This was just one part of an evil scheme to overtake the throne of Bren . . ." His voice trailed away in sorrow.

"Then that means . . ."

"Yes, that means my own son . . . my dear Lucian . . . set in motion a darkness that I had no power to overcome. But that darkness is soon to end," the old man said with confidence.

"What do you mean?" asked the boy.

"You are the way, my son. You will lead the way."

Chapter Fourteen

REGALION

Leonolis sat there in stunned silence with the reality that Regalion was indeed alive and well. Many questions began to stir in his mind, first and foremost of which was, "Lord Regalion, how can you be father of Lucian when it is said that no one knows his age? How can you be father of the one who has tormented the land of Bren for all ages? How can it be that you are the father of the one who has sought to destroy our family and depose the royal line since time began?"

"Ah, yes. I suppose that is a bit confusing, my son. But what you must realize is that the spirit of Lucian has been around since the foundation of time. Each generation since the beginning of time has had to face its own incarnation of that spirit," replied Regalion. "It just so happened that a series of events led to the inhabitation of that spirit within the heart and mind of my own dear son. Before he was evil, he was my son . . . and I suppose that somewhere in that twisted mind a bit of my son and his true identity still remain. At least that is my hope. Why else do you suppose he would have kept me alive after all these years?"

"But how did the evil overtake him?" asked Leonolis.

"You need your rest, boy. You have been through much this day. And around here, one never knows what a day might hold. I would suggest you get some sleep. We will have plenty of time for talk," said the wise old Regalion.

And with those words, Leonolis began to drift into a deep sleep as he laid his beaten body down on the rough straw that served as bedding in the dark, dank room. As he slept, his mind was flooded with many wonderful, adventure-filled dreams. He saw images he faintly remembered from somewhere in his past—of swinging high into the air from a rope swing and diving deep into a cool, clear pool, of riding a horse fast as the wind, leaping every stream and downed tree he came to, of fishing with a long pole and grasshoppers, of running from a group of boys, of falling into a deep hole in a dark cave, of his friend Dreyden, of soaring through the air as Arolis leapt above the fray of mock battle, of Sniffum and Snuffim, of Jidgel and the swamp, of Galennia and Rania and the swine rats, of Moonrysin and the Chiroptera, of how he would one day free the people of Bren from the evil of Lucian and rule with kindness and bravery over the land.

Suddenly Leonolis was awakened. Gently shaking the boy, Regalion told him to "do as I do." Just then, the door of the cell swung open with a loud clank and the sound of creaking metal hinges in need of a bit of axle grease. By now, Leonolis' eyes had adjusted to the dim light. He could see two guards blocking the doorway. One stood there as the other entered the cell and sat two buckets down with a thud in the center of the small room. Regalion sat with his back against the wall, hands behind his head, face bowed to the ground. Leonolis followed suit. As the guard approached the prisoners, he kicked the old man's feet then did the same to the boy. As they were kicked, they naturally drew their feet toward their bodies, knees now touching their foreheads. This was the way the guards determined if a prisoner was still alive, the movement of their feet being the sign.

As the door slammed shut behind the guards, the boy and the old man remained silent until they could no longer hear the footsteps of the guards. In a whispered tone the old man said, "It is best to remain silent when they enter. They take great delight in inflicting pain for the most ridiculous of reasons. It would be wise to give them none."

"I understand," said the boy. "How long have I slept?"

"Ha! Ha! Ha!" laughed Regalion. "Slept? I wouldn't call it sleep per se! You have been dreaming for almost two entire days!" said Regalion. "You must have been through an incredible ordeal. You groaned and moaned and squirmed and wrestled with many unseen foes during your 'sleep.' You spoke of things I have not heard before: of some contraption, I suppose, called a 'piano'; of a magnificent rope swing that could launch one into flight; of great battles and mystical creatures. You were quite entertaining!"

"I myself do not know the meaning of many of the things I dreamt. Some, like the 'piano,' brought me great pleasure yet I do not know why, and most of the other I actually experienced over the past few days," said the boy.

"I would like to hear of all you have gone through," said Regalion.

"But you told me you would tell me of how the evil overtook the mind of your son, Lucian," countered Leonolis.

"I suppose I did, did I not?" said the old man. "I will tell you the story with the promise that you will tell me yours."

"I will! I will!" said the boy.

Crawling to where the guard had placed the two buckets, Regalion took a cup from the floor and dipped it into the first bucket, offering a drink of water to the boy. As Leonolis gulped the cup down, Regalion took a loaf of bread from the second bucket, broke it into two pieces, giving the boy the larger share. "Here, son. Eat this while I tell you the story of how the great evil took my son."

Leaning back against the wall with his bread and water, the boy listened, enraptured by the tale that began to unfold.

Regalion began. "Long, long ago—long before you had even been thought of—your grandfather, High King Lairdon, had two sons. The firstborn, Lord Regalion (that would be me) and a second son, Troyolin (that would be your father) were born into a wonderful time in the kingdom. We were trained in the arts of battle just as I suppose you would be going through even now, were you back home. As we grew, we always knew we would one day rule over the people of Bren. Your grandfather instilled in us the royal necessity of gaining wisdom and strength but tempering both with kindness when we did finally reign. I, being the firstborn, was the natural heir to the throne, being twenty years older than Troyolin with seven sisters born between our births. It is, as you know, considered a sign of wealth to have many children. You also know that my sisters were in line of succession to the throne after me, but as per Brenolinian custom, they may waive that right should they deem it is not their calling. And each of my sisters invoked that right, leaving your father, Troyolin, the rightful heir to the throne after myself. It was assumed that I would take the throne when your grandfather, King Lairdon, stepped down or slept with the fathers. It was also assumed that your father, Troyolin, would serve as a trusted chieftain when he came of age. I was crowned high king when your father was sixteen years of age.

Even though we were so far apart in age, we became friends through the years. Fast friends. When he turned twenty we realized the depth of that friendship that only two brothers can understand. Your father and I were brothers, but he was also my friend of friends."

When the words "friend of friends" came out of his mouth, the old man hesitated for a few moments, obviously emotionally affected by the memory these words brought back.

Swallowing down a huge chunk of dried bread with a gulp of water, the boy excitedly said, "Yes! My father often speaks of those days! Even though it has been many years since your supposed death, he still speaks of you with a most reverent fondness."

"Does he have another he calls 'friend of friends' now?" said the old man.

Not wanting to say anything, the boy hesitated.

"It's all right," said Regalion. "I would like to know who he calls 'friend of friends' now. A man needs other men to keep his heart pure and his mind focused. Tell me, son."

"My father's friend of friends is Justinian. They went through the HommeDressage together as well as the Testolamorphia," said Leonolis.

"Yes, yes! I remember Justinian well. There is not a better man than Justinian. Troyolin has chosen well!" replied the obviously pleased Regalion. "Let me go on!'

"As I was twenty years older than my brother, it was always assumed that I would rule and that any son born to me would rule one day after me. But my wife was never able to bear children, so according to Brenolinian law, it would be the son of Troyolin who would rule after me," said Regalion.

"But you said your wife could bear no children, yet you have a son—Lucian. How can this be?" said the confused boy.

"People call me wise, but I made many foolish mistakes during my early years. My wife, being unable to bear children, became so despondent and grieved over her barrenness that she was eventually confined to the royal infirmary. I, in my own sorrow, foolishly began a secret relationship with a woman from the Dark Lands. My needs were satisfied for companionship even though our trysts were brief and in secret. She soon became pregnant with Lucian and gave birth to him just a few months before your father was born."

"Then Lucian was the rightful heir to the throne and not my father?" asked the confused boy.

"No! No! No!" interjected Regalion. "The law of Bren is very clear when it says 'The heir to the throne is to be a male born to the legal spouse of the king.' Even though Lucian was my son, he was not from the loins of my wife—my legal spouse—therefore, he could not legally take the throne. This would prove most detrimental to his fall into pride and mystical power in the days to come. I foolishly tried to keep his birth secret for many years, but when he was seven years of age, his mother died. I could no longer keep his existence a secret, so I brought him into the royal household. But much damage had already been done. Even at seven years of age, he felt ashamed that I had denied his existence to my own family for so long. Trying to make it up to him, I unwisely doted on him, spoiling him beyond measure before your grandfather took me aside and showed me the error of my ways.

"As your father was Lucian's uncle (you are his cousin!), it was quite natural for them to become friends. They learned to ride together. They learned to read and write together. They played together, and they fought mock battles together as boys. And when they became old enough, they went through the HommeDressage and the Testolamorphia together. And simply by virtue of his kind nature, your father was the one who always rose to Lucian's defense should his royal lineage ever be questioned. Even when Lucian did not deserve it, your father was always there fighting on his behalf. I was so proud of Troyolin and so grateful for Lucian to have such a friend. And they were fast friends, but there was always a tinge of jealousy on the part of Lucian. He knew the law of the land well, having been thoroughly trained in all the legal teachings of the land. Feeling as if he had been denied what was rightfully his by some archaic law concerning 'being born to the legal spouse of the king,' he was constantly challenging the legality of his position, always searching for some loophole in the law that would give him what he saw as his rightful place on the throne one day.

"It did not help matters that his younger uncle was treated as the one-day heir to the throne of Bren. And things went from bad to worse when they both had their eyes on the same girl's hand in marriage," said Regalion.

"My mother? They both sought the hand of my mother, Melania?" said the boy incredulously.

"I'm afraid so," said the old man. "You see, Melania was considered the most beautiful girl in the kingdom, not just for her physical features but for her sweet charms and graceful kindness as well. Both Lucian and Troyolin were considered to be quite handsome, but your father had something Lucian did not possess."

"What was that?" asked the boy.

"Your father had the confidence and assurance of who he was, so he carried himself with the strength of gracious manners and kind heart. And Lucian . . . well, Lucian was strong, but his strength was born of arrogance and pride. It proved to have the opposite effect upon Melania. He drove her away from himself with every arrogant display and prideful boast. Poor Lucian drove her right into the arms of your father. Your parents were married and Lucian's relationship with your father became very strained."

"And then what? How did the evil come to pass?" asked Leonolis.

"Again, I am sad to say, it was due to my own foolishness," began Regalion. "Lucian's mother was called Toralan . . . or at least that is what she told me her name was. It was not until Lucian was twenty years old that I learned the truth. After Troyolin and Melania were married, it took only a few months before it was announced they had conceived a child. It was during the time before you were born that Lucian was approached by the evil wizard, Gothgol, Wizard of the Heights, the White Wizard of Endoria. It was Gothgol who planted in his tormented mind the possibility of ruling the land of Bren. You see, unbeknownst to me, Toralan was actually the sister of Gothgol, only she was known by a different name than Toralan to the people of Endoria. Her true name was Tormentia."

"You mean Tormentia, the White Witch of Endoria was Lucian's mother? I have heard tales of her treachery and how she tormented men with her great beauty and charms and that she secretly plotted to destroy the throne of . . ." The boy was in shock as his words gave way to the reality of what Regalion was implying.

Now in tears, the old man continued, "Yes! Yes! Yes! It was I who brought the evil into Bren simply by my unwillingness to wait for the proper companionship that truly should have come from my wife! Had I only been patient, she would have been there for me, but on the day she learned of my unfaithfulness, her grief turned to hopelessness and she lost her will to live. That same night, my beloved wife died in sorrow. And I vowed to my father, your grandfather the good king Lairdon, that I would end the torment brought on by my own thoughtless, imprudent ways. So I set out to find Gothgol.

"I searched far and wide with a full regiment of the royal cavalry until we came face-to-face with Gothgol and his cronies in the Dark Forest of Endoria. Imagine my grief when I called Gothgol to account for his evil deceit, and he called for my son to come forth, and Lucian walked defiantly out of the shadows. Standing there facing my own son, the realization of what a moment of weakness over twenty years before had now brought forth in the present reduced me to agony like I have never known," sobbed Regalion.

Giving the old man time to regain his composure, the boy finally asked, "And then what?"

Taking a long breath of a sigh, Regalion continued. "I asked Lucian why he was in the company of such evil. His response? 'What else could you expect, Father? You never told me of my uncle, the Wizard Gothgol. After all of the unkindness I have received by the so-called good people of Bren, I have finally found someone who understands my plight and seeks to help me gain what is rightfully mine.'

"I knew he meant the throne of Bren, so I reminded him that 'by the law of Bren you can never ascend to the throne, Son. But because you are my son, you have every right, every privilege, and every good thing bestowed upon the royal throne and, indeed, upon every citizen of Bren. The keys to the kingdom are yours already, my son!'

"'Not enough, Father,' he went on. 'In my heart I know the throne rightfully belongs to me. Gothgol, my good uncle, has designed a way for me to ascend to the place you say I cannot ascend.' And with those words, the minions of Gothgol seized me, slaughtered the entire regiment with some strange magic, and then cut off my royal ring finger and the signet it bore, sending them by evil messenger back to Castle Aerie. Soon after this your father took the throne, since all assumed I was dead, effectively leaving you next in line for the throne. It was upon that day that Lucian and the dark forces had made their first attempt at usurping the throne. It was in the moment of denying me, his own father, that evil darkness filled his heart. And thus, the spirit of deceit that entered our world so very long ago was grafted into Lucian, thus carrying on from generation to generation in this manner. And this is why it is said that 'Lucian has tormented the land from its foundation.' He was simply the next incarnation of the evil one."

Regalion went on. "On the day you were born, Lucian appeared and presented a legal challenge to the throne. He had found what he thought was that loophole he had been searching for. 'Since my father's body has never been found, it is assumed he is dead. By royal law of Bren, his heir should have been appointed 'King Temporary' to rule until his return. That is the law. That is what has been decreed from of old.' The Council of Chieftains gently yet firmly reminded Lucian that he was not considered a legal heir. At that point, Lucian brought out the ancient Rule of Right Passage that said that 'if a royal ascension to the throne is challenged, then the challenger has a right to the Testing of Blood.' This Testing of Blood was established before even the royal lineage had been established, so, in a sense, Lucian had a right to challenge Troyolin's ascension. The Testing of Blood was essentially a duel of succession—mainly feats of strength, agility, and logic—which Troyolin easily won. The thought was that only a true member of the royal lineage would succeed in the tests brought forth. Lucian had forgotten that it was the strength of Troyolin that had gotten him through so many of the trials of his life at Castle Aerie. In his arrogance and pride, he had taken credit for so much of what truly had come at the hands of Troyolin. His pride was no match for the wisdom and humility of Troyolin.

"In a rage," Regalion continued, "Lucian summoned the waiting forces of Gothgol and stormed Castle Aerie, besieging it and the people of Bren for days. He had already begun a secret campaign of rebellion by recruiting the downtrodden and outcast of Brenolinian society. When he lost the Testing of Blood, he immediately called for his followers to rise up and stand against Troyolin, but the dark magic of Gothgol proved no match for the good magic of wisdom and humility that emanated from the heart of your father and the good people of Bren. On the field of battle, defeat at hand, Lucian and his followers were banished from the kingdom and exiled in the Mountains of Endoria. Your birth simply added fuel to the flame of Lucian's jealous rage . . . but there is something you must know."

Almost in a trance, Leonolis was startled from his enthrallment at this statement. "Something I must know? What do you mean?" asked the boy.

"On the day you were born, Lucian prophesied your death by his hand, but I have since received word that another greater prophecy was set forth that day. One of the wise sages of our land, the oracle Augurian, foretold of the day 'a boy with the heart of a lion would stand against the forces of darkness and prevail against all odds, bringing light to the Dark Lands and hope to the downtrodden.' It was understood by all that the words he spoke were spoken of you, Leonolis," the old man said solemnly.

"If you were here when those words were spoken, how could you possibly even know of them?" replied the boy.

"Dear Leonolis, do you not remember who I am? That I am of the same royal line as you, and that those who are called to rule are bestowed a specific and special gift from the Founder? Even though I never officially held the throne, it was my place to do so had I not been taken captive. My gift is intact," said Regalion.

"What is your gift, sire?" asked the boy respectfully.

"I was given the gift of seeing what would one day be. I see the future, my son. I saw this day several years ago and have patiently waited for your appearance. What you perceive as darkness all around you, I perceive as the hope of light. Your presence here means the prophecies have been set in motion. Your destiny is at hand, as is the destiny of an entire nation," said Regalion.

Leonolis pondered the words Regalion had just uttered. How could a boy not yet even experienced and tested in the HommeDressage and not yet having passed through the Testolamorphia possibly defeat such evil and bring peace to an entire nation?

"Why has Lucian allowed us to live if he, too, knows of the prophecy of Augurian as I am sure he must?" asked the puzzled prince.

"I like to think he has kept me alive due to some spark of love he feels toward me somewhere deep inside of his heart. Somewhere in there I like to hope that some part of his true identity remains intact. And as for you, I am sure it is simply his own pride that keeps you alive—that, and the words of Augurian. He, I am sure, hopes to torment your father with the enticement that he might possibly spare you. His pride, while Lucian's downfall, is your protection," said the wise Regalion.

"Lord Regalion, why did no one ever tell me of this—of all that has transpired?" asked Leonolis.

"It was at my request that I asked my father not to divulge the circumstances of Lucian's birth. I suppose I was so ashamed at how I had brought disgrace to the throne of Bren. It had been my intent to reveal the entire story throughout the kingdom upon my defeat of Gothgol and his minions, but, as you now know, I was never able to return to Bren. Perhaps your father was trying to protect you. Whatever the reason, it was not your time to know . . . until now," responded Regalion.

For several minutes, the two prisoners sat quietly, contemplating what things were being set in motion simply by Leonolis' presence in the cell. Pondering all that had transpired concerning the tale Regalion had just shared with Leonolis, they did not hear the approaching footsteps of the guards. Both were suddenly startled into reality as the door to their cell opened.

Chapter Fifteen

THE CRYSTAL ORB

In the days that followed Leonolis' capture, he had learned much about his own family that he had not known simply by virtue of the countless hours spent in conversation with Regalion. The prince had known very little about Lucian's history with his own father. What he learned only caused him to respect his father even more. Leonolis had always idolized Troyolin. The king had a way of making his son feel as if he could accomplish anything. Even though Leonolis was not the fastest or strongest or even the cleverest of boys in the kingdom, his heart was full of an inner strength and perseverance that permeated everything he did and everything he thought. Troyolin had also instilled a great sense of wonder and adventure in his son, so it came as no great shock to the king when he received word that his son had gone after Dreyden himself.

As the days rolled by, Leonolis lost track of time due to the constant darkness of the dungeon. Though it had only been a week since the adventure had begun, it seemed much longer to the boy. When he was not talking with Regalion or avoiding angering the guards, he had much time to contemplate exactly how and when his father would come for him, and the thought of how the king might deal with Lucian brought much solace to the heart of the prince. He was sure the king would come with the full force of his army, since the kidnapping was an affront to the entire kingdom of Bren. And he was sure his father would not wait too long before mounting the actual attack, being the great battle strategist he was. He would first gather the entire Council of Chieftains, and they would discuss the options for attack. At the same time, his father would also have sent spies into the land from every possible point of entry to gain as much intelligence as possible on where the dark forces were amassed, where the supply routes in and out of the valley were, what might be the best points of attack upon the walls of Abysstine, and so forth. Such thoughts helped keep the boy's mind sharp and his spirits high. His father would come and good would prevail.

After a few days, the boy's wounds had begun to heal even though the guards paid no attention to the actual well-being of the boy. It seemed their only responsibility was in keeping him locked away and alive. Leonolis, as you know, was not one to sit quietly and wait for his rescue. As his body healed and his strength returned, his thoughts turned toward devising a way to get word to his father that he was well and in good spirits. Leonolis was nothing if not resilient and optimistic. He reasoned that if he could get word to his location and condition to his father, then the king would be able to make specific plans regarding the layout of the castle as well as the number of guards and Chiroptera Leonolis had seen as he was brought into Castle Jadon.

One morning soon after the guards had brought the day's rations of water and bread, the boy noticed a faint squeaking noise coming from the farthest corner away from the cell door. This was not a metallic sound as the squeaking of the door, but rather the sound of some wee animal in communication with one of its own kind. The slightest of rustling sounds came from the tiny feet as the creature rooted around in the straw. Growing very still and focusing his thoughts in the direction of the sound, Leonolis began to think-speak.

Who goes there? In the corner . . . who goes there? thought-whispered the boy.

Suddenly, the squeaks and the rustling stopped. Whatever was there seemed to have frozen in place. Again the boy spoke.

I know someone is there. I can hear you. You have no reason to be afraid, as I am a friend.

From somewhere in the dark corner a small, faint, squeaky voice pierced the air. *How can I know you are a friend? We have no friends here, only enemies.*

Laughing softly in thought, the boy continued. *You really have no worries with me. I am a captive here in Castle Jadon, and I am looking for anyone who can help me get word to my father, the good king Troyolin, that I am safe and well.*

You are a captive of Lucian? asked the voice with a hack and a spit. *Cursed wretch of a man. If you are his prisoner, we are your friends.*

Who is the "we" you speak of? asked the prince.

It is I, Muriday, prince of the kingdom of mice who rule the unseen passageways of Castle Jadon. Scurrying cautiously toward the prince, two small rodents jumped to the rim of the food bucket and stood there as Leonolis crouched down to their level. Continuing, Muriday said, *And this is my sister, Princess Dorimay. And who are you, friend?*

I am Prince Leonolis of Bren, son of the high king Troyolin. I was taken captive only a few days ago by the Dark Lord. I must get word to my father so that he will know I am safe. I must get word to him of what to expect by way of the enemy's forces when he comes for me.

Ah, yes. We had heard rumor of a new prisoner from the south but have only this day made our foraging rounds to this level of Jadon. We are but wee creatures, and this is a most massive fortress. Pardon our initial standoffishness, as we are not accustomed to being greeted with kindness by the likes of men, said Muriday.

Here. Take some of my bread in return for your kindness to me, said the prince.

Regalion had not taken much notice to what was going on in the cell until he spied out of the corner of his eye what appeared to be Leonolis giving some of their meager portion of bread to two mice!

"What are you doing feeding the mice, boy? We barely have enough as it is without you giving it away to rodents!" cried Regalion.

Just as the old man was making his way to shoo the mice away, Leonolis rose to his feet and stood between the mice and the man.

"They are our friends, Lord Regalion! They can help us get word to my father that we are safe—and they can get word of the lay of the land of Castle Jadon to better plan our rescue!" countered the boy.

Stepping back in silence, Regalion was in awe of the boy's gift. Even though he knew of the existence of the prince's gift, seeing it in action and recognizing the power and potential of that gift was quite something to behold. Turning back to the bucket where the mice had been perched, Leonolis found that his new friends had scampered away in fear at Regalion's outburst.

"Muriday. Dorimay. Come back. It was all a misunderstanding. Regalion is my uncle and he, too, is a friend," implored the prince.

"We get that a lot . . . misunderstanding," said a squeaky voice from some unseen crevice in the darkness.

"Please come back. We need your help desperately, my friend. Though I am so much larger than you, it is you who has the power to aid my freedom and the freedom of an entire nation. Please trust me. We will do you no harm, and it is our desire to help free you from the tyranny of Lucian," urged the boy.

"Yes. Yes. Of course we will help," came the diminutive reply of Muriday and Dorimay in unison. "How may we be of service?"

"Please get word through the realm of mice to the outside world. My father must be warned of what awaits him here in Abysstine. Tell him of the Chiroptera and of the many guards that patrol the walls and the Castle Jadon. Tell him the way through the corridors of the castle and of the many layers and levels beneath. If your people . . . er . . . mice . . . know of any weakness in the defense of Abysstine, please communicate that to my father," implored the boy.

"Friend Leonolis, how do we tell him? How can we make him understand? Does he speak as you do, in thought?" wisely asked Dorimay.

Leonolis had not thought of this. His father's gift was well known throughout the realm. From an early age, Troyolin had demonstrated the ability to immobilize moving objects in midair simply by focusing on that object, whether it be an arrow or spear. As he had matured and grown, so had his gift. Troyolin had gained the ability to immobilize the movements of several people on horseback at once. Of course he had to be within a reasonable distance of the moving subject to effectively stop them in their tracks, often in midair. The most famous demonstration of this gift took place when one of the turrets of Castle Aerie had caught on fire, trapping one of the guards with no way of escape save to jump from the window to the ground forty feet below!

As the flames grew too much to bear, and fearing being overcome with smoke, the soldier had lunged for a nearby ledge just as the king was summoned to survey the commotion. Hanging by one hand for a few seconds, the guard, already weakened by the smoke he had inhaled, could no longer maintain his grasp, and fell, plummeting toward the hard ground as the gathering crowd gasped in horror. The collective gasp instantly became a collective sigh of disbelief as the falling guard suddenly came to a stop a few feet from the ground. Slowly, King Troyolin lowered the now unconscious man gently to the ground as the crowd began to cheer. Although Leonolis had not seen this feat himself, he had heard the story time and time again, and he never tired of hearing it. But his father's magnificent gift would not help him communicate with a mouse!

"Lord Regalion! What should we do?" asked the now perplexed boy. It was obvious they had nothing on which to write a message. As the humans and mice contemplated how best to get word to the king, the footsteps of the guards could be heard rushing down the corridor.

"Quickly! Hide, my little friends!" said the boy. "Can you speak with horses?" Leonolis hurriedly asked.

"Why, yes. We can," replied Muriday.

"My friend, the great horse Arolis is being held somewhere on the castle grounds. He may be able to help us think of a way to get word to my father. Find him and let him know I am well and safe and that we are working on a plan to aid the defeat of Lucian and his evil dark forces," said the boy.

"We go at once, my lord!" said the mice. "We will see you soon, once we have made contact with the horse Arolis. May the strength of Bren be yours today!"

Hearing the mice use one of the sacred sayings of Bren brought peace and hope to the boy's heart as the door to the cell came crashing open.

"What is going on in here?" demanded the guard.

"We simply talk," said the calm Regalion. "Surely there is nothing else for us to do in these fine accommodations," he said in a facetious tone.

"You will not respond with insolence!" yelled the guard as he struck the old man across the face, knocking him to the ground.

"Come, boy! Time for you to get to work!"

And with that, Leonolis was shoved into the dark corridor outside the cell. Slamming the door shut, Leonolis was led away from his uncle and toward the surface of the castle grounds. It took several minutes for the boy's eyes to adjust to the bright midday sun. This also brought much confusion to the boy since, in his mind, it was nighttime. He had lost track of the days since he had been thrown into the dungeon. Disoriented and squinting, the boy was once again collared and leashed.

Soon enough he was forced to quickly regain his balance as he was pulled toward the outer courts of Castle Jadon. This time he followed willingly behind the guard who led him, deciding good behavior would serve his purposes, and keep him from being struck!

Heading into an alleyway of sorts, they came to a doorway where much commotion and busyness seemed the order of the day. This was the entryway into the castle kitchen.

"Pick up that bucket," demanded the guard.

Leonolis picked up the large, wooden pail and followed the guard as he tugged on the boy's leash. They stopped in front of a large rectangular bin that stood about three feet high and ten feet long by four feet wide. The incredible stench that rose from the bin greeted the boy's nose long before they were close enough for him to peer in. As Leonolis turned away in disgust, the guard pulled his leash and almost caused him to fall into the filth.

"Here's your new job, Your Highness," mocked the guard. "Take your royal bucket and begin putting all this slop into the transport wagon."

A small wagon yoked to a small workhorse was waiting near one end of the long bin. The slop was the refuse from the kitchen and represented one day's worth of grease, discarded food, animal parts, and whatever else came from the kitchen's garbage. Leonolis' new job was to remove all the waste from the large bin and place it in the smaller bin in the wagon. It took the boy several minutes for his nose to grow numb to the smell. The first time he dipped the bucket into the mess it felt warm and disgusting and nearly caused him to puke. Keeping himself from vomiting became his primary focus as he proceeded to fill the wagon's container. Once the wagon bin was filled, the guard directed the prince to lead the horse and to follow him to the castle garbage heap. Once there, the wagon was backed up to a large open pit in the ground. A small gate on the end of the wagon was opened and the entire sloppy mess poured into this pit. From there, the waste material was rendered into other useful materials such as tallow for candles and oil for lamps within the castle grounds.

Once the wagon was emptied, Leonolis repeated the process. Making so many trips to the rendering pit and overcome with the nastiness of his task, the boy had lost count of how many trips it had taken for him to empty the entire large bin from behind the kitchen. By the time he completed the last trip, the sun was going down behind the mountains. After washing down the wagon and bucket, Leonolis was instructed to feed and water the workhorse and to lead him back to the castle stable area. When he realized where he was headed, a tinge of joy went through his entire being. Perhaps he would be able to see or even speak with Arolis!

Heading into the dimly lit stable, Leonolis was preoccupied with making contact with his horse and did not hear the stable master say, "I'll take her from here."

Startled back to an awareness of where he was and whom he was dealing with, Leonolis heard the stable master say, "Boy! I'll take her from here!" Not wanting to appear too obvious by asking about Arolis, he simply began to crane his neck over the front stalls in the hope of seeing his friend.

"Out, boy! You've seen horses before haven't you?" said the stable master. "And go wash up! You're stinking up the stables!"

Leonolis did not respond. Instead, he backed away and began sending his thoughts out. *Arolis! Can you hear me? Arolis! Are you here? It's me, Leonolis!*

Nothing. He was sure that Arolis must be somewhere in the stable. If so, he would surely be able to make contact. The boy's heart sank just a little as the guard pulled on the leash and headed back toward the castle area. Stopping in the area where he had rinsed out the wagon and bucket, the prince was instructed to wash himself. This was actually a most refreshing experience for the boy. As he washed away the slime and grime of the day's task, he began to daydream just a little, the water reminding him of days spent swimming with Dreyden and the other boys back in the Runland with Castle Aerie within plain view. Although he was unable to wash the stench away completely, at least the water made him feel clean. Once he was cleaned to the guard's satisfaction, they began to make their way to the dungeon. After they made it to the elevation apparatus, Leonolis was surprised when they stopped short of the lowest level where he had been housed with Regalion.

"Why have we stopped here?" asked the boy.

"You have an appointment," was all the guard offered.

Curious, Leonolis was led down the dark hallway and into a side chamber where a long table surrounded by twelve ornate chairs filled the room. On the table was a small feast, complete with a huge roast, vegetables of all manner, desserts, and sweet red wine. At each end of the table stood two more guards with several more guards standing at attention along each of the side walls of the candlelit room. And seated at the head table on the opposite end was none other than Lucian.

"Have a seat, cousin. Have a seat," sneered Lucian. "I hope you have enjoyed your time with my father and trust that he has filled you in on all the happenings concerning our very precious family."

Nodding but not saying a word, it had taken the boy aback just a bit when the word "cousin" made its way through his mind to the place of understanding. Lucian was his cousin! Although he had known a bit of his family's history, he had never really contemplated what it truly meant to him personally since his only practical relation was the same as every other Brenolinian: Lucian was evil and determined to overthrow the throne. To now be forced into a conversation with Lucian in regard to his family was a bit much for the boy.

"And how do you like your new job, my prince?" said the Dark Lord. "Why so tight-lipped now? You were quite the talkative one when we first met, or should I say insolent and disrespectful? It doesn't matter now. Here we are, dear cousin. I wanted to spend some time with you over a meal as good families do. Have a seat."

Lucian directed the guard to loose the boy from his leash. Leonolis slowly made his way to the only other place setting at the table, just to the left and around the table corner from Lucian. After filling his own plate, Lucian filled the boy's, making sure he had plenty. It had not taken Leonolis much coaxing to begin eating. After all, he had only been subsisting on bread and water since the day he had arrived at Castle Jadon. As the two ate the meal, the conversation was one-sided, mainly Lucian recounting his many feats of daring and heroism that seemed completely fabricated to Leonolis. After all, the boy had heard of all the same adventures Lucian now spoke of from his own father and from his own tutor, Maison the Wise. It was very odd to hear Bren's history as told from such a deluded point of view. Several times Leonolis had to bite his tongue to keep from correcting Lucian; he had to concentrate on his meal so as to avoid laughing out loud!

After the meal was completed, Lucian called for his servants to begin clearing the table. As they moved in to their work, Lucian once again directed his conversation to Leonolis. "I trust you were growing tired of the bread and water, weren't you, cousin?"

Nodding, Leonolis simply stared ahead silently.

"Did you enjoy the fine vegetables we grew right here in the Valley of the Abyss? And how about that rich dessert? It was made from the finest juji fruit in the land, grown in the highlands of Endoria. And the meat? Did you enjoy the fine roast? I hope you enjoy roast horse. I know I do," said Lucian. "If Arolis had only been more obedient . . . more malleable and trainable, perhaps he would have made a very fine war horse for me rather than a few days' worth of meals."

Leonolis began to grow violently sick as he pushed away from the table in horror. Falling to the floor he began to wail uncontrollably as he cried out, "Arolis! Arolis! Not my Arolis! What have I done!"

Laughing hysterically, Lucian sat back in his chair and began picking his teeth with a small toothpick made of bronze. Between his giggles and the boy's retching, the sound coming from that room would have made the strongest heart cringe in revulsion. After he had completely lost the contents of his belly, the weakened, heartsick boy jumped to his feet and lunged for the throat of his evil cousin. "You evil bastard! You will pay for this!"

As he leapt through the air, Leonolis' flight was cut short as the butt of a guard's spear met his head and knocked him writhing in pain to the ground. Still laughing at the poor boy, Lucian had not even flinched at the prince's outburst.

As his right eye began to swell shut and as blood gushed from the gash in the bridge of his nose, Leonolis was pulled to his feet by two other guards. Lucian beckoned for them to bring the boy close to him. Reaching down, Lucian pulled up the scepter he carried with him wherever he went. On the end of the scepter was a small, round crystal, milky white in color but tinged with specks and sparkles of gold and silver.

"See this, boy? This is the Crystal Orb. With this magical device I am able to see all that goes on within my kingdom, and once I am crowned rightful king of Bren, my power will increase in such a way that I can use the orb to see all that goes on within the entire world! Imagine that. I wouldn't put too much stock in the archaic prophecies of old men if I were you, dear cousin. The power I now hold will transcend and overpower any magic that seeks to work against it. Here. Take a look," said the evil one as he nodded to the guards.

Leonolis only glared at Lucian, looking him squarely in the eyes. If hatred could be a blinding light, Lucian would have been instantly blinded. Taking the boy's head by one of his strong hands, another guard forced Leonolis to look into the orb.

"What do you see, boy?" asked Lucian.

As if he were seeing a ghost, the boy exclaimed, "It's my father! And he is leading the legions of the armies of Bren. My father is coming!"

"Ah, yes. Your father is coming. But look again," sneered Lucian.

This time, the picture was not quite so pleasant. What Leonolis saw caused him to turn away in tears. The orb's revelation this time was still of the boy's father and the legions of Bren, but this time the picture was one of terror and confusion. Leonolis saw the unfolding of an ambush that seemed to catch him and his armies off guard. In the orb's smoky glass, Leonolis saw thousands of men lying dead on the field of battle and his father being led up to a gallows where a chopping block and a hooded executioner stood, axe sharpened and ready.

"Power is mine, boy. The kingdom is mine. Your father comes, but he will regret his decision to come after you. How does it feel to be the one who leads to the downfall of one's own father?" asked Lucian. "Oh, and one more look now."

Leonolis had no more strength to even raise his head to look into the orb. As the guard lifted the boy's head to face the orb, Leonolis saw Arolis, alive and well. Leonolis collapsed in relief as the guards carried him to the doorway.

"Did you really think I would waste such a fine specimen of horse flesh on the likes of you?" snorted Lucian after them. Thus was the perverse mind of Lucian. Cruel and malevolent, enraptured with himself, he found great humor and satisfaction at the expense and in the pain of others.

The next thing Leonolis knew, he was being thrown into a cell somewhere other than the one he had occupied with Regalion. This time he was alone, and his only thought was not in how he might escape. This time his thoughts were consumed in how to warn his father of the impending trap, and certain doom.

Chapter Sixteen

TO THE RESCUE

T royolin and an entire regiment had set off toward Treacherin once they had received the tattered saddlebag that had been found with evidence of Leonolis' swine rat encounter. While the other troops were being summoned with the purpose of gathering at Menden Lake in the upper reaches of the canyon of Abysstine, Troyolin and Justinian would have time to strategize during the journey to Menden Lake. As the king's friend was about to command the troops to head out, the sound of approaching hoof beats could be heard coming from the south, giving a momentary halt to their plans.

"Yo ho! Yo ho!" said the short, round man with the long, grey beard who came galloping through the sidestepping cavalrymen with great deftness for such an old man. Clothed in the robes those in Bren would automatically recognize as the robes of a scholar, the little old man brought his horse to a sliding (and might I say, very skillful) stop.

"Maison? What are you doing here?" asked the astounded king. "This is no place for my son's tutor."

"I have need of a private conversation with the king," said Maison the Wise excitedly.

"You may speak with me and my chieftains. I have no time to hide any news you may have from them," said the king.

"Sire, have I not been trustworthy in the care and training of your son? Does that not earn me at least the trust of the king in this most dire of circumstances?" asked Maison. "No disrespect, my lord, but what I share, I share with no one but the king. Trust me, sire. You will understand."

"Very well." The King acquiesced. "Come with me."

Dismounting with the aid of a royal guard, Maison the Wise followed (waddled actually) after the king into the forest, away from the road. Making sure to be far enough away for his words to be unheard yet sure to remain within eyesight of the king's Royal Guards, Maison signaled for the king to bend to his level. Whispering into the ear of King Troyolin, Maison delivered his message. Jerking his head away from the teacher as if in disbelief at what he had just heard, the king once again leaned down toward his son's tutor but this time took him by the shoulders and gazed intently into the smaller man's eyes as if to say "are you sure?" After a few more moments, the king and Maison returned from their conversation.

Clearing his throat, the king said, "Justinian, you will lead this regiment on to Menden and wait for me there. I have need to make a small detour that may prove to be very beneficial to our cause."

Taking the king by the shoulders and glaring into his face just as the king had done with Maison just a few moments before, Justinian said, "Troyolin, my king to be sure, but friend of friends to the death, I cannot allow you to do that. I will go with you or you will not go!"

"As king of the realm, you will obey me, Justinian, but as friend of friends to the death, you must trust me. I must go, and you must trust me . . . and as your king, you will obey me," the king spoke calmly.

"Sire, if anything were to happen to you I would . . ."

"Enough, my friend. It is settled. Where I go may well prove to be the difference between victory and defeat. We must waste no more time. Go at once. I will take a small company of fifteen Royal Guards. Maison will go with me as well," said Troyolin.

At first, Justinian had refused to go one step without the king at his side, but through royal decree in the heat of the moment, he had been persuaded to carry on with the march toward Menden Lake. Troyolin was very mysterious as to the reason for this detour. The darkness of the Forest of Endoria was not a safe place for a good king to venture into without good reason. As the last of the regiment led by Justinian passed by, the king turned and headed east into the center of the woods, accompanied by the Royal Guards and the frumpy old teacher, Maison.

After several miles of steady trekking through the forest, it became very apparent that Maison was leading the entourage very deliberately to their secret destination. As the noonday sun made its way through the massive, nearly impenetrable canopy of trees, shafts of light every few feet gave the eerie impression of long strands of straight vines, which contrasted starkly with the gnarled vines that hung so profusely throughout the forest. As insects intersected these strands of light, they flickered as sparks from a campfire on a very dark night, giving the entire forest a very magical feel. As the king kept his gaze fixed straight ahead, the old man kept his eyes toward the flickering above. As they came through a small ravine, Maison suddenly stopped as he put his finger to his lips, signaling for silence. Pointing to the flickering overhead, it took the king several seconds to make out exactly what the old man wanted him to see.

The flickering effects of the insects would dissipate as soon as the bug had flown through the light shaft. The "insect" that Maison was pointing to did not disappear as it came out of the light. This was no insect at all, but rather a tiny flitting fairy girl of the forest. As the fairy drew closer to the old man, she seemed to recognize him. Buzzing up and down as fast as a hummingbird with excitement, the fairy began beckoning the old man and those with him to follow her. So they did.

As they followed the beautiful flitting creature, they crossed several shallow streams and traversed many narrow ravines. The deeper into the forest they went, fewer were the shafts of light. Even though this was midday, it appeared almost like dusk just before the sun goes down, making their ability to follow the fairy easier. The deeper into the forest they went, the larger the trees and the larger the trees, the larger the massive roots that jutted out of the ground. This gave the appearance of goblin arms reaching and witch fingers clawing. Quite unsettling. The men who followed Troyolin for his protection never wavered once, nor did they ever flinch at the quest before them. They would follow their king to the death.

Suddenly, the little fairy seemed to disappear just as suddenly as when she first came to them. Inching slowly forward, the king and his men, along with Maison the Wise, made their way through the growing darkness one slow step at a time. Coming to a small rise, they began to weave their way through the maze of roots that covered the hillside. The closer they came to the top of the ridge, a faint light began to rise from the other side. Once at the top, they were once again amazed at what they saw.

There before them was a small but grand clearing in the forest and sitting in the middle of that glade mingled amidst the roots that grew from the forest floor around, sat a quaint looking little cottage of a home. Coming from the stone chimney that jutted up from one end of the house was a wispy, almost lazy, plume of smoke, meaning the house was inhabited. Nearing the house, Maison signaled for the company to halt. He then dismounted and slowly waddled toward the door. As he reached out to knock on the door, it sprang open and out flew the Fairy girl almost causing the old man to fall on his bottom as he stumbled back in surprise!

"Maison, my friend! What took you so long?" asked a voice from somewhere in the small cottage.

Emerging ever so cautiously from the doorway came an old man with a long, grey beard that flowed almost to the ground. Dressed in the garb of a gardener, it was obvious the old man tended the garden that grew beautifully in the center of the glade. Taking Maison by the hand, the old man hugged the teacher tightly, patting him on the back as an old friend would greet a chum he had not seen for a good while.

Releasing Maison, the old man then gingerly headed in the direction of the king, moving much more spryly than one would have anticipated. This alarmed the guards, somewhat causing them to place their hands upon their swords and sidle their steeds a bit closer to the king's side. Reaching his hand out to his men, the king signaled the men to stand at ease.

"Augurian. Is it really you?" asked the king somberly.

"My son, it is I," came the response.

At those words, Troyolin leapt from the back of his horse and fell to his knees, embracing the weathered old man's legs as a servant would embrace a benevolent overlord. For several moments the old man simply patted the king's head. It was obvious to all that the king was very moved at the old man's presence . . . and even appeared to be crying! In an act of respect for their king, the guards all turned their heads away from Troyolin as was the manner of gentlemen of Bren. As the king's tears subsided, he looked up into the eyes of Augurian and rose stiffly to his feet.

"Dear Augurian, since the days of my father's reign, I have longed for our debates and encouraging talks and to hear your joyful laughter again. Just this day did Maison alert me to the fact that you were not dead as all in the kingdom had assumed," said Troyolin.

"Dear Troyolin, even a seer cannot live forever, nor can he maintain his sight as he once did as a young man," stated Augurian matter-of-factly.

"But on the day my father died, you were no more. You simply vanished. It was assumed that as your deep magic was somehow attached to his reign that you had passed away with him. The ways of magic transcend and baffle human ability to understand. It was simply easier to believe you were dead rather than to believe you left me upon my day of greatest sorrow," said Troyolin.

"Dear boy . . . my dear boy . . . I had been assigned to your father's reign and was indeed 'attached' as a warrior is attached to his sword. The deep magic was a binding force that neither of us could deny. But that bond was severed the day your father died. It is the way of magic that took me away for a season. It is the way of magic that now brings us back together," advised Augurian.

Going on, the old man said, "Maison the Wise is himself a seer. His magic involves the magic of the intellect—the mysteries and magic of the mind. I, on the other hand, am a seer whose magic involves the mysteries of power and the soul. Both are powers neither of us understands. What we do understand is that our powers were given as a gift to benefit and protect those we serve. In a sense, we are brothers."

Nodding his head, Maison the Wise continued, "Yes! Yes! We are brothers of the magical arts! Though on the day of his disappearance he was vanished to my eyes as well, I somehow had an inner knowledge that he was not dead but simply gone. Through the years, I have studied his writings and the history of Bren in correlation and came to realize that within the combination of those writings and the history of our nation that a prophecy had been foretold of a great disturbance and the capture of a prince, and that one day Augurian would again appear and help bring light to a great darkness. Just yesterday I discovered the final piece of that prophecy, which led me to the understanding that the time of Augurian's resurgence was at hand."

"Yes, of course! What took you so long to get here?" teased Augurian.

"Dear Augurian, what joy and gratitude flood my soul to see you alive and well!" said Troyolin. "You were more than simply the royal seer to me. It was you who taught me the ways of logic but trained me to season my logic with the salt of faith in the unseen—in mysteries beyond my own understanding—and it was you who always used your great power in submission to the will of my father and for the good of our great people. Your legacy has lived on, even when we thought you did not. How have you survived all these years alone in the Forest of Endoria?"

Laughing with a silly grin, Augurian looked at the king and said, "Alone? I have never been alone! Did you not remember I, too, could communicate with the animals just as many in your royal line have done? The birds bring me news from the outside world. The rabbits bring me clover and lilies for tea. The badgers bring me tasty roots of all manner for my stew, and the wolves . . ."

Just then, his words were cut off as the Royal Guards suddenly surrounded the king, swords drawn. Gazing toward the end of the glade where the garden was situated, a wolf made his way stealthily through the rows of corn and beans and onions and potatoes. Without saying a word, Augurian simply lifted his hand and made a waving motion toward the guards, and they were frozen in place as if they were statues! Eyes ablaze in fear, the guards could do nothing to protect their liege or to break the magical hold Augurian had upon them!

"It is a friend and not a foe," said the seer to the frozen men. "I will release you if you promise to lower your weapons." Nodding with their eyes, the men's arms dropped and their swords fell to the ground as the magician released his grip.

"Hollister, my friend! What do you bring me today?" said the old man to the wolf.

As the wolf drew close to the group, he began to walk upright on his hind legs. The closer he came to the cottage, the more his appearance changed. Just as Galennia had transformed from the form of a hawk to that of a human, Hollister was all of a sudden a man! In his mouth he carried a basket. As he became a man, he took the basket from his mouth and held it in his hand.

"A wolfman!" exclaimed the king. "I thought they were simply the imaginary monsters of old wives tales made up to frighten children! Yet here one appears before my very eyes! Incredible! Simply incredible!"

"Not a wolfman," corrected Hollister in perfect human voice and language. "I am of the Wolfen race. A wolfman—Werewolf, as you call them, is indeed a monster . . . and is indeed also not made up."

Extending his hand toward Hollister, Augurian asked, "What do you bring me today, my good friend?"

"This day have I traded in the village of Treacherin for a basket of eggs, good Augurian. I thought they would go well with the wild boar we trapped for you along with some of the fresh green onions from your garden," answered the Wolfen.

"Indeed they will!" exclaimed the old man. "Come in, my son, and let us talk of what is to come while I prepare a meal for us."

Leaving the Royal Guards to watch over the cottage, Troyolin, Maison, and Hollister followed Augurian inside. As Augurian made preparations for dinner, it was actually Hollister who took over the kitchen duties, allowing Augurian to converse with the king. This was usually the case, as Augurian was wonderful at getting things started but easily taken captive in conversation. Any good friend of the seer knew this and simply took over whatever task needed to be tended to in the moment. It was never quite known as to whether this was all simply part of Augurian's plan or simply a whimsical part of his personality. Whatever the case, it brought joy to those who were fortunate enough to witness it!

"Augurian, my son Leonolis has been taken captive by Lucian," began Troyolin.

"This I have seen," calmly replied the old man. "I have seen this day for quite some time and had hoped that my sight was somehow incorrect, but, alas, I have not only seen but I have felt a strengthening of the darkness in my own soul and have seen its effects upon this small forest glade I call home."

"How so?" asked the king.

"The magic that is such a deep part of my nature naturally repels the darkness. When your father died, I was suddenly transported to this place, but it was not a place of light then. As I waited in the darkness for a sign of what my next season of life was to be, the trees began to push away, the roots began to release their grip, and this glade was formed. I began building the cottage with the help of the Wolfen and other friendly forest fauna. As long as there is light, the darkness is held at bay. As it is with this pleasant glade, so it will be with the destiny of the land of Bren, and so it will be with you and Leonolis. Darkness will be repelled by the light you allow to permeate your rule, sir King Troyolin."

Pondering the words of Augurian, Troyolin asked, "What does that mean, good friend? I have known this truth since I was a boy, thanks to your tutorage and my father's ways, but what does that truly mean now, sir?"

Rising and walking to the stool where the king was seated, Augurian placed his right hand on the king's shoulder and said, "Lucian was once of the light, but he allowed the darkness of pride and selfish gain to displace the light. There is not one of us who is completely safe from that same possibility. What this means is that you must never lose sight of the light of goodness, even in the face of personal tragedy and heartache. Leonolis must never lose sight of the light even though his life and future be in peril. As a nation, the good people of Bren cannot and must not lose sight of the good regardless of the ebb and flow between good times and hard times. And my son, they will be watching you for the encouragement as to how to respond to such situations. Light wins over darkness if the light does not hide its face."

Troyolin knew the old man was right, and he knew what this ultimately meant. The heart of a king must make the hard decisions for the greater good—even if it means personal loss and tremendous pain. The heart of a king is the heart of both sacrifice and service and Troyolin embodied both, but this did not make the task any easier. If the time were to come, would he be able and willing to sacrifice his own good for that of the nation? Sensing the king's thoughts, Augurian simply said, "Let us take eat, my friends. And let us focus on what we have rather than that which we do not. In this moment we find good friends and good food, and neither should be wasted on worry. Chins up and hearts honest, men. Let us dine."

Hollister kindly served the king and his friends, careful to make sure every need was tended to. As the old friends ate, the conversation began to lose some of the somberness as old memories brought joy and laughter into this most dire of moments. As their hearts grew warm on the inside, so the borders of the glade extended even further all around the little cottage, proving once again that a little light can push back a lot of darkness.

As the afternoon grew into evening, laughter and joy wafted out of the little cottage, pushing the forest back for almost a mile from where it had been when the company had first arrived. As the men grew tired, they each found a place to curl up and rest for the night. Outside, the men had done the same, posting four sentries around the glade while the remaining men slept. After doing so, they took rations from their packs and prepared for the watch. At three-hour intervals, the sentries were changed, allowing all the men to get at least some sleep through the night. As Hollister finished his service inside, he slipped out of the cottage and into the night, morphing back into his true form as he, too, took a place of watch over the glade. Unseen by the entourage since she had led them to the cottage (she was rather shy, you know) a little fairy darted from the cottage through the chimney and made her way to others who would play an important role in the things to come. As the night continued, a glow could be seen coming from the glade—a sort of beacon of hope that, though planted far into the deep forest, was not unnoticed by others in the realm, both good and bad.

Chapter Seventeen

WHEN WORLDS COLLIDE

As the king and his friends slept in the tiny cottage, a strange uneasiness began to fill the hearts of the king's Royal Guard as if someone or something was watching them. The Wolfen, Hollister, felt it as well. All night long the forest had been oddly quiet. Gone were the sounds of the night birds and the howls of the hunting wolves and coyotes. Gone were the rummaging sounds of the wild pigs and badgers that foraged with their snouts for morsels of buried roots and fat little grubs. Even the wind had died down to a deathly calm. The feeling was one of foreboding, like a ship at sea whose sails are suddenly limp, signaling the calm before the coming storm. This was one of those pre-storm moments.

Just before dawn, the silence was broken.

At first the guards felt more of a vibration than actually hearing a sound. Underneath their feet a slight tremor shook their feet every few seconds. It was as if the ground beneath them was alive. As the trembling increased, one of the guards went to wake the king while the others stepped back from the center of where the shuddering seemed to be coming from. Just as the king bounded out from the cottage, the ground directly in front of the doorway erupted like a volcano. Surprised, the guards were knocked back onto the ground, as ogres—Terrebithians, to be exact—began pouring out of the tunnel. In the same instant, a great howl began to rise from the far end of the garden as Hollister, seeing what was taking place, sounded the alarm to the Wolfen.

No more had Hollister gotten out his warning than the entire surrounding forest seemed to come alive with the howling of what sounded like hundreds of wolves, but Hollister knew these were not the plaintive cries of the Wolfen. The howling that pierced the night sky were the wails of the Werewolves, which sent shivers down even the Wolfen Hollister's spine. Recognizing the king and his party were in grave danger, Hollister retreated back to the cottage and quickly joined in the fray between the ogres and the Royal Guards. Leaping onto the back of the nearest Terrebithian, Hollister dispatched him with one agile slash of fang to neck then moved on into the thick of the battle.

As the northern end of the glade was now left unprotected by Hollister's absence, the glade floor seemed to crawl with life. Upon closer examination, it became all too clear that the ground was indeed crawling, crawling with two dozen slinking Werewolves, snarling their way toward the cottage. Being the very observant king he was, Troyolin caught sight of this new movement between dodging the sword jabs and axe blows of the Terrebithians. As the pack of Werewolves inched closer, Troyolin stepped away from the battle with the ogres and headed directly for the oncoming wolf pack. Standing defiantly with the confidence of a man protecting his own family, the king lifted his right hand toward the Werewolves and summoned the power of his royal gift and froze the demon wolves in their tracks—one in midair as it leapt toward the king's own throat!

It had been quite some time since Troyolin had been compelled to use his gift, so he had assumed he would be quite rusty. But in the heat of battle, something had risen from deep within him infusing him with great power, like the passion he remembered feeling on the day his son, Leonolis, had been born. Perhaps it was just that feeling for his son that had brought forth this new vigor. Whatever the case, the Werewolves were stayed for the moment.

As Troyolin stood observing his surroundings, he noticed an odd thing taking place (as if the sudden attack of ogres and Werewolves were not enough!). The glade, which had grown in area at the onset of their brief stay in the cottage, was now beginning to shrink. It became apparent very quickly to the wise mind of the king that the light that had produced the broadening of the glade was now being reduced by the onslaught of evil, of darkness. As he observed this strange phenomenon, the king could hear the battle between his guards and the ogres beginning to subside behind him. The Werewolves had been subdued and the ogres were being contained, so why was the glade continuing to shrink? The answer soon became quite apparent to all.

Although the predawn was still windless, the air suddenly sounded as if a huge whirlwind was descending on the forest glade. Looking skyward, Troyolin saw the trees in every direction coming to life. Rising from above the treetops and headed down into the shrinking glade were hundreds and hundreds of huge birds. As the birds drew closer to the melee, Troyolin's heart was filled with horror. These were no birds. These were Chiroptera! Evil, flying, demon-birds, the giant bat people descended upon the Royal Guards. Most of the guards had never actually seen a Chiroptera. In fact, most had never even seen an ogre before. Their knowledge of these creatures had come from the many stories of old and from the illustrations from the military library during their training days back at Castle Aerie. The hearts of these brave men still did not waver even in the face of this flying menace. Flailing into the air like swatting at giant flies, the men were no match for the strength and claws of the Chiroptera.

"Hold fast, men!" shouted the king. The Werewolves had been able to inch forward ever so slightly as the king broke his concentration long enough to encourage his men. Troyolin knew he was in trouble. For a brief second, he felt his own heart waver with the slightest tinge of panic, but the face of his son, Leonolis, once again came to the forefront of his mind. This only intensified his focus upon the Werewolves. Keeping his right hand stretched toward the wolves, he dropped his sword and simultaneously reached backward toward his men and just above their heads, freezing the attacking Chiroptera in midair. Though this did not halt the onslaught of screaming bats, the sight of comrades frozen in midair seemed to confuse the entire flock, giving the men time to regroup in a phalanx near the cottage. Holding their shields above their heads, the guards became one unit, jabbing from the protection of the shields into the attacking bats.

Unable to get at the guards and unable to penetrate the airspace around the king due to the force of his powerful gift, the Chiroptera who were not frozen began to attack the cottage itself. Like crazed banshees, the bats dived at the thatch roof, grazing the top and ripping away huge patches of thatch with every swoop. It did not take long for the entire rooftop to be stripped, giving an odd skeleton-like appearance to the little house as the joists and support beams were exposed in the moonlight.

The next wave of bats sent the joists shattering and splintering like toothpicks as they crashed into the remains of the roof. Once the roof was completely gone, the flying demons poured in through the gaping wound of the cottage roof amid terrifying screeches and screams as if one were hearing a flock of vultures fighting over the carcass of one tiny rabbit.

As the screaming intensified, the glade began to close in even more around the entire fracas, giving the king and his men the thought of what one must feel like when finding himself locked in a cage with dozens of hungry lions. The picture was bleak to say the least. Whenever the king's concentration was weakened, the Werewolves were able to edge ever closer to the king, and the Chiroptera were able to shuffle a little closer to his men. Hearing the horrifying ruckus going on inside the nearly destroyed cottage and realizing his good friends, Maison and Augurian, had never made it out caused Troyolin to break his hold on the crazed beasts.

As the king's arms dropped, the Werewolves lunged toward the king and his men while at the same time the Chiroptera dropped onto his men, crashing through the protective phalanx. Somehow, Troyolin had been able to reach for his sword just as the leaping wolf he had frozen in midleap came flying toward his face. In one swift motion, the king lopped off the Werewolf's head and dispatched two more in the same instant. This bought him enough time to once again focus his mind, giving him the opportunity to freeze the perimeter directly around himself. Though his focus was now weakened, the king was still able to keep the circling Werewolves at bay while he watched his men being helplessly carried away into the forests one by one by the demonic Chiroptera.

Seeing the last of his men picked up in the manner of a hawk picking up and carrying away its prey, the king bravely held his concentration, spurred on in his own fight by the shear perseverance and loyalty of such brave men who gave their lives to protect his. Once again, the hole where the ogres had first broken through began to crawl with life. The Terrebithians had sent reinforcements. The small, ugly creatures seemed to slither out of the hole and soon the surrounding forest began to come alive as Werewolves and ogres began pouring in from every direction. Still the king held his ground, the power of his love for his son filling him with the strength to maintain the protective shield around him. With Werewolves circling him, Chiroptera hovering above him, and Terrebithians blocking any hope of escape, the king appeared to be the last man standing of his own company. Even the commotion in the cottage had come to a standstill. How long had it taken the Chiroptera to subdue and tear to pieces two old men?

After a few minutes of this strange culmination to the brief battle, the ogres and Werewolves that filled the now very small glade began to part from the northern edge. Making his way on two legs, a Werewolf dressed in a long topcoat of red, laced with golden paisley patterns, and wearing a tri-cornered hat complete with a long, white plume stopped within a few feet of where the king firmly held his ground.

"I am Lupistad, king of the Werewolves," declared the gravelly voiced creature. "Let down your guard, King Troyolin. You have my word, as one king to another, that no harm will come to you."

Holding his ground, Troyolin replied, "How foolish do you think I am, Lupistad? Your kind cannot be trusted, you who make your way through life at the expense and fear of others."

"We make our way at the expense and fear of others? How are we so different, you who pretend to be gracious and kind yet using your charms and magic to sway the minds of the 'good people of Bren' to do your own bidding," mocked Lupistad.

"I will not waste my time arguing with one who knows only evil. Let us cut to the chase. Why have you attacked us this night?" demanded the king.

"It seems I have made a most beneficial pact with an old friend of yours, Nephew Lucian, as you know him. It appears that long ago you usurped a throne that was rightfully his, and now he has the means to finally obtain that which was taken. In exchange for a homeland for my people (you see, we have grown tired of always hiding from the likes of men) we have offered our services to help bring about his coronation upon the throne of Bren," continued Lupistad.

"He will never be king of Bren. Never. And you will never take me alive," countered Troyolin.

"Oh, he *will be* king, and we care not whether we take you alive or not, but we will take you. We can wait as long as we need. You cannot possibly hold your ground forever, dear King," sneered the wolf king.

From somewhere behind him, Troyolin heard a murmuring and stirring sound among the Werewolves and ogres. Turning slightly to see what was going on behind him, Troyolin saw the parting of the beasts once again. This time an ugly, grotesque ogre came trudging toward the king, pacing around the perimeter of the king's position as if searching for a way to break through the magical shield surrounding him.

Wreaking of foul breath and surrounded by swarming flies, the ogre spoke. "I am Hadian, lord and king of the Terrebithians." And turning toward Lupistad, "My friend, thank you for saving the king until I arrived. I will take great pleasure in cutting to pieces the one who has tormented my people for so long."

"Tormented your people? We have never brought one instance of harm to you or your people unless it was to protect our own from your conniving and marauding ways. It is you who has tormented any who cross your path. You are no better than the Werewolves!" Troyolin declared defiantly.

As the words came out of the king's mouth, Hadian lunged at the king with his battle-axe, whose blow glanced off the force surrounding Troyolin, causing the ogre to fall on his face.

"How dare you compare us to the likes of the weak-minded Werewolves!" shouted the embarrassed ogre as he quickly picked himself up. "How dare you! You will pay, vile human! You will pay!"

"Calm down, my ugly and clumsy friend," interjected Lupistad. "Can you not see he is trying to cause us to turn on one another? May I remind you of the task at hand? If you truly desire to be free of these human wretches called Brenolinians, we must stick to the plan."

"What plan is that?" asked Troyolin, knowing they would never divulge such information.

"Normally I would say 'wait and see,' but since you will not live long enough to do that, I will gladly tell you the plan. Once you and your leaders have been immobilized, we will make quick work of your leaderless armed forces. Then we will make a systematic and triumphal march through Bren. Those who bow to Lucian will live. Those who do not will die. It's quite simple. Kill the head, kill the body. With you gone and your son a slave of the new king, where will the people of Bren be able to turn but to the long-lost and wrongfully treated Lucian, rightful heir to the throne . . . blah, blah, blah. As if I truly care what happens!" laughed Lupistad.

Amidst Lupistad's glee at the turn of events, a fluttering sound followed by a thud startled Lupistad and Hadian, almost causing Troyolin to lose his concentration.

"Falling Rocks, please be more careful in your landings. We have no time for your foolishness," grumbled Hadian.

"I had to see for myself the mighty Troyolin," screeched Falling Rocks, king of the Chiroptera. "So it is true. We have taken captive the great hero of Bren. I have long awaited the day I could taste his flesh."

"That will have to wait for a while longer, I am afraid," said Lupistad. "It seems he has some deep magic that surrounds him. We will have to wait until he tires.

"Hadian and Falling Rocks, let us gather our troops and continue with our assigned duties. I suggest we each leave five soldiers to guard the king. Once he tires, we will divide his body among ourselves and feast on roast king."

Each one assigned a group of their own kind to watch over Troyolin. Gathering his Werewolves, Lupistad headed back to the north. Gathering his ogres, Hadian headed back into the tunnel. Soaring high above the treetops, Falling Rocks led his flock in the direction of Menden Lake. As the dawn's first light began to peak through the treetops from the east, the little glade was now almost completely swallowed in forest and though the dawn approached, the night never seemed more dark than right now to King Troyolin. As futile as it seemed, the king still did not give up hope of rescuing his son. The power of love is the deepest magic of all.

While the king contemplated his dilemma, he became slightly distracted at a stirring and clanking that seemed to be coming from inside the debris that was once Augurian's cottage. Maintaining his focus, Troyolin began slowly edging his way toward the remains of the cottage. At first all he could hear was the clanking and rummaging sound of someone trying to make their way through the wreckage. As he came closer, he could make out muffled voices. From the timbre of the voices he sensed a familiarity, like someone calling for you through the sound of a storm, you know you recognize the voice but you can't seem to place exactly whose voice it is.

Yelling in the direction of the sound, Troyolin cried out, "Augurian! Maison! Are you there? Is that you?"

More muffled cries and more clanging and banging.

"Hello! Hello! Can you hear me?" cried the king.

Suddenly, the entire mass of debris exploded with a fantastic burst of light and energy, sending the entire hodge-podge straight into the sky like a reverse bolt of lightning! The explosion caused the king to lose his concentration and his grip on his evil guardians was broken. But the blast also sent the ogres and Werewolves reeling backward for several yards and caused the Chiroptera to crash clumsily into the earth. Before they were able to regain their composure and attack the king, Augurian emerged from the midst of the lightning bolt and instantly immobilized each of the would-be aggressors, freezing them solidly in place in every awkward position imaginable where the blast had left them.

"Augurian! You live!" exclaimed the king.

"Of course, I live! What did you expect? That I would give up without so much as lifting a finger?" replied the seer.

"But the Chiroptera . . . the cottage . . . there was nothing left in the course of the battle! No one could have lived through that!" said Troyolin.

"My dear king. Your assumption was that the chaos that ensued from the midst of the cottage was produced by the Chiroptera having their way with good Maison and myself. Did you not consider that perhaps the vile screams and confusion from within the cottage may have been due to the agonizing screams of the Chiroptera as they met the righteous indignation of two old and perturbed men?" said the seer with a slight teasing giggle.

"I am sorry for the loss of your cottage but extremely thankful for your timely stroke of lightning! I was growing weary of holding off the ghastly beasts!" declared the king.

"The cottage is easily replaced. Its demise serves as yet another sign that the time of my place in the destiny of Bren is finally at hand. Come. We have no time to waste," said Augurian.

"But what of Maison?" asked Troyolin.

"Maison! Stop dilly-dallying and come here at once!" demanded Augurian in a not-so-teasing manner.

As the seer's words ended, so did the blast of powerful lightning, as the tutor, Maison the Wise, let down his outstretched hands from which the blast was emanating!

Astonished, Troyolin exclaimed, "Maison! I thought your power was that of the mind! Yet here you are the source of this mighty delivering blast. I thought only Augurian possessed such power!"

"The power of the mind is rivaled only by the power of love, my king. Of course, when that power is coupled with a little tutorial magic it does tend to get a bit loud at times!" sniggered Maison—the wiseacre!

"I appreciate the humor, my wise old friend, but we must be off at once," said the king. "Augurian, just how did the Terrebithians, Werewolves, and Chiroptera all get the same information that we would be here on this night?"

"I am afraid that those we call friends may not be as friendly as we may hope," began Augurian. "And I have seen in the many omens coming forth that one with dark power has in his service one of the three ancient crystal orbs."

"Lucian has a crystal orb?" asked the bewildered king. "It has been passed down through the lore of Bren that the three orbs were held in secret by three of the ancients."

"That is the story, my king. But reality is that somehow someone has found one of the ancients and managed to obtain the orb," replied Augurian.

"So Lucian saw our every movement!" said Troyolin.

"Not exactly. He saw what you would understand as 'impressions,' revealing that you were on the move with a small company of men, but he had no way of knowing exactly where that might be. Were you followed, my king?" asked the seer.

"No . . . I do not think so. Even my trusted leadership knew nothing of where I was headed nor did they have knowledge of my business here," explained the king.

"Someone is not as they seem, good king. You have been betrayed. I have seen it. Time and circumstances will reveal the truth. It does not matter now. We have no time to waste. We must get to Menden Lake as soon as possible. Maison, let us revive the king's men," said the seer.

Chapter Eighteen

WHAT HAPPENED TO
OLLIEMAN

O llieman had flown for his life while trying to help Leonolis find his way to Abysstine. The Chiroptera had been relentless in their pursuit, but Ollieman had been cunning in his escape. Flying through the dark of night was much easier for an owl than even a salivating Chiroptera intent on having a fresh owl for dinner. While Chiroptera resembled large bats, they did not possess the natural radar ability of true bats. They relied more on their sight yet without the optical agility or ability of a wise old owl, and, of course, they possessed none of an owl's wisdom!

The frantic owl headed straight through the dense upper branches near the forest ceiling, knowing the much larger bat people would have a very difficult time keeping up with him. After only a few minutes of very intense bobbing and weaving through the treetops, Ollieman spotted an opening in an outcropping of rocks near the ground, jutting from the wall of the creek bed. Heading for the opening he was sure the Chiroptera could not possibly see, much less squeeze into, he made it into the chasm. Outside he heard the muffled cries of several bat men unable to pull up in time to avoid crashing into the wall, into each other, and into the razor-sharp stones jutting out from where the owl had found refuge.

Ollieman was able to crawl into the empty crevasse and make his way ten feet from the opening. He would simply wait out the hungry Chiroptera. He didn't have to wait long. After only a few minutes of whining and clawing at the opening, the hungry crash victims began to lick their wounds and clumsily take flight back to their commander in hopes of getting a piece of the prince, Leonolis.

The owl waited for quite some time before finally venturing anywhere near the opening of his shelter. What to do? Should he risk taking flight while the darkness still held sway? Could he risk waiting until morning light when he knew the Chiroptera would be less willing to reveal themselves? What was now happening to Leonolis and to Arolis? What could one owl do to help deliver the boy and the horse from so many with so much power? This was one of those rare moments when the wise little owl was at a loss as to what wisdom would do.

Just as he had gotten up the nerve to finally step to the opening, the raptor was startled from his own questions by a tiny wisp of twinkling light that shot into his dark hiding place. Revealing herself to the owl was none other than Rania, the Fairy the small band of wanderers had first encountered while running from the pig rats.

"Follow me, brother owl. We can waste no more time!" exclaimed the girl.

"But what of the Chiroptera?" questioned the still fearful bird of prey.

Rania replied, "They are long gone. They have taken the boy and his steed to Abysstine. There is nothing more we can do here. But there will soon be need of your service to good King Troyolin."

"Troyolin? How can I help the king when I have no way of communicating with him?" asked Ollieman.

"Leave that to me. Communication is one thing. Your wisdom is quite another. We have need of your astute insight, brother owl. Fly now! Answers later!" demanded Rania.

At that, the Fairy girl tore into the still-dark night sky, sans the glitter by which she had approached the owl (lest the bat people see her starry trail and follow), and Ollieman after her. Again flying near the upper growth of the trees for cover, the fairy and her feathered companion were off. Ollieman was full of questions by this point, but felt more need for vigilance in watching and listening to the night than for finding resolution for his thoughts. After flying for several nights (they had to limit their travel to the cover of night and found the rest sketchy at best during the day), the duo eventually made their way to the realm of the southern forest through which Ollieman had not so long ago traversed with Leonolis and Arolis.

So unlike the usually meticulous-about-time Ollieman, the now-weary owl had lost track of time—so much so that he had not even noticed the wafting scent of freshly harvested juji fruit, which could mean only one thing. Treesants!

The tiny fairy-guide once again began emanating a trail of glittery radiance as she alit near the top of a massive juji fruit tree. Coming to light next to Rania on the same branch, it took the normally visually aware bird a couple of seconds to realize they were completely surrounded by a massive throng of Treesants. The movements of the tree people were very obviously less flowing than the last time he had been in their presence. There was an air of agitation, fear, worry . . . fretting.

As Ollieman's eyes adjusted to the scene, Sylvan himself stepped into the owl's awareness as if from nowhere. "Where is the boy?" asked the Treesant leader.

"I'm afraid he is now in the clutches of the dark lord, Lucian," stated the owl very matter-of-factly.

"As I have felt. As I have feared," said the Treesant.

"What do you mean 'as I have feared'?" asked the owl.

Sylvan went on. "Just this night we have sensed a deep stirring of evil in the land. My scouts have laid their own eyes on a massive gathering of Werewolves, ogres, and Chiroptera moving through our domain. A great darkness is overtaking our land, but not just our land. The entire realm, from the Dark Lands of the north to the Bright Lands of southern Brenolin, is slowly yet surely being engulfed in this darkness. A great evil has been unleashed. The signs are more than apparent. Something evil is coming upon us. We have sensed a great disturbance in the balance of all that is good. Betrayal. Deceit. Treachery of all manner. Though we do not necessarily count him as our king (we are a sovereign people), our seers have seen that this very day a great evil will befall good King Troyolin. And as Troyolin goes, so goes the entire realm."

"We must warn the king at once!" demanded the owl.

"No time! What has begun has begun!" said Sylvan.

Going on without allowing time for Ollieman's response, Sylvan said, "Even now we have received word that the king and his men have been besieged this very night by a marauding band of evil. He is safe but his numbers have been severely diminished. With this loss, the darkness has already begun to fall."

"What must we do?" asked the owl.

"I suggest we who love the light—regardless of who our king may or may not be—join our hearts with all others who love the light. If the light goes from the land and darkness prevails, all life as we know and love will cease to be the same," replied the tree king cryptically.

"Those who love the light? That is a most wonderful idea," said Ollieman, "but how do we do that . . . join our hearts?"

"I will send my emissaries to Sandovar, king of Larovia. They are well situated to the north and west of the land of Bren and would be strategic in their proximity to Abysstine. Surely they have also seen the signs of darkness, and we will present our case in adamant fashion," avowed the Treesant.

"Rania will fly to the Dark Forest of the Fairy realm and reveal herself to the human inhabitants of the land of Larovia where she will enlist the aid of Sandovar, king of the realm. My hope is that he will have sensed the growing darkness just as we have and will join us in our quest to put an end to the darkness. Fly, little one! Fly!" commanded Sylvan. And the little fairy was gone in a flurry of whirling fairy dust.

Turning back to Ollieman, Sylvan spoke with great gravity. "Brother owl. Go to good King Troyolin. Tell him of what has transpired. Tell him the Treesants are at his disposal, that Sandovar leads all of Larovia to his side, that we will rally those who seek to end the coming darkness, be they great or small, hidden or seen, Wolfen or Hawken, man or beast."

"Tell the king? How can I tell the king when I cannot speak as a man speaks?" moaned the now confused bird.

In a suddenly reverential tone, Sylvan spoke the prophecy. "It has been seen in the leaves by our own prophets. It has long been spoken that 'One will rise who rides the sky to whom a king will bow, and darkness cannot hide in light when wisely cries the owl.'"

"What now? I am to believe an old Treesant wives' tale?"

"Believe what you will, wise owl, but the prophecy is the prophecy, and this is the time spoken of so long ago. Will you not be wise enough to dare to believe?" responded Sylvan.

Ollieman perched quietly as he mulled over the Treesant's words. Wisdom does not respond lightly when the fate of an entire nation and way of life are weighed in the balance, and Ollieman knew the gravity of his situation.

Slowly the owl began to speak. "Logic does not always equal wisdom, my good tree king. After all I have experienced over the past two days, logic has flown out the window, and the realm of passion and righteousness and wonder and awe have taken its place. Though I do not see how the things we are facing are even possible at times, I cannot deny the power and substance of the fulfillment of so many prophecies at such a blinding pace. I will go to the good king Troyolin. I will worry about how to convey the message once I find him."

"We must move at once, good owl," said Sylvan. "We have no time to waste. I will send a company of my people to help assure you a safe and speedy passage to the king's party. Even now we have received news of his last known whereabouts. As long as we have trees through which to move we will be with you."

"Hold it right there!" Ollieman cried. "Why can't you speak these words to the king?"

"It has been foretold that the king would receive help from the owl. We do not question the prophecy. We simply uphold the word and allow the power of that word to bring forth what it will," said the Treesant.

And with that, Ollieman knew there was no more arguing with the tree king. As he lifted his wings into the air, a small band of Treesants stirred beneath him into formation. Flitting back into view, Rania made herself known.

"I will lead you to King Troyolin but must leave you there and make my way to the land of Larovia. To their high king, Sandovar. To the north we fly!"

The fairy led the way, followed by the owl, followed by the Treesants. This time, the entourage did not worry about travel in broad daylight, the situation becoming more and more dire with every tick of the clock. Over hills and through villages, soaring over mountains and traversing valleys, the Treesants were able to actually glide through the air for a few hundred feet when crossing rivers or streams or rocky crevasses. Traveling all day and all night they soon found themselves on the southern borders of the Dark Lands of Endoria. At this point, the Fairy girl bid her farewell and began her lonely journey toward Larovia to deliver the message to King Sandovar.

As the forest glades began to thicken and grow ever darker, the band of Treesants and owl slowed their pace in order to maintain a stealthy approach into the Dark Lands and the realm of Abysstine and the dark lord Lucian. Passing through the forest, even near the tops of the trees, began to grow treacherous due to the mangled growth of vines and thorny outcroppings of sinister-looking plant life. It was as if they were in some windless maze that reeked of mold and decaying plant life. Soon this moldy, decaying smell began to give way to the smell of smoke and burning sulphur, and then the air itself began to cloud with wisps of smoke emanating from somewhere below. As the smoke thickened, a clearing came into view . . . and the wreckage of a small cabin below.

From their high vantage point the band of would-be defenders of the light could see many bodies strewn about the clearing—bodies of Wolfen and Werewolves, bodies of Chiroptera and Terrebithians, and humans. Being aware that some great conflict had obviously just taken place, they warily made their way to the glade.

"From the looks of this, we are headed in the right direction," noted Ollieman to Sylvan.

"How can you be sure?" asked the tree king.

"Do you see these humans?" responded the owl. "They wear the uniform of the king's guard. See the royal insignia on their armor and on their shields? The king was here . . . and I fear has met some great evil."

Just at that moment a trumpet sounded from the northern edge of the glade, startling the entire group and causing the already hesitant Treesants to fly back into the cover of the trees, leaving Ollieman alone on the glade floor. As he flapped his wings to join his comrades, the owl was suddenly frozen in midair! Hovering not of his own power, the little owl was at once amazed and mortified at his dilemma. As the trumpet blare gave way to silence, a small band of soldiers began to emerge from the darkness in the direction from which the sound had come, followed closely by two short men wearing the robes of scholars and a towering figure clothed in regal armor normally seen only in kingly processions. As they drew near the owl, the tall, regal figure began to speak.

Are you friend or foe, brother owl? Friend or foe?

And before the stunned owl could even answer, the voice continued. *And who are the strange creatures we saw you with, the ones now hiding among the branches and leaves above and around us?*

Gaining his composure, Ollieman had no time for small talk and did not even stop to ponder that yet another human could think-speak to him just as Leonolis could.

Release me at once. I have urgent business and a grave message to deliver to the high king Troyolin, protector of the realm of Bren! Release me at once!

At this, Augurian interrupted in thought-speech. *One does not speak to the high king in such tones, even one as wise as brother owl! Watch your tongue, bird. This is the high king Troyolin to whom you now speak.*

Augurian, it is of no consequence. I will release you, brave owl. Please give your message, said the king in perfect thought-speech.

Sire, forgive me! I did not know to whom I was speaking! And how is it that you can speak with me in this manner? Few humans I have ever encountered have such ability! Only one boy before today had ever spoken to me thusly . . . and now two more! Incredible! The prophecies are *true!* exclaimed the owl.

What boy? What boy do you speak of? demanded the king.

Why, the boy Leonolis, of course, replied Ollieman.

My son! You have seen my son? Where is he? I had just received word that he was in the hands of the Dark Lord, but you tell me you have been with him? Where may I find him, owl? Where! responded the king.

Alas, it is true. I was with the boy . . . your son . . . but I am afraid it is all too true that he is even now in the clutches of the Dark Lord, sire, said the owl hesitantly. *But I have news. Even now word is being spread throughout the realm. The fairies are relaying word to Sandovar in the north and to the animal realms throughout the land. The Hawken and the Wolfen are gathering their kind for battle against the dark forces and are, even as we speak, rallying to join arms, shoulder to shoulder with the forces of Bren against the legions of Abysstine. They await us at Menden Lake, sire,* said Ollieman.

Seemingly satisfied with the owl's explanation, the king turned his gaze toward the trees and asked, *And what of your strange traveling companions, bird? Could they be the Treesants that are rumored to exist?*

Yes! Oh, yes! They do exist! They stand for right against the Abyss! rhymed Ollieman. *Come out, dear friends! Come out and bring your pledge of friendship to the king!*

With that, the trees began to shimmer as if suddenly illumined by translucent beams from some unseen sun in the very canopies of the forest. Transforming before the eyes of the king and his entourage, the Treesants made themselves visible, forming a semicircle around the king.

Bowing before Troyolin, Sylvan spoke. "Dear good King Troyolin. Until now we have done our best to keep our existence in the realm a legend, thinking it the better part of wisdom to keep to ourselves for ourselves. But as the events of the past few days have begun to unfold, we have come to realize that we are indeed part of a much larger picture concerning the land of Bren and its surrounding environs. We are a peaceful race at heart, but we understand there is a time to stand for what is right and against what is of the darkness. Let it be known. Let it be thus. We, the race of the tree people, the Treesants, humbly pledge our lives to you and the people of Bren and will stand with you against the dark lord, Lucian, and those foolish enough to fall under his spell."

With his eyes glimmering with what some would say were tears of both awe and gratitude, Troyolin responded in a humble yet resolute tone. "To my good new friend Sylvan and to all those of the race of tree men: friends, I pledge to you my utter gratitude for this kind and most sacrificial act of service. May the kindness you are about to show to the people of Bren and to the uttermost ends of this world be returned upon you one hundred fold from generation unto generation. As we say in Bren, 'This day we conquer! This day we overcome the Dark Lord! This day we live or die for the king!' We are this day one people with one purpose. Let us overcome darkness with the light of truth. To Menden Lake at once!"

With that, the king and his troop, along with the shimmering waves of Treesants, led by a brave little owl, headed north for the shores of Menden Lake.

Chapter Nineteen

AROLIS AND THE MICE

Muriday and Dorimay made their way through the dark recesses in the hollow places within the Castle Jadon's walls, finally making their way to the capital mouse city of Rodenthe—a literal city among many mouse cities within the grounds of the Castle Jadon. Once there, they quickly scurried to the great hall of the mouse palace—the Mouse House, as the residents of Rodenthe called it. Here in the great hall were the thrones of their father and mother, King Forsythe and Queen Hyacinth.

Quickly approaching the throne, but desiring to follow proper mouse protocol, the brother and sister came near the throne of Forsythe and bowed reverently, even though they were addressing their own parents. This act of respect was born of deep love and admiration for their parents as much as from the many years of etiquette training that was required of the royal lineage.

"Rise, my son. Rise, my daughter. Why do you approach the throne?" asked King Forsythe.

"Th-this day! Th-this d-day!" stuttered and squeaked the excited mouse siblings in one simultaneous voice (as mouse siblings often do).

"This day what?" asked the amused king.

"This day we have spoken with a prince of Bren who is even now being held captive by the dark lord, Lucian!" squeaked the pair.

"What do you mean you spoke with a prince of Bren?" responded the king as he looked now at Muriday, which in the tradition of mice indicates that only the one to whom he looks should respond.

"Prince Leonolis, son of the high king Troyolin, is being held captive in the deepest dungeon of Castle Jadon! He has, this day, asked for the aid and assistance of the people of Rodenthe in alerting King Troyolin of his predicament!" said Muriday.

Looking to Dorimay for confirmation of what Muriday had just relayed, Muriday's sister went on. "Lucian has taken him captive as part of his plan to overtake and rule the entire realm of Bren. Prince Leonolis has asked that we take word of his predicament to his father, the high king Troyolin. He has urged us to find his friend, the good horse Arolis, who is also being held against his will, to help in this endeavor," replied Dorimay.

Holding up his hand as if to say "enough," the king sat back in his throne for a few seconds. After a few moments, he turned his gaze to Queen Hyacinth, and they both nodded as if they knew some great secret had just been understood between them.

Rising, King Forsythe began to speak in a solemn manner. "This day, my son and daughter, the prophecies of old have been set in motion. It was told long ago of a brother and sister of our race helping bring rescue and freedom to the race of men. As is with the customs of mice, once we know our task we waste no time. Let it be told throughout Rodenthe and the other mouse cities of Castle Jadon what has been set in motion this day. Muriday and Dorimay, you must go at once to the stables and seek out this Arolis. I will send a small band of warriors to accompany you."

Clapping his tiny mouse hands, the king summoned his royal guard, a small troop of twelve mighty mice, to accompany his children to the stables. He also gathered his quickest mouse emissaries to deliver word to all the mouse villages within the castle realm to gather in the great mouse war hall to prepare for the onslaught that King Forsythe knew was coming. After all, if it were one of his sons or daughters that had been captured by the Dark Lord he knew what he would do, and he knew that King Troyolin would do no less. And with a final clap of his hands he sent his children and the emissaries to their tasks. From there he withdrew to the great mouse war hall to meet with his battle strategists to lay out a plan that he hoped would benefit all of Bren.

Winding their way quickly through the many unseen inner roadways of the castle walls, the group made it to the main courtyard of Castle Jadon. Though there was another way that offered much more safety, time was of the essence—and going right across the courtyard in the open was the quickest way to the stables of Jadon. Beckoning the children to follow and cross the open area in a stealthy manner, the leader of the troop crouched behind a bucket that was just outside the crevice from which they emerged from within the castle wall. Staying close to the outer wall and in the shadows, the courtyard was abuzz with castle servants going about their duties. There was much shouting and scurrying from the patrons of the king who were trying to get passage onto the castle court for a meeting with the Dark Lord. Muriday and Dorimay looked at each other as if to say "And we thought mice scurried about frantically. Just look at these people. They are not so different from us!"

Once they came to the corner of the castle itself, they came upon a small drainage ditch submerged within the cobble-stoned courtyard. About six inches across and four inches deep, this conduit was meant to carry rainwater from the rainspout that opened up from the corners of each castle wall. Quickly hopping down into the channel, the tiny band hugged the wall that was shaded from the daylight and quite quickly managed to make their way all the way to the stable entrance. It was as if no one was even paying attention to what was right below their feet. Only once, when a maiden dropped a basket of apples did they fear detection. Even though she saw the group of mice when she reached down to pick up the fruit that had fallen into the trench, she feared the wrath of her superiors at her ineptitude more than she feared the sight of a group of mice! Just as they were about to climb up from the trench, a sudden movement from above froze them all in place.

Mice are instinctive as it is, but these mice were well trained in the art of predator detection, and there was no doubt what they were facing now. Only a few feet away, hidden by the bale of hay that lay at the entrance of the stable, was a very large and hungry-looking barn cat. Yellow with streaks of white in its fur, this cat was well known to the entire mouse world. Though only one of the twelve small troops had actually seen this legendary mouser, they knew all too well his reputation for killing mice. There was no doubt. The steely, glazed look in his eyes, the notch torn in the right ear from the great battle for the mouse city of Edam, the slight hint of a sneering smile, the claws long and as sharp as butcher's knives. There was no doubt. This was Hades, the cat from hell according to mouse legend. Few had ever returned from an encounter with Hades, and now that reality was not far from any of the small band's minds.

Without any time to devise a plan, Mostel (leader of the royal guard) leapt into action. He knew that the only hope for getting the message past the cat was for one to distract Hades while the rest made a run for it. Scrambling up from the trench, the brave little mouse wielding his sword began to shriek at the top of his lungs as he ran straight for the fiery glare of Hades! As Mostel charged the cat, the rest of the mice began to head for the bale of hay , hoping to find refuge within the straw from the fury of the beast.

Making it to the bundle of hay, the group froze within its dusty recesses while just outside they heard a furious squeak followed by the most terrifying, blood-curdling scream any of the mice had ever heard before. And just as quickly as the battle had begun, it was over. Silence. And they dared not move. They each knew that Hades would wait for them—that he could hear the smallest rustle of hay, that he could smell their very presence. At least now they had time to gather their breath and try to devise a plan of escape. So they could do nothing for the time being.

After several minutes, Muriday signaled to Dorimay that they needed to do something, as indeed the entire band of mice knew that time was of the essence. But something began to move the hay. The sound of faint rustling and frantic clawing caused them all to huddle even closer together. Should they dare to move away from the sound and risk sure detection or should they stay right where they are and hope they were deep enough to make the cat grow weary of digging through the dusty, sharp-edged straw? Every few seconds the rustling would stop. Of course they all knew this meant one thing, that Hades was listening for them. Instinctively they all knew that once the cat reached them they were all willing to respond with the mouse code of honor, just as Mostel had done. In the kingdom of mice, a mouse shows his love by being willing to give up his life for another. Whomever the cat reached first was the one that would respond, allowing the rest of the mice to scamper away to safety.

Now the rustling began to take on a whole new fury, as if the cat was suddenly given a burst of new energy. The hay was being ripped through and the stale dust within the bale was being stirred to the point of causing suffocation. The sound was coming straight for Muriday, who bravely stood up between the sound and his sister. While the others prepared to run at first pounce, Muriday stood defiantly, ready to give his life for that of his sister and the troops under his command. And once again, the rustling stopped. Silence.

Not being able to stand it anymore, Muriday did a very brave thing. He began to tear at the hay directly in front of him, going straight for the area where the sound had been most intense! Those behind him began to slowly dig their way away from the sound, knowing this was part of Muriday's plan. The brave little mouse, now furious in passion to save his sister, began to dig and shout at the same time. "Here I am, oh loathsome cat! Come and get me if you can!"

The battle was on. As Muriday fought his way through the straw, the cat began clawing furiously toward him. While the others slipped out of the straw and into the safety of the stable walls, they could no longer hear the rustling of hay, and that was a merciful thing for Dorimay. At least she would not hear her brother's flesh being torn apart by the sharp fangs of the cat.

For just a few seconds, the company of mice took time to catch their breath from the narrow escape, but during the course of their respite they were startled to terror when two small figures burst through the wall opening into their midst!

After all the squeaking and shrieking (as mice are prone to do) settled down, they all fell to their knees in laughter, some rolling on the floor holding their mouse bellies in jolly delight as they realized the two figures were Muriday and Mostel! It had been Mostel, not Hades, who had been frantically tearing through the hay with his sword in search of his friends! Hades, the cat of legend, was not quite as fast as Mostel when it came to swordplay. As the cat had taken a quick swipe at him, Mostel had let out a mighty squeak as he hurdled and flipped over the cat's paw and squarely planted his sword in the right eye of the fearsome cat, thus eliciting the blood-curdling scream they had all heard. Hades had shot out of the stable in agony without touching even one whisker on the mouse warrior's body!

Now highly elated, and spirits boosted by this unexpected turn of events, the entourage began traversing the many hidden corridors of the stables, stopping only long enough to inquire of the stable mice whether they knew of the mighty horse Arolis or not. After several inquiries they finally came to a mouse with knowledge of a magnificent black stallion being kept in the royal paddock, a special area of the stable reserved for the Dark Lord's most prized horses. Surely this must be the horse Leonolis was referring to.

After only a few minutes, they came to an opening in the stable wall that opened directly into the paddock stable room. The horse was not there, but they noticed a door that led from the stable out into a small open area, the paddock, and that door was open. Still wary of moving out in the open, the mouse band stayed close to the wall, finally coming to the open doorway. Standing right in the middle of the paddock with his head held high and his eyes closed as if taking in the sunlight was a mighty steed, jet black in color, with a spectacular flowing mane and tail. His coat was so brilliant it seemed to reflect the sun, glistening with beauty. This had to be the one.

Still not daring to reveal themselves in such an open area, Muriday began to call out to the horse. "Brother horse! Brother horse! Down here!"

Slowly cocking his head downward in the direction of the sound, the horse gazed intently as he opened his eyes. At the same time the horse began to walk toward the doorway. As he neared the tiny group he began to speak. "Brother mouse. What do you need?"

"Are you the great steed Arolis?" shouted Dorimay excitedly.

"There is no need to shout, little sister. I hear you loud and clear," chuckled the patient horse. "And how do you know my name?"

"It is he! It is he! Hurray! Hurray! It is he!" sang Muriday and Dorimay simultaneously.

"We have a message for you from your boy, Leonolis!" continued Muriday.

"You have spoken with Leonolis? Is he alive? Is he well? What does he say to me?" said the normally unexcitable stallion in a rapid, almost stammering pace.

"His words were thus. 'Please get word through the realm of mice to the outside world. My father must be warned of what awaits him here in Abysstine. Tell him of the Chiroptera and of the many guards that patrol the walls and the Castle Jadon. Tell him the way through the corridors of the castle and of the many layers and levels beneath. If your people know of any weakness in the defense of Abysstine, please communicate that to my father,'" said Dorimay in one single breath.

"How well do you know these corridors?" asked the horse.

Looking anxiously at one another, Muriday and Dorimay shrugged as they said, "Well enough, I suppose."

Haltingly, Mostel began to speak. "If I may, lord and lady mouse. Warrior brother. I have traversed these very halls on several occasions as the mouse king's business has required. I can guide you if you can carry me."

"I can carry you all. Quickly. Climb on," said the horse as he lowered his nose to the stable floor.

The entire mouse band scurried up his head and positioned themselves inside his mane. Muriday, Dorimay, and Mostel found a place directly behind the horse's ears while the rest of the troop went further down the neck, taking cover. One even scampered all the way to the tail of Arolis to keep watch from the horse's blind side. Walking toward the stable gate, the mighty horse stealthily slid his head over the cutaway door and lifted the latch as he pushed against the door. Opening the door and walking out into the corridor as if he owned the place, Arolis spoke softly. "Lucian told Leonolis that he was going to end my life. He did this to frighten the boy into submission. The truth is that he values me for horse stock and has pampered me to no end, much to my embarrassment. The result has been that I have been given access to this hallway to come and go in this area of the stable as I please, but I have gone no further. Which way to the castle courtyard and main gate?"

"I would suggest we go another route, horse," said Mostel. "There is actually a secret military entrance that leads directly out of the castle. It is used occasionally as a service entrance but mainly for the many spies Lucian sends out to do his bidding."

"Then lead me there at once," said Arolis.

As they made their way through the stable, Mostel guided the stallion with great expertise. It was quite obvious this mouse warrior had indeed become keenly acquainted with the stable on his missions for the mouse king, Forsythe. Only once had they even been approached by a stable hand, and he had only stopped the horse to pat him on the head and neck, admiring the mighty horse he had only seen from afar before. Coming to a wall at the end of the stable hall, the horse came to a stop, saying, "Where do we go from here?"

"Lower your head, brother horse. Lower your head to the railing. There you will see a small metal hook protruding from the wall."

"Do you mean the small hook from which the bridle hangs?" asked the horse.

"Yes. Yes. It is more than it appears. Pull down on the hook. You will find that it moves," continued Mostel.

Arolis pulled down on the hook with his chin. As he did, a small puff of air was released as the wall began to open. The doorway had been cleverly concealed to appear as a wall. The horse quickly stepped into the darkness behind the opening, turning to pull the door closed behind him. Allowing his eyes to adjust to the dimness, the troop found themselves in a tunnel bored through the rock. As quietly as possible, the horse began to move toward the dim light ahead. Approaching the opening of the tunnel, and stepping through the branches of the trees that concealed it from the outside, the horse and mice were suddenly standing in the open air outside of the castle walls.

"Where do we go from here?" asked the horse.

"There is only one way to go—up the valley to the headwaters at Lake Menden. From there we will devise a plan. We must go at once," said Mostel.

With that, the horse became like the wind. All that could be seen was a black streak moving away from the castle with fourteen small mice flying behind, flying like screaming kites in the wind as they held on to the horse's mane and tail for dear life!

Chapter Twenty

THE GATHERING AT MENDEN LAKE

K ing Troyolin, Augurian, and Maison, along with the Royal Guard, had arrived at Menden Lake, fending off the occasional Chiroptera and Werewolf through their long night's journey through the forest. Throughout the day they waited for news from the Fairy people as to the response to the king's request for aid. During the midafternoon hours, the king's men were rallied to surround the king as the sound of hoof beats neared them from the direction of Abysstine. Soon enough the men lowered their spears as a lone, riderless horse approached the encampment with regal boldness. There was no doubt. The soldiers knew this steed by his size, demeanor, and stride. There was only one Arolis.

The horse slowed from his gallop and walked straight to the king. Face-to-face the two began to nod to one another. Until this moment, no one in the kingdom had ever suspected that King Troyolin could speak with the animal races, but it was made obvious by the king's knowing nods and understanding look in his eyes as he locked eyes with the stallion.

Dear King, spoke the horse, fighting to catch his breath yet determined to convey the state of things to the king. *Dear King, this day Forsythe, king of the mouse domain of Rodenthe, has bid me to find you with word of Leonolis.* Stopping to catch his breath, the horse was silent.

What of my son, Arolis? What of Leonolis? urged the king.

Not missing a beat, Muriday chimed in. *My lord, good King Troyolin. I am Muriday, son of Forsythe, prince of the realm of Rodenthe. This day, my sister Dorimay and I have spoken with Leonolis—have seen him with our very eyes. He and the old man, Regalion, are well and in good spirits.*

As if he had seen a ghost, Troyolin reeled back a little, dizzied from the apparent news that his brother, Regalion, was still alive! At this, Arolis instinctively caught the king by the shoulder, helping him maintain his balance.

My brother? You tell me my brother is alive? he asked, reliving for a fleeting second the very moment so long ago he had opened the box sent to him supposedly by Gothgol containing the ringed finger of Regalion as proof of his death. *Are you sure? How do you know this to be true? And what of my son? Is he well?*

Both are well. Your son, the fine young man, spoke with us, telling us to get to you any word we know concerning the grounds of the castle and the environs of Abysstine. We heard him call the old man Regalion on several occasions whenever we were near his cell. Only today did we meet them, said Muriday.

Turning to Augurian and Maison, the king said, "My good advisors. Set a council with these leaders of the mice realm and devise the best plan of attack for freeing my son and putting an end to the schemes of Lucian for once and all."

Extending his arms up to the shoulder of Arolis, the mice hurriedly scurried down to the shoulders of Augurian. Together with Maison, they began to gain an understanding of the lay of the land they would soon encounter. While the council took place, Troyolin continued to converse with Arolis concerning how to free Leonolis. As the day wore on into evening, the forest surrounding Menden Lake began to come alive with the gathering forces of Bren.

From the south came the mighty army of Bren itself, setting up a myriad of tents that completely engulfed the northern rim of the lake, creating a barrier between the forces of Abysstine and the king. From the west came the forces of the Treesants along with the wolf tribes of the Wolfen race, who immediately took the form of men so as to set the race of men at ease with their presence amongst them. Also from the west, having made their way around the northern mountains separating Abysstine from Larovia (being led by the flitting Rania), a royal entourage came from Sandovar, king of Larovia, with the pledge of support King Troyolin had hoped for. At the king's signal, the special forces of Larovia, trained in the art of mountain warfare, would come from directly above Castle Jadon. Able to cross and make their way through even the most treacherous of mountains, the special mountain forces of Larovia would prove most helpful if Lucian was to be defeated.

As if stars were falling from the skies, all present at this mighty gathering were in awe as the legions of the Fairy people began to descend, led by Kelsin himself, high king of the Fairies! At his side was the beautiful and mysterious Galennia, winking at Arolis as she floated down from among the Hawken, taking the form of a maiden as she landed. As soon as the fairies had made their descent, the skies once again began to come alive—this time with a faint yet mighty rumble as the legions of the Hawken race descended, taking the form of men as they alit on the ground!

As each legion of every tribe and race assembled around Menden Lake, King Troyolin gathered the kings of each tribe for a council at the great fire of meeting his men had lit on the northern shore of the lake. The king was regal and serious as he called the council to order.

"I have no need to tell you what we are up against," began the solemn Troyolin. "We have each had our own dealings with the treacheries of the dark one, Lucian. We know the evil that rises against us, the evil that would have dominion over each race and realm represented in this great circle should he have his way. We know he has amassed a mighty force from the realm of Abysstine and the Dark Forest. With him are the Terrebithians, the race of the underworld. We have word of the Chiroptera doing his bidding, the race of bat people who rule the Dark Mountains of this realm. With him are the Werewolves, the ravenous beasts who leave none alive who cross their paths."

Turning to face the north, the king continued to speak to the council of the races of Bren. "We know Lucian expects to command the high ground since Castle Jadon rests against the impenetrable Northern Mountains. Evenhawk, lord of the Hawken, before dawn, you and your legions will fly north, stationing your forces on the surrounding peaks. You will also alert the forces of Larovia, along with King Sandovar, of the plan of attack. At my signal, you will descend with the fury of fire upon the Castle Jadon and city of Abysstine."

After addressing the Hawken, Troyolin turned his gaze to Caniday, lord of the Wolfen. "Good King Caniday, the forces of the Wolfen will assemble with the corps of horsemen of the men of Bren, stationing one of your people between each of my horsemen. Your task is to dispatch the horsemen of the dark forces in tandem with my men. You will trouble the feet of their steeds while my men take their surprised horsemen from the backs of their horses. Work as a team. The archers of Bren will begin the siege with a triple barrage of arrows. This will decimate the ranks of darkness and will also serve as the signal to the Hawken and the forces of Larovia to begin their attacks.

"Treesants," continued the king, "you will infiltrate the tree-lined city of Abysstine with the goal of gaining access to the Castle Jadon itself. Once you have gained control of the castle you will station guards among the shrubs and trees of the castle grounds, holding fast until my forces can gain access to the throne of Lucian. If I know Lucian at all, he will not involve himself in actual battle, the coward that he is. He will prefer to play chess master with his own men, forcing his whims upon them to do his bidding by some dark magic."

As Troyolin spoke, the solemnity of the moment was broken by shouts and the sound of approaching hoofs. As the ranks of the forces of the races of Bren parted, Justinian and a small contingency of men approached the king. Dismounting and bowing, Justinian, Troyolin's friend of friends, stood and embraced the king.

"Sire, my friend of friends, even now the forces of Lucian gather," said Justinian matter-of-factly.

"Justinian, we are not alone. As you can surely see, the deeds of Lucian have garnered much support in our favor. We have nothing to fear," assured the king.

Before Justinian could reply, a frantic shrieking began to rise from somewhere in the mane of Arolis, who was standing attentively near Troyolin. "I have seen this one! I have seen this one! This man is one of the dark ones! I have seen him!" squeaked Mostel.

"What do you mean 'He is one of the dark ones?'" demanded Troyolin.

Standing between the ears of Arolis, Mostel went on. "This day, even this day, I have seen this one. As I dispatched the cat from hell, Hades, the commotion startled the horse upon which he had been riding. His eye caught my own as he gazed down from his mount to see the cause of his horse's fear. I saw him see me as well. He was in the stable of the Castle Jadon this very day."

"Fie!" countered Justinian. His face suddenly red with anger, the friend of the king drew his sword and raised it to strike. "You lie, filthy rodent! You lie!"

Stepping between Mostel's position on Arolis and Justinian, Troyolin looked Justinian eye to eye. "What is the meaning of this, friend? He is but a small creature. Do not allow your anger to bring you to the level of darkness from which you will find only regret," the king stated wisely.

"Sire, this day I have spent in reconnaissance and in the gathering of intelligence concerning our enemy. I was, indeed, in the stables of Castle Jadon . . . gathering information, having infiltrated the castle grounds," replied Justinian. "I take great offense that one so small could level such a great accusation toward me!"

"Speak, Mostel. Could what you have seen be true?" asked the king.

Not waiting for the mouse to respond, Justinian said, "Was I wearing the uniform of a soldier of Bren or was I not dressed in the garb of a horse trader?"

Mostel, in a most humble tone, responded. "Of course you were dressed in the garb of a horse trader. But my concern was in this. As I hid beneath the bale of hay after my brief battle with Hades, I silently listened for my well-hidden friends. As I strove to hear their whereabouts, I could not help but hear part of your conversation with the soldier of Lucian. You asked of the location of the boy, Leonolis. You also said that Lucian would have that to which you agreed . . . that by nightfall you would have relayed the location of the forces of Bren to Lucian in exchange. In exchange for what I could not discern, as I heard my friends stirring and I began making my way through the hay to them. Good King Troyolin, I heard what I heard and I stand by my word. From my perspective, he is one with the Dark Lord."

Troyolin turned his attention back to Justinian. Without having to say a word, Justinian knew that Troyolin expected an explanation.

"My friend of friends, I indeed spoke the words this one has said. But what he did not hear and what he could not know was that I was offering false information in the hope of producing the exact location of prince Leonolis. Nothing more. Nothing less."

Without speaking a word, King Troyolin continued to look directly into the eyes of Justinian. After what seemed like an eternity of awkward silence, the king spoke for all the council to hear.

"We attack at dawn."

Chapter Twenty-One

THE BATTLE BEGINS

King Troyolin knew that something was troubling his friend of friends. The gaze into his eyes told him so, but at the same time he could see the intensity of his friend's faithfulness to him and to the realm of Bren.

Justinian placed his hand on the king's shoulder and said, "I fear we do not have the luxury of waiting until dawn, my lord. The attack is upon us."

With a sudden and unrelenting fury, the forest and skies grew loud with the clamor of rushing wings, clashing teeth, clanging metal, and anguished screams. At first, the forces of Bren stood still in shock at the sudden fury with which the battle ensued, but quickly went into battle mode once they realized what was taking place. Not having a chance to put his battle plans in to motion, King Troyolin called out for Kelsin, king of the fairies.

"Kelsin! Quickly! Your forces must relay this message to all the forces of Bren. Push back against the darkness! Force the darkness into the abyss! Force the darkness into the valley of Abysstine! We will gain the upper ground by forcing them down into the valley!" shouted the king.

With only a nod of understanding toward Troyolin, Kelsin was off like a bolt of lightning. Without the need for spoken words, the Fairy king shot from fairy to fairy in his nearest vicinity. Each fairy he touched, in turn, sped off like streaks of electricity to fairies near them until the entire Fairy contingency was off, filling the raucous night air with thousands of lightning bolts of sheer energy. Within a few minutes the forces of Bren had been alerted and the battle was fully on!

Without any hesitation, the Treesants had been the first to recognize the coming danger, not quite in time to warn the others but in plenty of time to conceal themselves and begin making their way to the city of Abysstine, knowing full well their duty had not changed—that the city of Abysstine was vital to the success of the siege. Like wisps of night smoke, the Treesants were gone.

The Wolfen, much more cunning and aware of their surroundings, because of the constant danger presented to them due to everyday life in the forest, had also taken quickly to their task. As the army of darkness had swarmed in like a plague of silent roaches, the Wolfen literally leapt into action, assuming their full wolf form and easily taking down the first line of Lucian's soldiers with swipes of their mighty claws to the exposed throats of the dark forces.

In the midst of all the chaos, no one had noticed the rumble beneath the forest floor. No one noticed the ripples on Menden Lake caused by the rumble. All assumed it was the oncoming armies of darkness, but it was something else. Like multiple volcanoes exploding from the forest floor, dozens of chasms opened beneath the feet of the armies of Bren and up from their darkness rose the forces of the Terrebithians, the fierce earthen ogres of the underworld. Swords drawn and shields flashing dull grey in the dim firelight that remained, the ogres seemed to come from everywhere, causing much disruption to the ground forces of Bren.

With the onslaught of Terrebithians, Augurian and Maison went to work. Using the combined magic of both wizards (as they later came to be understood and identified), the small, wise men cast a spell of sleep upon the ogres and one by one they began to drop their swords to the sides of their bodies, slumping clumsily into hairy clumps on the ground, adding noisy snores to the din of the ongoing battle! The minds of ogres are quite easily overtaken by magic. This was common knowledge.

No sooner had they dealt with the ogres than the skies began to be filled with that eerie flapping they had just the night before been confronted with in the glen of Augurian. Chiroptera! Swooping down like insane missiles, the bat men began to swipe at the unsuspecting horsemen of Bren, causing many to tumble to the ground beneath the feet of their own horses. In the confusion King Troyolin had stumbled, falling backward when he tripped on the outstretched feet of a slumbering ogre. Dazed from the slight bump on his head, the king was slow to rise and the group of three Chiroptera made their way directly for him. Seeing his fallen friend in trouble, Justinian removed the head of the Werewolf he had been facing and ran to the side of Troyolin. As he reached the king, Justinian turned to face the diving bats, easily separating the left wing of the first Chiroptera to reach him. Becoming tangled in the writhing limbs of the badly injured bat man, Justinian had not been able to fend off the other two, and they quickly lifted the mighty man of Bren into the night sky, clambering upward, each one holding one of Justinian's arms in its talons. Troyolin was safe and recovered enough just in time to see his friend being dragged helplessly into the sky and out of sight.

As the battle went on, the surrounding forest continued to exude all manner of loathsome creatures. Werewolves, ghouls, witches, temptresses, and every demonic form one could imagine. Yet, the forces of Bren were able to hold their ground. The Hawken had been able to confuse the Chiroptera by taking the form of the Chiroptera themselves. The way the Hawken were able to distinguish between themselves and the real Chiroptera was that they retained the red feathers from their hawk forms so as to tell each other apart. The Wolfen had taken such a strategy against the Werewolves as well, retaining a small, white patch on their foreheads along with a small, white patch at the tips of their tails.

Just as the Treesants had headed for Abysstine at the first hint of trouble, a small party of Hawken had headed for the mountains to the north for the purpose of relaying the news of battle to King Sandovar and the Larovian forces.

The battle went on through the night. At times the darkness would push back against the forces of Bren, but the now fully engaged forces of Bren were beginning to make some headway. As dawn approached, the battle had indeed gone the way Troyolin had hoped. The entire mélange was now encompassing the whole of the Valley of Abysstine. The battle reached from the shores of Menden Lake in the south to the regions around the walls of Castle Jadon and from the river Runland to the east and to the Dark Forest of the west. Endless battle. Battle in the air. Battle on foot. Battle on horseback. Battle. As dawn neared, the two small wise men of Bren, Augurian and Maison, took leave from the battle to make their way to a high bluff overlooking the fields of battle.

From there they turned back toward the south, gazing intently toward the badlands area, toward the Sleeping Giant. And they began to chant:

"Great Founder, Maker of all that exists,
Hear our cry for mercy.
From days of old, before the abyss,
Before the days of worry,
Our need is great
Our strength grows faint
We have need of righteous fury!
To the ways of life
To the ways of hope
To your ways we stand compliant
Release the fire
Release the power
Of the mighty Sleeping Giant!"

Repeating the incantation three times, the wizards kept their gaze fixed on the south, aware of the battle behind them, but intently fixed on the south. Nothing. Not a rumble. Not a stirring. Nothing. Turning to look at one another, Augurian and Maison nodded in silent agreement that they had done all they knew to do according to the ways of magic. They had called upon the Founder, spoken a prayer not uttered in over a thousand years, and beyond that there was nothing they could do but go back and rejoin the battle at hand and hope the Founder heard them— and hoped the prophecies had been true.

The Treesants had successfully made it to the city of Abysstine and had quickly taken root within the walls of Castle Jadon itself. Although most of Lucian's dark forces had been sent into battle with the forces of Bren, there was still quite a large contingency left to guard over Lucian and the castle grounds. This was no major threat to the Treesants, who were largely able to move about unnoticed. As the forces of darkness were pushed back within shouting distance of the wall surrounding Abysstine, many of the remaining soldiers had been dispatched to guard over the city walls, leaving the castle grounds in the hands of only a hundred or so men. One by one, the Treesants simply waited for one of Lucian's men to walk beneath a tree. Silently they would slip down upon them and, from behind, take them out of commission, hiding the bodies in the trees to avoid detection.

From high above Castle Jadon, the special mountain forces of Larovia were steadily and stealthily making their way from the pinnacles high above the castle grounds. Any Chiroptera that had been sent to guard over Castle Jadon had been taken out of commission at the hands of the clever Hawken. Like dozens of spiders sailing through the air buoyed by their threads, the men of Larovia slowly descended in complete silence from above. They had been able to take out several sentries that had been posted in the three main turrets. The legendary Larovian prowess with a bow and arrow was more than legend. It was very much reality.

By the time the main battle began to spill through the gates of Abysstine, the Castle Jadon had all but been rendered useless as a place of refuge for the dark forces, having commandeered the grounds and sealed the gates from within. The castle had been captured except for the palace and throne of Lucian. By now, Lucian had summoned the White Witch of Endoria to assist him. As the battle grew near the castle gates, the White Witch cast a spell on the palace rendering the doors and windows impenetrable. But for this area, the castle had been taken for all intents and purposes.

Lucian spoke to the witch. "They are playing right into our hands just as you said they would."

"Humans are all too predictable. Thinking they stand on the side of right, they blindly go where their passions lead them without giving one whit of consideration to the consequences. Some would call it chivalry. I call it foolishness," cackled the hag. "Bring the orb," she demanded of Lucian. "It is time we end this. Do as we discussed and all will end well. They will not know what hit them until it is too late."

As the pair stood and walked toward the palace doors, the spell remained unbroken. No one would be able to enter the palace until the spell had been lifted. As they continued out from the palace and began to cross the castle courtyard, the Treesants and the Larovians began to move toward them. As the first Larovian soldier swung down from his perch atop the eastern turret, the White Witch lifted her hand and sent an arc of light to sever the rope from which he hung, sending him quickly to his death. As the evil witch and the Dark Lord walked beneath a tall oak tree, a gang of Treesants began to fall upon them like a cloud of falling leaves. Without even losing one stride, the witch simply lifted her hands, stopping the Treesants in midair. Carrying them along in this suspended state, she calmly walked up the stairs leading to the top of the castle wall, Lucian close behind her. Once they reached the highest point in the wall, she guided the now terrified groups of tree people out and above the ground. And she let them drop to the ground. Even a Treesant cannot survive a fall from one hundred feet.

After killing the helpless Treesants, she stood defiantly gazing out upon the raging battle below for several minutes. The battle, which had now spilled into the streets of Abysstine itself, did not seem to cause her any fear at all. She continued to watch and actually take delight in what was taking place. Lucian simply sneered his satisfaction; a wicked smile and obvious blood-lust made him appear truly evil in nature. After a few more minutes, the White Witch lifted her hands high above her head and the forces of darkness suddenly bowed to their knees and lowered their weapons, some while in the middle of striking a deathblow to a soldier of Bren!

"Silence!" she screamed. "Silence!"

The din of battle completely subsided. It was as if someone had commanded a howling thunderstorm to be still and quiet, and that storm had obeyed! This miraculous display of power was lost on no one. Uneasiness filled the air from the Castle Jadon all the way to the furthest flank of battle near Menden Lake. And, whether any of the forces of Bren would like to admit or not, a tinge of fear began to creep into every heart.

"We call for a truce! We will parley with your leader!" she demanded. "Now!"

Turning from her perch atop the castle wall, the White Witch and Lucian confidently made their way back down the stairway, across the castle courtyard, and back into the palace and the grand throne room of Jadon where they waited patiently for High King Troyolin and the other leaders of the forces of Bren.

Chapter Twenty-Two

PARLEY

W ord reached Troyolin. It was true. A truce had been called and a demand for parley had been made. On the fields of battle this generally boded well for the one from whom the parley had been requested. The bad news was that the mythical White Witch of Endoria was in consort with the dark lord, Lucian. Summoning both Augurian and Maison, they slowly gathered the other leadership from among their ranks and began to make their way toward Castle Jadon. Kelsin, the king of Fairies; Caniday, king of the Wolfen; Sylvan, king of the Treesants; and Evenhawk, king of the Hawken all joined the slow march into Abysstine and up to the darkness of Castle Jadon. It was decided along the way that King Troyolin would handle all negotiations for the realm.

As they passed into the castle grounds, the courtyard was riddled with the bodies of dark forces. There were also many bodies of brave Treesants and Larovians strewn about as well. Only a handful of living, breathing dark forces seemed to remain within the castle walls . . . and they still knelt in eerie silence just as they had done when the White Witch had lifted her hands to call the truce.

Entering the castle, the leaders walked down the center of the very ornate palace. The grandeur of the room was astounding. As dark as the castle appeared from without, it shone with equal brilliance from within. Still, the feeling of darkness permeated the room and filled the hearts of the leaders of Bren with dread. To a man they were each inwardly grateful that it would be Troyolin handling the parley rather than they.

Nearing the grand staircase that led up to the level of the throne, the group stood silent as they came to a halt. "You will approach the throne," said the White Witch, breaking the awkward silence.

"We will not," succinctly replied Troyolin.

"You will approach the throne! Now!" screeched the witch.

Still, Troyolin stood his ground. "It is customary for foes to meet for parley on common ground. And besides, it is with Lucian that we have business."

"Nonsense!" scorned the hag. "Who do you think gives Lucian his power?"

Turning her head toward Lucian, the witch said, "Tell them, Lucian. Tell them with whom they have business."

"Yes, Mother. I will tell them," calmly replied the Dark Lord.

Suddenly, Troyolin's memory flooded back to the days before the darkness had fallen—to the days before Lucian had been born, to the sorceress Toralan and the baby she bore, Regalion, to the sorceress who would be forever banished from the realm of Bren due to her conniving and cunning ways, to the sudden and horrific realization that she had become the mythical and sinister White Witch of Endoria!

It was obvious to all that Troyolin had been taken aback at this revelation—causing even more fear among the ranks of the leadership of Bren, much to the witch's delight—but he quickly came to his senses and gained his composure, saying, "Toralan . . . or should I say 'Tormentia' when addressing you?" said the king.

"Mock me if you will, Troyolin of the realm, but I believe I have something you desire, so I would watch my tone were I you," snorted the witch. "You *will* come to me, oh King," she said in her own mocking tone. "You will want to see this. Looky, looky at what we tooky," she jeered. "Show him the orb, Lucian!"

Turning around to the other leaders of Bren, they all nodded in agreement. They all knew what he would see, and they all would have acquiesced to this demand if it were they in his shoes. So Troyolin humbled himself and walked up the massive steps and came face-to-face with his nephew, Lucian, and Lucian's mother, Toralan. Extending the orb for Troyolin to see, the king shuddered visibly at what he saw within the orb.

The image seen in the Crystal Orb was one of Leonolis bound and hanging from a thin rope from the ceiling of the Cavern of What-Might-Have-Been hundreds of feet above the Needles of Regret, a crystalline formation rising up from the cavern floor. True to their name, the massive spikes of razor-sharp crystals grew from the floor, rising some thirty feet from their base to pinpoints of teeth that showed no mercy to any who fell upon them. There were dozens of spikes in the formation. And scattered among the crystalline spikes were the skeletal remains of hundreds of Lucian's victims. What Troyolin had no way of knowing was that this was merely an image and not reality. It would not have mattered to the king had he known, knowing well that the mind of evil is capable of such wickedness. His response would have been the same, one thought in mind—to save his son.

"Lucian, there is no escape for you. Whether you slay my son or not, you are defeated," began the king. "I ask that you spare my son. He has done nothing to deserve this. Your quarrel is with me and with the law of Bren."

"You are correct, dear uncle, that my quarrel is with you, but much has been taken from me that was rightfully mine. A throne. A kingdom. A family. Honor. Respect. My life. These were all taken from me and so much more. What price does one place upon a life so robbed of all it deserved?" whined Lucian.

"This is not about honor or respect or family or life! This is about hurting me and anyone else you hold responsible for your life. This is about pride and power, Lucian! Do you honestly believe that by taking the life of my son you will suddenly gain all you lost? Do you think that hurting me will miraculously erase all that has happened? Do you not take any personal responsibility for the paths your life has taken?" reasoned the king.

"The paths my life has taken, as you say, were by no means any choice of mine whatsoever!" screamed the Dark Lord. "I was never given a choice. I was *told* what my choices were!"

"Life is like that, Nephew," said Troyolin in a suddenly compassionate tone. "Sometimes the choices are made for us, but a man always has a choice as to how he will respond to those choices. A man may choose, as you seem to have done, to respond with hurt and bitterness and to lash out in pride and vengeance, or a man can choose to respond with forgiveness and creativity, to open his eyes to the realities faced, and from the ashes create something beautiful out of what he has been given. Lucian, you could have found a life of privilege and honor—a life full of endless possibilities—yet you could only see the possibility of power, power that was never rightfully yours to begin with. I am sorry for the way your father responded to you and to your mother, but do not hold an entire nation responsible. Do not hold a boy responsible for what he had no hand in."

Lucian could not hear the compassion of his uncle or see the truth in his words, so blinded by many years' worth of bitter loathing at the thought of all he perceived had been done to him. Like a fire that was now burning out of control, the flames of his bitterness had been fanned for all those years by the constant reminders of his own mother, herself consumed with acrid hatred toward all those who had wronged her, whether in reality or in the recesses of a mind gone mad from envy so many years ago that she could not even remember all the reasons for her own bitter feelings.

Sneering with rage now, Lucian responded, "Dear uncle, how dare you lecture me on what I feel or think. You cannot possibly know or even begin to understand the hurts and humiliations I and my mother have suffered. About one thing you are right, though. I can see the possibility of power, and thanks to my long-suffering mother, that power will soon be fully realized."

As Lucian turned to his mother for affirmation of all he just said, Troyolin asked, "Why have you kept your father alive all these years?"

"My father? How do you know this? Indeed your spies have done well for you," began Lucian. "This knowledge is of no consequence. Your brother, my father, was too ashamed of me to stand up for me in regard to all that should have been mine. When given the opportunity to avenge my loss I felt his punishment should fit his crime. Rather than get to enjoy the privilege of his royal position, I would make him suffer in solitude much as I have had to. It actually brings me great pleasure to know he has been robbed just as I have. Would you agree, Mother?"

Laughing deeply at the thought of Regalion's suffering, Toralan replied, "I agree with every word, dear son. What has happened to your father and now to all those who have brought such degradation and deprivation to you and me is now returned to them! Whether you rule from the throne of Aerie or here from the throne of Jadon, we . . . er . . . *you* will rule and rightfully so!" As she seemed to take great delight in the situation, the witch began to laugh uncontrollably.

Troyolin interrupted her spiteful laughter. "Laugh as you will, Toralan, but neither you nor Lucian will ever rule this land. Even if you held the reins of power in the realm, you would never find the honor and respect you so crave. Honor and respect—indeed, the love of a people—is earned. It is the wise ruler who leads by example and as a servant to his subjects. This is the true power of the king."

Expecting some retort, Troyolin waited for a response, but the room seemed to brighten with some sort of solemnity at the thought of where true power lies. After allowing the words to soak in the atmosphere for a few more moments, Troyolin continued.

"Lucian, I will never cede power to you or to a bitter, old woman who has absolutely no claim to the throne. What you could not possibly know or even remotely understand is that a true member of the royal line would gladly give up his life for the sake of the kingdom. I know my son, Leonolis. I know him deeply. And I know his heart, Lucian. Even this young boy knows that true and real power emanates from the heart of a servant. If Leonolis must die in order to save Bren, he will not hesitate. But mark my word, whether he lives or whether he dies, Bren will stand. And this day I will stand with my foot on your neck. You will never rule over Bren. Never," said the king calmly yet with great authority.

"Ha! Ha! Ha!" laughed Lucian. "Dear uncle, there is no need for such theatrics. I knew well that you would say every word you have said. I assumed you would have brainwashed your son into believing all that drivel about the higher calling—that servant-of-the-people, lead-by-example poppycock. There is no need to sacrifice your own son. Don't you think we've had enough of that in our family?" Lucian asked rhetorically in reference to himself.

"The greater reality is this, Uncle. Leonolis does not have to die. There is another way, but not without a price," said the conniving Dark Lord.

"And what would that price be?" asked the king.

"A life for a life. The life that was rightfully mine was taken from me, thus I require a life be given in exchange. The life of your son will satisfy my need for payment on that debt. Yet there is another way. I will free Leonolis in exchange for the life of another."

"What 'other?' Whose life?" asked the king.

"Your life," responded Lucian.

Without asking for permission to speak, the long-silent group of leaders had waited patiently during the parley but now broke their silence.

"Good King!" began Evenhawk. "Do not even consider this! We have the leverage! We have subdued the dark forces! Just say the word and my people will fly to your son's rescue! Do not listen to him!"

The others all nodded, shouting in agreement as Troyolin pondered the words of his nephew.

Holding up her hand, Toralan began to speak to the group. "Fly to him! Indeed, fly to him, graceful Hawken, but you will never make it in time. I have but to close my eyes and the boy falls upon the spires."

As the words oozed from her lips, the group suddenly became aware of an odd thing. Although they had all kept a corner of their eyes focused on her, they had never seen her blink. This was not something they would have thought twice about until she had spoken the words: "I have but to close my eyes and the boy falls upon the spires." They had all noticed but had thought nothing of it, and now that same sense of knowing told them all that what she said was true.

"Sire," began Augurian, "Maison and I can break her spell and her hold upon the boy, and you, sire, you can hold him in suspension above the spires from where you stand."

"Go ahead, little wizard. Make your spell. Do you honestly think I would not have prepared for such a possibility? Your magic will not work, and the gift of the king will never be able to penetrate the granite between this place and the boy," replied the witch. And with a wave of her hand in the direction of Augurian and the others she, by some dark magic, turned them all to stone. Leaving them alive yet rendering them helplessly frozen, each of them could still see and hear the proceedings, but could do no more to help the king.

"You cannot turn everyone to stone, Toralan," replied the king. "Even you do not have that much power."

"I have enough for now, though," came her retort. "And that is all I need. Let us continue the parley."

"The offer stands, King. A life for a life. I will give you Leonolis in exchange for your own life," said Lucian.

"You may take a life, Lucian, but it will have no effect on your ability to take the throne of Bren," said the king.

"Then we have a deal?" asked Lucian.

"I will exchange my life for that of my son, but I must know that he is safe and restored to his rightful place on the throne of Bren. There is no other way. You will place him in the hands of a trusted royal guardian who will, in turn, return him safely to his mother and the royal court of Castle Aerie. Upon that transfer you have my word. My life will be freely offered to you," said Troyolin.

Looking triumphantly to his mother, Lucian nodded, and with that nod, the curtains behind the throne began to move. Stepping from behind the throne of Lucian came a small group of soldiers. In their midst was a bound soldier of Bren. Justinian!

Overjoyed to see his friend of friends, Troyolin rushed to embrace this one he thought was dead. As the soldiers of the Dark One leveled their spears at Troyolin's approach, Lucian placed his hand between the spears and the king, saying, "Let him pass. This should be quite touching."

As Troyolin embraced his friend, Lucian motioned to one of the guards to unbind Justinian's hands. Free of his fetters, Justinian returned the king's embrace.

"Justinian, I thought you were dead!" said the king. "So you heard all that has transpired?"

"Yes, my lord. I heard it all," replied Justinian.

"Then to you I transfer guardianship of Leonolis. Once he is free, return at once to Aerie and relay to the realm the gladness with which I lay down my life for the sake of the kingdom!" exclaimed the king. "And help my son establish his rule, and tell him of all that has transpired, and tell him that just as his life was worth mine, the life of the kingdom of Bren is worth his . . . worth every soul of Bren."

"Tell him yourself," snorted the witch.

And to everyone's surprise, the witch clapped her hands, and, once again from behind the throne, the curtains opened. Being led from the darkness by a leather leash, Leonolis was brought to stand before his father.

Chapter Twenty-Three

LIFE FOR A LIFE

L eonolis!" cried the king. He rushed to hold his son but was abruptly stopped as two guards stepped between the king and his boy.

"That's close enough for now," said Lucian. "There's no time for such frivolities." Lucian was quite jealous of this display of father and son affection, having never received much from his own father.

"It is time for the exchange," continued Lucian. "Release the boy. Bind his father."

As his hands were being bound, Troyolin spoke to Leonolis. "My son, are you well? Have they harmed you? You're going to be safe now!"

"Father, I knew you would come for me! I knew it! I am fine, and I will be fine whether I live or die. Father, I heard the words you have this day spoken, and I will gladly give my life for Bren. There is no need for you to take my place. I gladly accept this fate if that is the wish of the Founder," bravely spoke the boy.

"Dear son, you are a true son of Bren, and you speak with the heart of a man. It would seem I see the visage of a boy but behold the heart of a man! How proud I am of you, but I am still king and I am still your father. What's done is done. Life for a life," said the king.

Turning to Justinian, he spoke. "Friend of friends, I hereby grant you guardianship of my son. Take him at once directly back to Castle Aerie. The Royal Advisors will commence with the necessary training and rituals for rightful ascendancy to the throne."

Lucian had watched this entire exchange with such glee that he could no longer contain himself, responding with, "Yes, good Justinian. Take care of the boy just as we agreed."

A chill ran down Troyolin's spine, and he looked back to his friend, Justinian. He watched reality revealed as the redness of shame enflamed the face of his friend of friends.

Justinian could not look at Troyolin but began to speak with shame and disgrace. "My friend. Even as we have ridden together these past few days, Lucian has managed to take captive my wife along with my children—my sons and my daughters all. In the Crystal Orb he showed me their fate should I not do his bidding."

"And just what is that bidding?" shuddered the betrayed king.

"That upon your agreement to hand over the guardianship of your son to me I was to, in turn, assign that guardianship to Lucian in exchange for the lives of my wife and children. Yet I am ashamed to have ever agreed to this, my friend," wept Justinian.

And just as quickly as his heart filled with joy at the release of his son, it was crushed by the weight of the betrayal he now felt. While he understood his friend's desire to preserve the lives of his family, he could not comprehend why Justinian had ever kept his predicament from him. A friend is to share their burdens with their friend of friends. That was the basis of the bond, and that bond had been broken.

"Bind his hands, good Justinian. Bind the hands of your friend of friends," commanded Lucian. "To the dungeon with him. Put him in the cell with his brother. It is time for a little catching up for old time's sake!"

Turning back to the boy, he commanded his guards to take him at once to the Cavern of What-Might-Have-Been and suspend him above the spires.

"But you exchanged my life for his! What of our agreement!" exclaimed the king.

"I exchanged your life for his just as we agreed. I never agreed to allow him to go free. I agreed to turn him over to the care of your guardian, and your guardian has agreed to return him to me in exchange for the lives of his family. Seems like a very equitable trade to me. And now I have the pleasure of extending to you the many years of retched torment you extended to me, dear uncle," scoffed Lucian. "To the dungeon with him . . . and to the cavern with the boy. We seal my ascension to the throne this day!"

Without so much as a touch, the boy and his father were again separated. Troyolin was led away to the inner recesses of the dungeon while Leonolis was led to the cavern. "Justinian, you are free to go," began Lucian. "Tell all of Bren what has transpired. Tell them that this day their king has fallen. Tell them that this day the transfer of one life for another has ceded to me the throne of all of Bren. Tell them this is a good day. And tell them that I join with the entire land in saying 'May the strength of Bren be mine today,'" said Lucian, quoting the oft-used motto of the land.

Justinian wept uncontrollably as he ran from the palace. He had no other choice. At least his family would be safe.

Troyolin was thrown violently into the cell with Regalion, causing the old man to be startled awake from his midday slumber.

"Who goes there?" asked Regalion.

"Brother, it is I . . . Troyolin," responded the king.

Embracing his little brother whom he had not seen in years, the old man said, "How has this come to be, little brother? Why are you here?"

Filling in his brother as quickly as possible, Troyolin then began to bombard Regalion with questions. "Dear brother, what resources for escape have we?" began the king.

"I am afraid there are few resources available in this dank abyss," replied Regalion with sadness.

"There are always resources, Regalion. There are always unseen avenues. Perhaps you have been behind these walls for so long you have forgotten the words of our father. 'There is always another way. Learn to see every circumstance of life from another perspective. Answers lie in the new point of view.' Remember, Brother?" implored the king.

"My point of view became blinded to any others far too many years ago, little brother. One can only see with physical eyes when the spirit has been denied for as long as mine, and even then, age has clouded even that. Do not chide me, Troy (as the older sibling used to call the younger). I have not forgotten . . . I have just been beaten down into the mire of captivity for so long I forgot what hope looks and sounds like, but even now, seeing you and hearing you has sparked a place in my heart that was only recently sparked to life again by your son, my good nephew, Leonolis," said the now emotional old man.

Continuing, the old man said, "What of *your* resources, Troy? What do you see?"

"I see we must find our way from this hellish prison if we are to save my son. Even now he is being led to the Cavern of What-Might-

213

Have-Been. He told me of mice who came to your rescue; even they tried to warn me of Justinian's betrayal. Surely one of the citizens of Rodenthe would be within distance to hear our cry for help," responded Troyolin.

Without missing a beat, the king knelt to the mouse hole in the corner of the dark cell (his eyes having had time to adjust to the lack of light) and began calling out with the language of thought. Rising he said, "I will continue to cry out for help should we hear no response, but in the meantime, what of the guards? How many are there? When do they make their rounds? Perhaps we could coax them near enough to disarm them and escape."

"They do not have rounds, Brother. Mistreatment is the normal treatment around this place," said Regalion. "They sometimes respond to my cries for water should they forget about me for a day or two, and since the boy was taken and the battle you spoke of has taken place, I have not received food or water for two days now. Perhaps they would respond."

So the old man began clanging his empty water pail against the bars of the cell, crying out as loudly as his dry voice would allow. "Water! I have been now two days without water! Will someone please have mercy on an old soul! Water!"

Nothing . . . except for a rustling sound near the mouse hole and a faint squeaky voice saying in thought, *Who called upon the Kingdom of Rodenthe for assistance this day?*

Bending down near the opening, Troyolin responded. *It was I, Troyolin, king of Bren, who this day has been betrayed and abducted by the dark lord, Lucian. I must find a way from this captivity. The life of my son is at stake.*

Do you mean the good and kind Leonolis? answered the little mouse.

Yes! Yes! Good and kind Leonolis! He is my son, and Lucian is, even now, leading him to his death. I must find a way out of here! Can you help, brave little mouse? asked the king.

I think I can! Though I only saw Leonolis briefly from afar. The legend of his kindness to the prince and princess of Rodenthe is already well-known in our realm! It would be my honor to serve his father! said the mouse. *I'll be right back!* And with that, the little rodent disappeared into the darkness of the mouse hole.

Taking up his clanging again, Regalion once again began to cry out, "Water! I must have water! What must an old man do to get a drink of water? All I ask is one small drink!"

As the clanging continued, Troyolin kept watch over the mouse hole, having a distinct intuition that somehow the tiny creature he had spoken to would come through with help—of what sort, he knew not. Soon, Regalion grew tired of his task and took a seat on the cold floor in order to catch his breath. No sooner had he sat down than the little mouse appeared in the mouse hole once again.

Without waiting, the wee creature excitedly said, *I know it is not much, but perhaps they will be of use!*

What will be of use? asked the already grateful king.

These, responded the mouse.

Hopping back into the hole, he emerged with a small skeleton key, saying, *Even this day I have seen this key unlock the door behind which the witch resides, the place where the Crystal Orb is kept. Whoever has the Crystal Orb wields great power. I regret to tell you it was impossible to retrieve the orb itself, being as that I am but a mouse, but I can tell you that even now the witch has laid it within the glass casement in this room. Perhaps it would be of use to you, father of good and kind Leonolis.*

Yes! Yes! This is a most wonderful gift, good mouse! replied the king.

Disappearing into the hole once again, the mouse reemerged, this time dragging a small dagger, twice the size of his own body. *Though it seems immense to me, I know this dagger would be a mere pittance in size compared to the sword you most assuredly carry when not confined, good king.*

Not small at all, dear mouse! Not small at all! Anything larger would be impossible to conceal! What such a weapon lacks in power it more than makes up for in its ability to remain hidden until the proper moment of use! What a heroic and mighty mouse you are . . . er . . . you must forgive me, my new mouse friend. I did not even take the time to inquire as to your name! Please forgive me for this slight! begged the king.

I understand the nature of our meeting, sire. It is no slight and certainly of no consequence. I am Reedincourt, humble servant of Rodenthe at your service! said the furry little creature, who suddenly darted back into the hole for no apparent reason.

"Someone this way comes, Troy," said the old man nervously.

"See if you can gain his attention, Brother, while I weasel my way close enough to him to subdue him and win our freedom," said the king in a whisper.

Obviously perturbed at the disturbance, two guards reluctantly approached the cell, one protesting loudly all the way while the other carried a bucket of water, most of which he had clumsily sloshed onto the floor with his cavalier attitude.

"What now, old man? No wonder the dark lord locked you away! You are never quiet, always complaining about something," said the first guard.

"Back away from the door, old man. And you . . . (speaking now to Troyolin) don't try anything or you'll not see another day of living," said the second guard.

As one guard slipped the key into the cell door, the other kept a wary eye on Troyolin. It was not lost on them how important the new prisoner was to Lucian. In no uncertain terms they had been warned. Should he escape, they would be separated from their heads—immediately.

As the door creaked open, Troyolin prepared to attack, determining the guard with the bucket would be the easiest to subdue. Needing both guards inside the cell for his plan to work, the king crouched in the corner, pretending to cower at the sentries. As the guard set the bucket in the corner, Troyolin made his move. Lunging at the guard with the newly provided dagger, the king flew through the air . . . and was met squarely in the jaw by the water bucket as the guard rose to defend himself. What Troyolin could not have known is how expected such behavior was, that every new prisoner tried the same ploy at some point in their incarceration.

The guard quickly stepped on the hand with which Troyolin held the knife. Reaching down to remove the weapon from the dazed king, the guard's jaw was met with Troyolin's fist, easily taking the guard down and rendering him unconscious. By this time, the guard at the door had slammed the cell shut, quickly locking it before Troyolin could get there.

"Foolish imbecile!" said the guard. "Do you not realize who you are dealing with? Do you not think we are foolish enough to not be prepared for such incidents of rebellious behavior? I will be back with more than enough help to free my comrade." And turning to head back down the corridor, the guard suddenly froze in his tracks.

He slowly returned to the cell door, slipping the key in and quickly unlocking it! Troyolin could not believe his eyes, and knew he and Regalion must take advantage of this strange occurrence at once. Surely this must be the magic of the Founder . . . or perhaps Augurian or Maison had suddenly been freed from their stony prisons and had sent a magical incantation to free them.

Turning to help Regalion out of the cell, Troyolin was met with the outstretched arms of his brother. "Now you will come inside the cell." And the guard obeyed! "Now you will give the key to the king." And the guard obeyed. "And now you will remain silent and continue to keep your brother sentry here silent while we make our escape," commanded Regalion.

Locking the door and leaving the guards to the silence (and leaving Troyolin silent in amazement), the brothers hurriedly made their way up from the depths of the dungeon. With each sentry, Regalion performed the same feat, rendering the guards silent and gaining information as needed. As they subdued the final sentry between them and the castle courtyard, Troyolin whispered to his brother, "Of course! I had forgotten! Your gift! The gift of mind control! I wrongly assumed you had lost it through the years of confinement! Praise be to the Founder, Brother! You have gained for us our freedom! Let us make our way to the cavern at once!" said the king.

"I cannot go with you, Troy. There is unfinished business I must attend to here—a son who needs to hear my heart and a scorned woman who needs the same. I go to seek their forgiveness, whether they grant it or not. This is what must be done, or I fear the darkness will continue to wreak havoc upon this fair land. Go to your son, dear brother, as I go to mine." And with those words, Regalion headed for the room of the Crystal Orb to find Lucian, and Troyolin headed for the Cavern of What-Might-Have-Been to rescue Leonolis . . . if it was not too late.

Chapter Twenty-Four

THE RECKONING

L eonolis had gone quietly. Knowing well his father was proud of him for standing in honor for the sake of all that is good and righteous to the people of Bren, yet knowing well that his father also had an expectation that Leonolis conduct himself worthy of the blood coursing through his veins—that arguing with one's captor or lowering oneself to the place of meaningless argument held no honor. There was an unspoken rule of wise silence. A saying of the land. "Even a fool, when he is silent, people will think him wise" had been deeply ingrained in the boy's mind by example. He also had heard his own father say on more than one occasion, "Son, never answer a fool in the same manner he argues with you. Always remember this: he who argues from the foundation of anger has no leg to stand on." In watching how the men of the royal lineage conducted day-to-day dealings with the people of the land, Leonolis had come to understand the wisdom of silence—the wisdom of surveying one's enemy by his conversation and surmising the best route for getting into his mind. Leonolis was even now becoming more of the man his father had called him to be. His father's words had filled him deeply with strength.

As the group of ten guards led him through the long labyrinth of tunnels from Castle Jadon that would convey them to the Cavern of What-Might-Have-Been (they had wisely chosen to not go by the above-ground route so as to avoid detection should they enter through the main opening of the cavern), Leonolis had begun to listen intently to the conversation. Even though their conversation was mostly small talk, he soon realized that these men carried a great bitterness toward their master, Lucian.

In a strident, mocking tone, the lead guard said to the one who held the leather leash guiding the boy, "'To the cavern with the boy! Go at once!' said the great dark lord. 'And send word to my mother when the boy is in place above the spires.' And what a brave leader we have, allowing the king of Bren to talk to him as if he were a child."

"What else can you expect from a momma's boy?" said the leash handler with a chortle.

"And he expects us to feed our families on the pittance of pay he gives us while living the lavish life of a king as if we cannot see! It's almost as if he expects us to applaud his arrogance!" said the first man.

"I'll show him what he can do with his arrogant attitude," said the second.

"Hold it down, you two," said the captain of the guard. "We are nearing the scaffolding. And minions of Toralan wait for us there. You wouldn't want her to hear how much you despise her and her son, would you? Just do your job and be glad for the work."

The final few yards to the scaffolding were covered in complete silence. In reality, Leonolis had not been suspended from the cavern ceiling at all. Toralan had merely conjured up the vision to manipulate her plan, but now that plan was becoming all too real for the boy. The scaffolding was a large, wooden frame standing roughly twenty-five feet high. From the base a series of steps rose, going back and forth until it reached a platform at the top. From there a series of ropes and pulleys had been assembled with which to raise victims into position above the Needles of Regret. This system of death had been devised by Lucian and his mother long ago as a means of torture—a means of gleaning information from less-than-willing informants.

Waiting for them at the base of the gallows were three sorceresses, the minions of Toralan. These women had each been kidnapped from the realm of Bren as young girls and pressed into service of the White Witch. Long ago they had lost the will to escape and through the constant berating at the hand of Toralan, had come to believe this was their lot and purpose in life. Graceful in beauty at one time, they were now eerily graceful yet unemotional in preparing the boy to be hoisted up.

Seeing an opportunity to speak, Leonolis said to the lead guard, "Why do you continue to serve a lord who treats you as less than the garbage he throws from his daily feasts?"

"Hush, boy! You do not know of that which you speak. You are but a boy . . . a boy who understands only privilege," rebutted the guard.

"Even in my privilege," continued the boy, "I know that my privilege comes at a great price. As a child of privilege I must understand that all I have been given is but a means to an end. All I have and all I am are given in order that I may serve my people. Were you a citizen of Bren you would know this; you would know the security that those in our military know. The king of Bren takes care of his people. He does not use them for his own vainglory. Why else have you witnessed this very day the many men of Bren who valiantly and willingly laid down their lives for country and king? They do as they see their king do. Can your army say the same thing?"

At the guards' lack of response, Leonolis knew he had struck a chord. Just what that would gain for him was yet to be seen, but at least he had gotten a foot in the door.

As the boy tried to speak again, his voice was suddenly muzzled as the three minions stuffed a piece of cloth in his mouth and then secured it with a piece of rope tied around his head. Harnessed around his chest, a rope was attached by a hook that had been equipped with a special release lever that could be pulled from an adjoining rope once the boy was in place above the Needles of Regret. As they began to winch him up to the highest point of the cavern ceiling, Leonolis kept his gaze on the lead guard, eyes locked until he had been pulled too high to matter anymore. Once he had reached the apex of his ascension, the minions secured the ropes, the main weight-bearing rope as well as the trigger rope, to a mooring post on the platform. Next, they began to turn a large wheel (it reminded Leonolis of the wheel of one of the many merchant vessels that sailed up and down the Runland each day). This wheel set in motion a series of cogs and gears that served to move the massive wooden arm like a crane into position above the spikes. Once in position, they secured the crane in place and quietly made their way back to the trigger rope . . . and waited for word to release it.

From this height, Leonolis could not see the cavern entrance due to the direction his harness put him in, but he could see the light filtering in from somewhere behind him. Because of this vantage point, he could not possibly have seen his father slinking from boulder to boulder, which were strewn about the cavern floor. He had somehow made his way through the tunnels and into the cavern unnoticed. Now that he was here he had no plan other than to be prepared to suspend his son in midair should the release lever be pulled. How he would get him down once that had occurred he would figure out as the time came. If he could remain undetected in such a scenario, the longer he would be able to keep Leonolis aloft. After coming to within a hundred feet of the scaffold, he dared not come in closer lest he be exposed.

Meanwhile, back at Castle Jadon, Regalion had used his gift to gain access to the wing housing the royal sleeping chambers of the castle. From what Reedincourt the mouse had told them, the Crystal Orb was housed in the chamber of Toralan. If Leonolis was to be saved, the White Witch must be stopped, and Regalion was certain that somehow her power was connected to her control of the Crystal Orb.

As he walked down the corridor, he stopped at each door, listening intently to try and determine which one might be hers, gingerly and as quietly as possible placing the key into each keyhole. With each door came a sense of thrill to the old man's soul. Having been in utter seclusion for so many years with only the insensitive prison guards to occasionally speak to him, any contact with another person was better than no contact at all—even contact with an evil hag who wanted nothing more than to pierce his heart through with the end of a blade.

Finally coming to the last two doors after no success at the previous twenty-two, Regalion heard voices. Coming from the door to his right, he chose to go into the one on his left, hoping that perhaps the witch had left the orb unattended. Sliding the key in and turning it gently, the mechanism unlocked with a muted *click*. Gently rotating the doorknob, he slowly pushed the massive door just enough to get in. Squeezing through the opening, he slid the large door closed as quietly as possible. Turning around, he walked toward the center of the room where he saw an ornate wooden pedestal, crowned with a square case composed of expertly cut glass, and encased inside the glass lay the Crystal Orb. He had not imagined it would be so easy.

And he was correct in that summation. As the old man reached to lift the case from the pedestal, the clearing of a throat from somewhere behind startled him.

"*Ahem.* Would you like some assistance, dear *father?*" Lucian said sarcastically. "Perhaps you need some help. It would appear you are pale and weak from your long stay in the guest room I prepared for you below."

Stepping away from the orb, Regalion turned to face his son, taking a few steps toward him. "Lucian . . . let us talk."

"How is it that you are no longer in your cell?" said Lucian, completely ignoring the words of Regalion. "And what of the king? I assume he has escaped as well."

As he turned to summon the castle guards, Regalion rushed to his son, taking his right hand in both of his as he fell to his knees.

"Do not touch me!" sneered Lucian as he tried to pull his hand away.

"Hear me, Son. Please just hear me," said the old man, his voice hoarse and cracking with emotion. "It was I who wronged you all those years ago. It was I who was more concerned with power and appearance than with doing what was right, than in showing you the love you deserved as my son."

With those words, Lucian stopped pulling away from his father. Feeling something he had long forgotten—a feeling once familiar yet conjuring up far too many hurtful memories to linger long. Feeling a tinge of pity for the old man, perhaps . . . he ceased pulling. Whatever it was, he allowed the old man to continue.

Sensing this might be his only chance to give voice to these words, Regalion continued. "All the bitterness and jealousy you feel is understandable. All the hatred you feel toward me for abandoning you is understandable. All the power you crave, the desire for respect and honor is understandable. You come by those feelings naturally . . . because . . . because you learned them from me."

Trying to pull away again, yet not with quite as much passion as before, Lucian's curiosity was now aroused. "What do you mean, old man? I learned nothing from you!"

"I did not teach you these things in a formal manner. No, no, no. You learned them in a much more insidious way. You learned to fear the rejection of others by watching me. You learned to crave power and position by watching me. You learned to mistrust and despise and manipulate by watching me. Everything you now have become is simply a reflection of my inability to put others before myself. Everything I did in moderation you have become in excess."

Angered at these words, Lucian jerked his hand from the grip of Regalion saying, "I am nothing like you, old man! Nothing!"

Rising, Regalion again approached Lucian, this time placing his hands on the dark lord's shoulders and gently turning him toward his own face. Face-to-face now with his son, Regalion looked him in the eye. Staring back at his father in bitter rage, Lucian seethed. Yet the anger once again began to subside as Regalion continued.

"Son . . . my son, dear Lucian. I have had much time to relive all the ways I have wronged you, and trust me, they are indeed many more than I care to admit. For this I am ashamed. I did truly abandon you, and I know words will never replace all that my actions have taken from you. But there is one thing I need to say to you, one question I must ask. Let me ask it and then you may do with me as you will."

Glaring with indignation, yet feeling that tinge he felt earlier—it was indeed more than pity. Perhaps love, perhaps longing to be embraced. Whatever it was, it was some sort of emotional connection with the one he loathed, and he could not find or feel that loathing in this moment— Lucian began to soften his gaze. "Go ahead, old man. Say what you must."

Not breaking his stance or his grip on Lucian, Regalion continued to gaze into the eyes of his son. After what seemed an eternity, he began to speak. "Dear son . . . there is only one to blame for all the wrong done to you. Only one, and I am that one . . . and I know it too well. Hear me well. Hear me deeply. Hear me beyond the anger and beyond the bitterness. Hear me beyond the confusion that surely now courses through your mind, but hear me nonetheless and know that even as I say these words I expect nothing from you in return. Not one thing."

Waiting for his son's response, the old man continued when none came. "There is need for but one question. I offer no excuse or explanation for the rebellion of my ways toward you and I take full responsibility for every wrong word, every wrong attitude, and every wrong deed I have ever displayed concerning you. My question is this:

Lucian, for all the wrongs I have done to you . . . for *all* the wrong . . . will . . . you . . . will you . . . will you forgive me?"

Now speechless, Lucian's mind began to reel at the words his father had just spoken. As if by some magical spell, some glorious incantation from some unseen wizard, his heart began to soften, and his mind began to relive every hurt and every rejection and every wrong ever done to him. But as he did, it was as if the hurt and bitterness he had always attached to those memories was now flying away from his mind, as if the talons of hatred that had for so long gripped his thoughts were releasing their hideous grasp of his mind and he was being set free! Lucian could not even form the proper words in his mind and could not have said them anyway had he tried, so overcome with this strange magic now winding its way through every fiber of his existence.

He was forgiving.

Whether he consciously meant to forgive may never be known, but forgive he did. From some long-ago place where he had suppressed the hope of ever truly being loved or of ever truly loving, he had dreamed of this moment, and now it had flooded his heart and mind beyond repair. Once forgiveness seeps in, icy cold hearts tend to melt, and Lucian melted into his father's arms a crumpled mess of emotion.

And Regalion sat back on the step that led up to the bed stand, gently cradling his son in his arms, enjoying in a moment what had been lost for years—a father finally giving his son a place in his heart.

From the direction of the door this very unforeseen yet fortuitous moment was abruptly cut short by a slow and deliberate series of handclaps. "What a magnificent performance, Regalion! I must hand it to you. I expected force and magic to come against us, but did not expect our son to crumble at the first sign of weak emotional sentimentality! Bravo!" mocked Toralan.

Speaking now to an embarrassed Lucian, she said, "Get up, fool! Get up at once! If the old man is free then the king is lurking about somewhere most assuredly up to no good!"

Lucian, as if he had no strength in his body, simply sat beside Regalion with his head bowed, propped up by his hands on his knees, quietly sobbing to himself. Looking up at his mother, with a sense of relief and with great calm, he simply said, "I am done, Mother."

With great disdain and disgust she turned toward Regalion, shouting, "What have you done to him? Reverse this magic at once or I will slay you on this very spot! Reverse it!"

Looking up toward the witch, Regalion calmly responded. "Toralan, I wronged you as well. I should have taken responsibility and should have done what was right. But I didn't. Just as I have spoken thus to our son, I speak it to you. I expect nothing. I deserve death if anything but simply and humbly ask, will you forgive me?"

"Forgive you? Is that it? Forgive you and suddenly all will be made right and well and good? You have gone mad, old man! Simply mad! If forgiveness looks like me on a throne ruling over this pitiful land . . . if forgiveness looks like the lavish life of a queen that I rightfully deserve, then let forgiveness flow! Forgiveness for everyone, I say! Forgiveness! Fie on forgiveness old man. I, too, am done with the lot of it."

And with that, Toralan headed for the Crystal Orb. Lifting the glass casement from it and dashing it to a thousand pieces against the hearth, she lifted the orb. But before she had time to begin her incantation, the hand of the old man subdued the witch's arm and, thus, the orb.

"Toralan, let the boy go. It is done. You cannot win," said Regalion without loosening his grip, a surprisingly strong grip.

"It is not done!" screamed the witch. "It is done when I say it is done!"

With her free hand she drew a dagger from its sheath between the folds of her gown and plunged it deeply into the old man's chest, causing him to release his grasp and fall back toward Lucian. Gasping for breath, the old man crumpled to the floor as the witch began her incantation.

"O, spirits of the dark domain
Release the hounds of hell and pain
And let the captive fall"

As she raised the Crystal Orb above her head, it began to emit a brilliant beam of light. As the beam intensified, it exploded with a clap of thunder, sending a flash of light through the entire castle that was visible all the way to the Canyons of Callay to the south and to the land of Larovia to the north.

The light disappeared as quickly as it had come. The witch turned toward the dying Regalion and said, "*Now* it is done."

Chapter Twenty-Five

THE CAVERN

While the confrontation between Regalion, Lucian, and Toralan had been coming to a head at Castle Jadon, Leonolis had become concerned with the small tremors that had begun shaking the earth a few moments after he had been suspended from the cavern ceiling. His father below had felt them too. They had been going on with a steady, rhythmic pattern for several minutes and now small bits of earth and fragile stalactites began to crumble away and fall from the ceiling.

Not daring to venture any closer to his son for fear of being seen, Troyolin stayed low but kept his son constantly in his line of vision. His plan was to suspend the boy in midair once he had fallen, but now he pondered whether it would be more prudent to simply lift the three minions and suspend them in midair, keeping them away from the release mechanism until he could somehow lower the boy. He never got the chance.

As the tremors increased in frequency and magnitude, the entire cavern began to echo from the vibrations. The crystalline stalagmites that grew from the floor began to do as crystals are wont to do. Resonating in brilliant tones, the vibrations at first sounded like low rumblings, but as the tremors increased, the pitch began to rise until the room echoed with what sounded like a chorus of fairies at midnight in the Dancing Meadow on the night of a full moon. Eerily beautiful and captivating, the sound seemed weirdly juxtaposed against the backdrop of evil that this cave was so used to.

Just as the quaking ground reached its highest peak, a blinding burst of light filled the chasm, knocking the guards, the minions, and King Troyolin to the ground. With stalactites falling perilously close to him, all Leonolis could do was hang on for the ride. As quickly as the light had filled the room, the cavern went pitch black in darkness. All assumed the level of darkness was due to the sudden blinding effects of the burst, but it was something more, something blocking the massive cavern's entrance, something that would change everything.

Fumbling around in the darkness, Troyolin tried desperately to regain his bearings but could see nothing. Groping for a boulder to steady himself, his sight was drawn to a small flicker of light emanating from the direction of the scaffolding. It was a minion striking a flint with a piece of metal. She was trying to ignite a torch.

Within seconds, she had accomplished the task. Surveying the scaffolding she made a beeline for the release lever. Before she could get her hands on it, Troyolin stood, still concealed behind a large boulder, and stretched his hands toward the woman, lifting her up and away from the lever. Suspended in midair, she served as a sort of light pole filling the room with a faint glow. What Troyolin had not seen was the minion who had been knocked to the scaffolding floor at the burst, landing very near to the mechanism. Without being seen by the king, she crawled to the lever, grabbed the small release rope, and pulled.

As the boy plummeted toward the spires, the cavern erupted in a massive tremor, ground shaking, people falling, boulders rolling, stalactites crumbling, air filling with dust, and Troyolin losing his grip on the minion. As the king fell to the ground, he instinctively looked toward Leonolis. All he could see was the helpless falling body of his son, falling toward the crystal spikes. His heart sank.

And all went silent.

Leonolis had not screamed, had not made a sound. Due to the settling of earth and debris, Troyolin had been spared the sound of his son's body striking against the sharp blades of crystal. He had not been able to save his son. He had not been able to say good-bye. He would never see his son alive again. Never had the king known such despair as in that moment. Never had he known such sorrow. Never had he been filled with so many thoughts of times he had missed with his own boy. Even in Bren one does not know how much they have been given until what they have been given is gone.

Back at Castle Jadon chaos ensued. As the blast of light filled the castle grounds, the leaders of Bren had been released from the stony spell the witch had cast upon them. Augurian immediately took command, charging Evenhawk to fly to the armies of Bren and call them back to battle, directing Caniday to search the castle grounds for the whereabouts of the witch, sending Kelsin to fly to the dungeon and seek out and release King Troyolin, and calling the Treesants to once again secure the castle grounds. Without even saying a word, all went directly to their tasks as Maison and Augurian set out for the Cavern of What-Might-Have-Been.

As Evenhawk flew above the still-amassed armies of the combined force of the races of Bren, he called out for the heads of each legion to assemble at the city gate—the main gate—of Abysstine. Within thirty minutes, all had assembled and each commander given the assignment to secure a certain region of the Valley of Abysstine. Among those gathered at the city gate was Justinian and Arolis. Justinian, though he had betrayed the king, had made it as far as Menden Lake before his shame had driven him to the point of complete abandonment of all that was Bren, right and good. He had turned around and headed back toward Castle Jadon, intent on righting his wrong no matter the cost. Slipping away from the crowd, he quietly made his way to Castle Jadon to seek out the White Witch.

Arolis had been caught up in battle until the parley had been called. Even in battle he had kept an ear open for the thoughts of his boy, Leonolis. And since the parley had begun, he had been constantly calling for the boy. Calling. Listening. Calling. Listening. Nothing. He, too, slipped from the ranks and began making his way around the outer city wall in the direction of the cavern, though he did not know where he was going. By some deep instinct, he just knew he should go there.

Throughout the land, the burst of light had been seen, and with that burst of light had come both fear and hope. All had heard and felt the tremors as well. Some would tell later that they had seen a mysterious streak of grey presence streak by as the tremors grew more intense. No one knew what they had seen. Some even considered they had been hallucinating. Whatever the case, something had happened outside the realm of normal this day. Call it magic. Call it mystery. But something great and mystical was taking place.

Augurian and Maison quickly found the entrance to the tunnels that would lead them to the cavern. Without hesitation they coursed their way through the tunnels, casting down with magical waves of their hands any guard who would dare stand in their way. Coming into the cavern they were confronted with the silent darkness that filled the room. Augurian pulled a small wand from his robes and lifted it, saying,

"Shine, O shine good hope of light
Pierce the dark
Replace the night."

And with that, the tip of the wand began to shine a magnificent light that filled the entire cavern. Leaving not one shadow, it permeated every nook and cranny. Not too dim yet not too bright, the light of Truth (as Augurian called it) exposed all darkness to light.

At first, Troyolin had not even noticed the light, too distraught to look up, not wanting to see the body of his son impaled and torn apart upon the crystal blades of glass. Not even caring that there was light, the king simply sat there on the ground where he had fallen when the earth had begun to quake. His sorrow was broken only by the sound of laughter. Still the king did not even respond, did not even care that someone could be so callous as to laugh at the loss of another's son. Leonolis was all he could think about. He no longer cared about anything else, especially his own feelings.

As the laughter grew closer, the king recognized the source, or should I say, sources. Having known these laughs for as long as he could remember, the king recognized the jolly belly-laugh of Augurian and the contagious twittering laugh of Maison. At this recognition the king's sorrow began to give way to incredulity. How could his friends respond like this? It did not make sense, and he would ask them to stop immediately.

Before he could rebuke them, the pair of wizards was upon him.

"Look up, good King! Look up!" said Maison.

"Let me grieve the loss of my son, Maison. Have you lost your sense of propriety? This is not proper, even for such old friends . . . especially from old friends. Have respect, Maison. Have respect," implored the king.

"Sire, look up. Look up. Now is not a time for sorrow. Now is a time for great joy," said the patient Augurian.

Standing to give the pair a piece of his mind, the king was frozen by what he heard next.

"Father . . . Father, look up," spoke the voice of a boy from somewhere above the king's head.

Turning his gaze toward the last place he had seen his son in freefall, the king turned and stumbled backward in awe and amazement. He could barely make out the face of his son peeking out from the edge of some massive apparition. Having to allow his mind to come to grips with what he was surely seeing, the king could say nothing as tears of joy began to flow down his bearded cheeks.

There, holding his son on his outstretched palm, was a giant. Lying on his belly with arm extended, he had bounded into the cavern just as the light burst through. His very magnitude had been the reason the tunnel entrance had been blocked and the darkness had fallen. Now the giant lay dead, pierced through the heart by the very spikes that would have pierced Leonolis.

"Leonolis, can you see a way down?" Augurian called.

"Yes! I can see a way across his arm and rappel down from his hair!" shouted the boy in answer.

As the boy deftly crossed the arm of the giant, he came to the shoulder. Using the shoulder as a launching pad, the boy grabbed several locks of the giant's hair and slowly glided to the ground.

Running into his father's grateful arms, the boy asked, "Who is he, father? Who is the giant man who would do such a thing?"

Rubbing his head in wonder, the king replied, "I have no idea, Son . . . no idea."

"He is Reuben of Old," said Maison as he gazed in awe at the body of the colossal giant.

"*The* Reuben? *The* Sleeping Giant?" countered the unbelieving boy. "The one you told me of in the storied legends of Bren? The Founder himself?"

"Yes, boy! *The* Sleeping Giant!" responded Maison excitedly. "Do you remember the things I taught you concerning the legend, Leonolis?"

"Of course! I have dreamed of great adventures many times that involved the Sleeping Giant! But I did not know he was any more than a story sparked by a mound of dirt in the Canyons of Callay!" said the boy.

"But think about what the very meaning of his name is," said Maison as if to illicit the answer from his student.

"Reuben means 'behold the son,' good Maison. I do not understand what that has to do with anything," queried the boy.

"It was told that one day the Sleeping Giant would rise and rescue the son of a king. 'Behold the son,'" said the teacher to the pupil as he held out his hands toward the boy.

"I am the son in the legend?" asked the astonished Leonolis.

"Yes! Yes! Yes! You are the son! Behold the son, Son! You have been delivered, this day, by the great Sleeping Giant, Reuben of Old. The Sleeping Giant is more than a myth and more than a mound of dirt in a barren place. He is the very spirit of faith, the spirit of goodness, the spirit of righteous anger, the spirit of the Founder all wrapped up in one. This is the spirit that rises up to face evil when the people have had enough. This, my son, is the spirit of Bren!" said the now reverent Maison.

As they all stood in awe of the giant lying dead before them, they all grew very solemn as the reality of their place in history began to sink in. The legend of the Sleeping Giant had been told for the past thousand years, but no one really believed it to be true. It had been assumed (wrongly, everyone now realized) that this was a figurative prophecy and that the Sleeping Giant represented the spirit of Bren. All assumed from the prophecies that the spirit of Bren would come upon some great leader for some great time for some great deliverance, but now they beheld a literal giant!

"Wait a minute," said the boy, breaking the solemnity. "Do you mean to tell me that this mighty giant of a man that lies before us now is the same Sleeping Giant—the hill near the Canyons of Callay?"

"One can only assume it is one and the same, my lord. Perhaps we will have the answer to that question on the trip home," said Maison.

"Why now? Who awakened him? Why did he not come sooner?" continued the boy.

"We had very little faith to believe the prophecies were literally true ourselves, Leonolis," began Augurian. "But as the battle raged on earlier this day, both Maison and myself felt a deep yearning to call out the ancient prayer of incantation to the Founder. From a rise near Menden

Lake we turned our gaze and our hearts and our faith toward the south and recited the prayer. Thinking nothing of it again, we returned our attentions to the battle at hand . . . and here before us lies the proof that the prophecies are indeed very true."

"Why did he have to die, Maison?" asked Leonolis.

"Freedom comes at a price, my lord. As you have heard through the years, freedom is not free. Life requires life to continue to exist. The absolute greatest expression of love is death, that one would be willing to sacrifice his or her self for the object of their love is the single greatest manifestation of true love. Today you have witnessed that expression. Your life—indeed the life of an entire world—has been spared, has been given by this One who gave his," said the wise little man.

"Come. We cannot tarry here any longer. Leonolis, I have unfinished business to attend to. Lucian and Toralan still have the Crystal Orb and who knows what they will do once they see their plans to take your life and seize the throne have been thwarted," spoke the king.

"This time, you are with me, Son. Augurian and Maison, please attend to the body of the Founder. Prepare the ritual of burial commanded in the ancient writings. I dare say we cannot move the body, but we can entomb him here as is only fitting. No longer let us call this place the Cavern of What-Might-Have-Been. From this day forward, let this be known as the Cavern of Dreams Realized," commanded Troyolin. With that, the king and Leonolis set off back to Castle Jadon to confront the Dark Lord and Toralan.

Chapter Twenty-Six

THE MATTER OF THE WITCH

A s Troyolin and Leonolis came to the place where the tunnel back to Castle Jadon should have been, they found their way blocked by a mass of debris. Looking ahead to the feet of the giant, they could see a ray of light coming from between his very large feet. Climbing over the giant's leg, they were able to squeeze into daylight between the feet. Once in the open they were met by a small contingency of Brenolinian infantrymen and a beautiful black steed.

Arolis! the boy shouted in thought as he ran to the horse.

Leonolis! returned the horse in a simultaneous neigh.

Nudging the boy toward his side, Arolis said, *Up! Upon me and let us fly!*

But what about my father? said the boy.

"I believe he was speaking to me as well, Son!" shouted the king to his surprised son.

"You have this gift too, Father?" asked the boy.

"Yes . . . I suppose I do!" said the king. "Enough of this! To Jadon, horse!"

And the three sped toward the city gate of Abysstine. As they entered the city they careened through the streets, carefully avoiding collision partly due to the populace staying away from the heat of battle and partly due to the horse, his riders, and their combined prowess. Charging through the castle gates and across the courtyard, the horse did not wait for the palace doors to open. Rearing up on his hind legs, Arolis used his front hoofs to pound the doors open with a single ram of his feet! Then through the palace they flew, coming to the residential wing of the castle grounds. Arolis slid to a halt on the marble floor as his riders instinctively slid off his back in a graceful dismount.

"Arolis, take the western hall! Cry aloud should you find the witch or Lucian. Leonolis, come with me!" barked the king.

Away clopped Arolis down the western wing while the boy and his father headed down the eastern hallway. Coming to the end of the hall they could see streaks of light coming from beneath the last door on the left. "Arolis, this way!" shouted the boy. Immediately, the horse turned around, arriving back with the king and Leonolis just as they were about to enter the room.

Opening the door slightly, the king saw a pool of blood on the floor near the bed . . . and saw the witch on the opposite side of the large room, speaking to someone facing her. Troyolin could not see to whom she was speaking because he was concealed behind the vanity partition. But he could hear, and his heart leapt for joy.

"Enough, Toralan! We end this! Use your magic! Use your lies! Use what you will, but you will no longer use me!" spoke the voice.

"Justinian!" muttered the king to himself.

The White Witch was still very defiant, saying, "You fool! I needed very little magic to convince you to turn on your own king! I never held your family . . . only made you believe I held them! How easy it was to move you this way and that by simple suggestion. Such a weak mind comes only from a weak man!" With those words she directed a small bolt of lightning from the Crystal Orb, striking Justinian in the left shoulder.

As Justinian stumbled forward, he came into Troyolin's view. Bloodied and limping, yet wielding his sword, the man lunged for the witch. Once again she hit him with a mighty charge, this time sending him to the floor.

"Are you serious?" asked the witch incredulously. "Do you seriously think you stand even a smidgen of a chance against me? Not only will I take your head this day, but I will take the heads of your wife and those five little rats you call children. In fact, I shall let you live long enough to allow you to watch the beheading party I will throw on your behalf!"

Now confident she had won, Toralan moved in for the kill. Lunging toward the witch, sword raised—having discreetly picked it up while no one was looking—the king was met with a mighty bolt that sent him flying to the ground.

"What a wonderful day! Two mighty men for the price of one!" boasted the witch.

As she came to Troyolin, she kicked the sword from his hand, proclaiming, "I have waited a lifetime for this moment and now it is come!"

Toralan directed the orb toward the heart of the king and as she prepared the charge, Justinian summoned up his last ounce of strength, stood to his feet, and swung the sharp edge of his sword toward the neck of the witch. As the head of Toralan rolled to the opposite wall, and as her body slumped to the floor, Justinian rushed to the side of his fallen king.

Cradling his head in his hands, Justinian said to the semi-conscious man, "My king! My friend of friends! Please hear me! I have wronged you this day! Please forgive my rebellion! Please forgive my insubordination! Please forgive me for not trusting you upon my first contact from the White Witch! Had I come to you, none of this might have happened! My friend, I am sorry! I am so sorry!"

Having no more strength, Justinian sat there holding Troyolin's head in his lap.

"My friend of friends, fret not. What's done is done. You have more than made restitution to me and to all of Bren. Evil would have been evil with or without you, my brother. It could as easily have been me she manipulated," said the wise king.

"But—" began Justinian.

"No more, Justinian. No more talk. It is finished," said the king.

Arolis and Leonolis had witnessed the entire exchange, from the witch's lightning strikes to what had just transpired between Troyolin and Justinian. After a few moments, Leonolis went to the Crystal Orb and picked it up. Instinctively, he placed it on his father's chest. As they watched, the orb began to pulsate, exuding a glow that seemed to permeate the king's entire body, emanating through the king and right into the beaten and torn body of Justinian. This was the proper use of the orb—for healing and for the good of the kingdom. Any other use of the orb to this day, is considered perversion of that which is holy.

As the two revived men rose to their feet, the attention of all was drawn back to Lucian.

"Where is he?" Troyolin said to Justinian.

"He was here when I first confronted the witch. There, where the pool of blood lies, he was there tending to the wounds of an old man when last I saw him. The old man seemed very near death. In fact, my first reaction was, 'Do not bother with the old man, he is gone.' And strange as it may now seem, Lucian did not appear the same Lucian as before. The rage and fury of bitterness were gone from his countenance. I saw pity—actual pity—coming from him toward the old one. While I dealt with the witch, he must have slipped away," replied Justinian.

Going to the pool of blood, Leonolis followed the bloody footprints that led to the far wall. At the wall they suddenly disappeared, as if the ones who had made the tracks walked right through the wall!

"There must be a secret passage!" shouted the boy. Pushing on the wall where the tracks came to an end, Leonolis could feel the wall give way. Sliding inwardly away from the room, the door indeed opened to a secret passage that led down a long, spiral staircase. Allowing his son to go no further, the king commanded a team of Royal Guardsmen to follow the trail and find Lucian. They were able to follow the trail all the way to the underground River of Abysstine, but could only assume Lucian had drowned. For several weeks afterward, the Royal Guardsmen continued their quest to find Lucian. But they never did.

Lucian, along with his father, Regalion, had managed to slip away, never to be seen or heard from again, at least that was the legend. All that was known for sure was that the land of Bren was never again to face Lucian. Of course, evil is always around . . . and evil always has a way of manifesting itself in various and devious ways. Bren would face evil of all manner through her ages, but never again would they encounter the darkness of Lucian.

For many years after the battle of Abysstine (as it came to be called) there were sightings of Lucian and his father. With each sighting came an investigation, but always with the same result. No Lucian. Still, the legend persisted and that legend says that a kind old man named Lucas lived in a small glen high in the northern mountains, caring for his elderly father, Royal, until the day the old man passed away . . . and this Lucas spent the rest of his days going about doing kind deeds for others.

Chapter Twenty-Seven

BACK TO AERIE, THE LONG WAY HOME

I t took three days of intense meetings between Troyolin and the leaders of the other races of Bren to set in place a treaty that would serve as a powerful settler of disputes. From the time of the Great Treaty of the Races of Bren, all disputes were peacefully settled due to the very simple and clear foundational principles set forth in the document, the greatest of which read: "All men and women, all children of the Founder, are equal in worth; let the law of each nation be founded on the bedrock of this perspective: always treat another in a manner you would hope to be treated." It was simple yet profound and used to this day as a basic principle of living taught throughout the land of Bren for many generations since the time of Lucian.

As it relates to the history of Bren, Abysstine soon rebounded from its many years of darkness and learned to live without the oppressive control of Lucian and Toralan. King Troyolin had established the rule of Bren over the land and set a most benevolent and wise man in charge over the realm. Justinian the Redeemed ruled over the land for the rest of his days, followed in succession by his son, Moralion, followed by Moralion's son, Rightman, followed by generation after generation of descendants. The house of Justinian, as this succession of rulers came to be known, was revered for its kind benevolence and fair hand of justice.

During the three days of meeting, emissaries from all the tribes and races of Bren made their way to Abysstine to make a sort of pilgrimage to the Cavern of Dreams Realized to pay their respects to the Founder, laying garlands of flowers at the feet of the body of Reuben. Since the body was too large to remove, it had been decided that the cavern itself would serve as the tomb of the Sleeping Giant. The official ceremony of ratification (the ritual signing of the treaty by the emissaries of all tribes and races) was to be held on the morning of the third day outside the tomb entrance. This solemn Day of Commemoration was set as a national holiday from that day forward.

Until the tomb could be properly sealed, a massive cloth woven of purple velvet had been draped from the top of the opening all the way to the ground. After all the dignitaries had taken their places around the table of signing and as soon as the crowd from the city of Abysstine and the surrounding villages (thousands upon thousands) gathered, Augurian rose, and by some sly magic, caused the throng to quiet and turn their attention to High King Troyolin who stood to speak.

"On this day we remember the Founder and give honor to whom honor is due!" he began. "We have also come to celebrate our national freedom. This freedom—your freedom—has come at a great price. The loss of many lives has served to secure the lives of many more. Though we are many colors, from many races, of many tribes, destiny has brought us together this day as one. It has been as one that evil has been put down this day, and it will be as one that we continue to fight any darkness that would seek to destroy that unity! To all the tribes and races of Bren I say let us live as one!"

At those words, the massive crowd erupted into applause and loud cheering. The dissonant clashing of thousands of whistles (Brenolinians love to whistle) was at once grating but intensely joyous! Again, Augurian stood and brought silence.

Continuing, Troyolin said, "Let us always quickly settle our dispute with kindness. Let us always be fair and honest in our dealings. Let us be slow to anger and quick to forgive. Let us as one nation, seek to bind up the wounds rather than inflict them. Let us as one people, always strive to set those in bondage free. Let us as one righteous body, put down evil and lift up all that is good!"

Again with the applause and whistling, the crowd sounded like a roaring ocean, rising and swelling with raucous, exuberant joy. This time, Augurian allowed them to go on for several minutes, realizing the need for this moment of national bonding.

"In honor of the Sleeping Giant, whose body lies behind me, we will set a royal seal upon the outer stone of the tomb," the king said solemnly as he motioned for Leonolis to rise and release the small curtain covering the ornate plaque that had been placed near the entrance of the cavern. As the veil fell, Troyolin continued.

"The inscription reads:

> In this place, life was given
> That life might go on.
> In this place, freedom's price was paid.
> Let us never forget the cost of freedom.
> Let us always be willing to pay the price.
> This most solemn ground is
> A testament to freedom for all
> Brenolinians of all races and every creed,
> Of every tribe and every tongue.
> For life and for freedom this site is declared
> Solemn Ground to the good people of Bren."

As his father was reading the inscription, Leonolis could not resist taking one more peak behind the curtain that hid the body of Reuben. As he stepped back slightly, he could just manage a small bit of room between the stone and the curtain. Allowing his eyes to adjust, he strained to see the feet that had jutted out from the entrance ever so slightly, but he could see nothing. As curiosity took over, the boy lifted the curtain and stepped behind it. Walking quickly toward the place where those massive toes should have been, the boy bolted into the cavern as far as the light would allow . . . and saw nothing! Nothing but the place the giant had once lain and the mounds and mounds of flowers and funerary preparations the Royal Burial Ministers had used to prepare the body for entombment remained. The Sleeping Giant was gone!

Frantic, the boy ran from the cavern, tripping over the rope that held the enormous curtain in place, causing it to flutter like an immense purple cascade of water to the ground.

"He's gone!" shouted the boy. "He's gone!"

As if one giant mouth voicing one giant moment, the massive throng of people let out one colossal gasp.

Troyolin, Augurian, and the others had all felt the gush of wind as the massive curtain had fallen to the ground, and they could see that the Sleeping Giant was certainly not sleeping here!

"Who could have taken the body, Augurian? Why would someone do this?" asked the king.

One last time, Augurian quieted the crowd and began to speak, not waiting for the king's approval.

"Let us behold a mighty deed that was long ago foretold. You all. Whether Brenolinian or Hawken, Fairy or Wolfen, Treesant or Larovian; to a person you have all heard the stories. From childhood you have all read been told the prophecies. So why do we gasp in wonder? This day you have witnessed what was told long ago:

> When the giant falls
> Life is spared
> And many becomes one
> In death he sleeps
> But rises up
> The third day's rising son.

"There is nothing more to say. Believe if you will what you will, but know this: the prophecies are true and this day you bear witness to this. Go now from this place. Go in silence and awe but in your going, as you enter the realm of each homeland, proclaim to all you meet what this day you have seen. Let this day be remembered as the day Bren became one and the prophecies were fulfilled. And let us never forget the words yet to be fulfilled:

> When the land unites in freedom's name
> The day has just begun
> Though evils come and evils go
> But Bren remains as one
> When words revealed have come to pass
> Great blessing takes the land
> But words denied by selfish greed
> Turn blessings into sand."

Standing alongside Augurian, Troyolin spoke. "Go now, my brothers and sisters. Go and let the happenings of this day be known. Tell the story to your children and to your children's children and for generations to come. From now and forevermore, let us gather each year on this day and let us renew the pact our hearts have this day made. And let us embody the creed of Bren in all we say and all we do. I thank you all for your brave service to our land. Thank you! Thank you! Thank you! May the strength of Bren be yours this day!"

The crowd began to walk toward the empty cavern, each person filing by in quiet reverence to see for themselves that, indeed, the Sleeping Giant was gone. Some would whisper they felt small tremors in the night. Others would say they thought they had caught a glimpse of a giant figure slinking through the valley as the barely felt tremors faded away in the darkness. Whatever the case, he was definitely not there!

As the king and Leonolis rode past Menden Lake, leaving behind the Valley of Abysstine, Troyolin said to his son, "Show me."

"Show you what?" asked the boy.

"Show me how you got here. We have time. I have heard you and Arolis and Ollieman recounting your adventures of the past days . . . so show me. Retrace your steps, boy! We have time," said the king with a gleam in his eye. So off they went, the boy on the black stallion, with the little owl perched on the saddle horn in front of the boy.

They came first to the Dark Forest, talking all the while about everything they had experienced. The boy, the horse, and the owl did not even seem to notice the king or the regiment of Royal Guards that patrolled behind. They were enraptured in the retelling of their mighty deeds, and the king loved every minute of it!

As they came to each place of importance, the story would be acted out by Leonolis. "Father, it is right here that we were surrounded and I was led away by Lucian's men!"

"Arolis! Arolis! There! There it is! The cave where we found shelter from the storm. And look! The very place where we first encountered Falling Rocks and Moonrysin duped him into letting us go!" exclaimed the boy.

Each time they came to a place of importance, the king and the trio of friends would stop long enough for the story to be retold, often from three very different perspectives. There was, of course, much laughter amid the various versions!

Passing through the small city of Treacherin they remembered the streambed where they had camped. Passing by the narrows they recalled the feeling of dread that came over them.

Passing through the Forest of Endoria, Leonolis recounted their first meeting with the Hawken, Galennia, and the Fairy, Rania, and they retraced their steps as they told of their brave encounter with the swine rats and their first glimpse of the Dancing Meadow.

Then they all grew silent as they passed into the Canyons of Callay, knowing they would pass by the mound called the Sleeping Giant. Silently they had all wondered the same thing. Would the mound be gone? Would they see Reuben in the flesh? Would there even be a Sleeping Giant? As they came to the place of the mound, they could see it seemed to be exactly as they had left it—a hill that looked like a giant man lying on his back, covered with a veil of earth and plants. Still silent as they passed by the form of the giant's right arm, they noticed a stream bubbling up from the mound that made up the outstretched palm of the right hand. Reddish in color, the brackish water formed a small rivulet that ran down the length of the giant's "body" and formed a small pool where a few birds gathered to bathe and drink.

Was that here before? asked Leonolis of Arolis.

It was not, sire, said the horse matter-of-factly.

"What does it mean, Father? Why is it red?" asked the boy.

"I believe it is yet another sign from the Founder, Son. Perhaps it signifies the blood that was given to save a life. Look at the birds. Even now that 'blood' sustains life," responded the king. "What shall we call this pool, Son?"

Thinking for a few minutes as he slid from the horse's back and walked around the pool, the boy returned to his father's side and reverently said, "I think I would like to call it 'Life Gate,' Father, because it was through this very passage that my life was threatened yet through this same passage that my life was sustained."

"Then 'Life Gate' it is," said the king.

Continuing their journey home, the group was much more solemn yet still quite joyful as they passed through the Great Forest and smelled the sweet aroma of the juji fruit, greeting the occasional Treesant as they flurried in the treetops.

Leonolis even convinced his father to go through the Forbidden Swamp rather than around it, introducing the king to Sniffum and Snuffim and stopping for a meal of fried catfish with the creature, Jidgel.

Coming to the Crystal Cave where Leonolis had begun his journey, the king looked at Arolis and nodded. The horse knew he could not continue with the boy and his father. Dismounting and patting his horse, the boy said, "I'll see you in Aerie, my good friend."

Walking into the cave, the boy and his father looked at each other as they ripped away their leggings and shirts. Leonolis bolted into the water first, shouting to his father, "Race you!" And they swam back through the cave, stopping at each air pocket to laugh and catch their breath. All the way to the Castle Aerie the father and son simply relished in being together, each with a newfound depth of love and respect for the other.

After drying off and putting on fresh clothes, the king and the boy had joyous reunions with their family members. A grand ball was held that very night and the evening culminated in the official close of the Testolamorphia, installing the boys who had begun the journey into manhood into their official place of men in the kingdom. And just as they had begun, Dreyden and Leonolis completed the journey—together! These young men remained friend of friends for the rest of their days. Leonolis stood as best man at Dreyden's wedding and Dreyden did the same at his. Each helped in the training of the other's sons, and both rejoiced at each son's Testolamorphia. And the descendants of both Leonolis and Dreyden remain friends even to this day, held by a bond set forth in the days of Leonolis and Dreyden.

After many years of rule (after he succeeded has father's reign), Leonolis made a trek to the pool he had named Life Gate as he had done yearly since the days of his Great Adventure (as it came to be known in legend). This being the year of his fiftieth birthday celebration, he, at the advice of Augurian, had brought with him the Crystal Orb. Following Augurian's instructions, King Leonolis walked to the edge of the pool. Bending down so as to see his reflection, he touched the tip of the orb to the water, reciting the words Augurian had given him precisely:

"A life lived well is a life of joy
Each day lived as if one's last
Each memory sweet
And love's pool deep
Through sorrow's waters passed
With thankful heart through all these days
Through pain remains the joy
Of living deep and living well
The man remains the boy."

Leonolis had always known he was different, that somehow, somewhere, there had been another realm of existence even Augurian and Maison had not been able to explain to him. He just knew . . . knew that the long life he enjoyed in Bren had somehow been reflected somewhere in another world a universe away. Having long ago learned to put away such thoughts for the sake of his own sanity, Leonolis tried to stand up from his crouching position, but his feet had gone to sleep, causing him to lose his balance. And in a completely nonroyal manner, the king fell headlong into the pool!

Even as he fell, he had seen his reflection as he braced to painfully meet the bottom of the shallow pool. But the bottom never came! And the reflection he saw and knew as his own somehow seemed to recall another life in another place in another time. As the king continued to fall, he could feel his body begin to transform. He suddenly felt young again. He felt those old boy feelings begin to race through his veins! He suddenly felt the memories of Bren give way to the memories of a small town and life on a farm, and he felt warm sunlight hitting his face as he gasped for air at the surface of the old shale pit!

On the bank, taunting him, was a group of boys, and there, with a freshly bloodied nose, stood Ryan, Lee's nemesis!

As Lee climbed up onto the bank, Ryan rushed toward him, fist raised in anger, relishing his revenge, revenge that would have to wait for another day as he was dropped by the perfectly landed right hook to the nose! Buoyed by some inner strength, some inner heroism as if he were someone brand-new, the boy, Lee, never took another bit of guff from Ryan or anyone else. He didn't know why, but he felt strong and lived the rest of his days determined that not one drop of who he was depended on what anyone else thought of him.

This truth would serve him well in the days—and adventures—to come . . .

THE END

BONUS FEATURES

Dive deeper into the world of Bren with bonus materials only available at **www.thechroniclesofbren.com**:

- Listen to songs written and performed specifically for each book's journey. Unlike any series before, each book has a series of custom songs written and performed by the author as part of each book's story and journey. You won't want to miss these FREE songs that add so much to the story!
- Original sketches of each main character rendered by the author and available for you to connect deeper with the world of Bren.
- Updates about a new book series: The Bairn of Bren. This collection of stories features the grandchildren of King Leonolis and Queen Abila in daring adventures of their own! You won't want to miss this continuing series of adventures in the world of Bren.

GLOSSARY

Abysstine—Capitol city of the region of Endoria; also called Dark City

Almighty King of Creation—The Founder, God-figure

Arolis—Faithful black steed of Leonolis

Augurian—Oracle; seer; wise sage of the reign of Lairdon

Beezlebird—A buzzard used as a messenger by the dark lord, Lucian

Belimond—Young boy Lucian used to trick Troyolin

Bren—The shortened, less formal name for Brenolin

Brenolin—The formal name of the land founded by King Bren

Brenolinian Battlecry—"This day we conquer! This day we overcome the Dark Lord! This day we live or die for the king!"

Brenolinian Saying—"May the strength of Bren be mine today."

Brestling—Town of the northern realm of Bren

Princess Bria—Early royal heir almost captured. Her near-capture was the catalyst behind creating the secret escape tunnels beneath Castle Aerie

Caniday—King of the Wolfen

Canyons of Callay—Barren region between Brenolin and the Dark Lands

Castle—Castle Aerie

Castle Jadon—Fortress of Abysstine; home of Lucian

Cavern of Dreams Realized—What King Troyolin renamed the Cavern of What-Might-Have-Been

Cavern of What-Might-Have-Been—A massively huge cavern with a ceiling hundreds of feet high. This cave is located directly to the east of Castle Jadon in one of the granite mountains; see also Needles of Regret

Center Isle—Solid ground in the center of Forbidden Swamp

Chiroptera—The bat-like people of the Mountains of Endoria

Cleft of the Rock—Secret royal hiding place beneath Castle Aerie

Corellian—Royal commander of the King's Guard

Council Hill—Where the treaties unifying the many provinces of Brenolin were signed. This meeting place became the earliest known place where the leaders of the land met in council to discuss the welfare of the good people of Bren

Crooked Way—A secret passage through the Canyons of Callay into the Dark Lands; discovered by Leonolis

Crystal Orb—Magical crystal used for conjuring up the deceitful images Lucian uses to trick his victims. The orb adorns the top of his riding staff

Dancing Meadow—A large, secluded opening in the Dark Forest where the local denizens meet for their moonlight festivals and dance the night away in graceful abandon on the first night of every full moon

Danwyn—Bodyguard for Leonolis

Dark Lands—Dark Lands (another name for the regions of Endoria)

Destrin—Second in command of the King's Guard behind Corellian

Dorimay—Princess of the mouse kingdom of Castle Jadon

Dreyden—Best friend of Prince Leonolis

Evenhawk—King of the Hawken

Falling Rocks—Lord of the Chiroptera

Forbidden Swamp—Abandoned marshy area once used for Bren's supplies of peat moss; also known as Maudlin's Marsh

Forsythe—King of the mouse kingdom of Castle Jadon

Friend of Friends—The Brenolinian term for a man's best friend

Galennia—Maiden of the Hawken

Gothgol—Wizard of the Heights; the White Wizard of Endoria

Graymon—Dreyden's horse

Hadian—King of the Terrebithians

Hangman's Rock—A place of execution from the early days of the kingdom.

Hawken—Hawk people of the Forest of Endoria; preservers of all that is good. They can transform themselves from their true hawk nature into a human form

Heath—Royal gardener; father of Dreyden

Hollister—Friend of Augurian; of the Wolfen race

HommeDressage—Four additional years of constant training in the arts of military strategy and warfare for boys thirteen years of age and the horses they ride

Hyacinth—Queen of the mouse kingdom of Castle Jadon

Juji Fruit—A sweet, pithy apple-like fruit that grows in the treetops of the trees found in the higher elevations of the Great Forest; the main foodstuff of the Treesants

Justinian—Friend of friends to King Troyolin

Kelsin—King of the Fairies

King Bren—First High King of Brenolin

King Lairdon—Father of Troyolin; grandfather of Leonolis

Larovia—Peaceful kingdom lying north and west of Brenolin

Leonolis—Prince of the realm

Lucian—Dark lord of Endoria

Lupistad—King of the Werewolves

Maison the Wise—The tutor assigned to teach Prince Leonolis

Maudlin's Marsh—Abandoned marshy area once used for Bren's supplies of peat moss. Also known as Forbidden Swamp

Melania—High queen of the realm

Menden Lake—Lake high in the mountains overlooking Abysstine

Merrywell—Second of Lord Dreyden

Messenger's Gate—A special passageway through the fortress wall where royal messengers could come and go during all hours of the day or night

Miraculin—Fifth king of Brenolin; the miracle king; creator of the secret passages of Crystal Cave

Moonrysin—Trapper/hunter from the Forest of Endoria

Moralion—Son of Justinian; ruler of Abysstine after the reign of his father ended

Mostel—Leader of the Royal Guard of the mouse kingdom of Rodenthe

Mountains of Endoria—Northern boundary of Brenolin

Muriday—Prince of the mouse kingdom of Castle Jadon

Narrows—Narrow gorge near Treacherin

Needles of Regret—A crystalline formation rising up from the cavern floor of the Cavern of What-Might-Have-Been

Oriana—The first high queen

Phrygian Crystals—Crystals that emit a low-grade light and were thought to contain healing powers

Protected Place—Another name for Cleft of the Rock

Queensland—City in the southern area of the Forest of Endoria

Rania—Princess of the race of Fairies found in the Forest of Endoria

Reedincourt—Mouse; rescuer of Troyolin and Regalion

Regalion—Son of King Lairdon; brother of Troyolin; father of Lucian

Reuben of Old—The name given to the Sleeping Giant; the spirit of Bren

Rodenthe—Capital city of the mouse kingdom within Castle Jadon

Runland—Main river of Brenolin

Sandovar—King of Larovia

Sea of Arabon—Southern boundary of Brenolin

Second—Military assistant; expert in military etiquette

Sleeping Giant—A hill whose outline looked like a giant sleeping man from a distance; see Reuben of Old

Sniffum—Turtle of Forbidden Swamp; brother of Snuffim

Snuffim—Turtle of Forbidden Swamp; brother of Sniffum

Stirling—Royal messenger of the king

Sylvan—King of the Treesant people

Terrebithians—Underground-dwelling race of earthen ogres

Teslin—Olden king of Bren; gift of seeing events before they occur

Testing of Blood—A duel of succession; feats of strength, agility, and logic meant to reveal royal lineage

Testolamorphia—The ceremony in which boys are welcomed into the fellowship of manhood at the turn of their thirteenth birthday.

Toralan—Mother of Lucian; also called Tormentia, sister of Gothgol; a sorceress who would become the White Witch

Tormentia—Mother of Lucian; also called Toralan, sister of Gothgol; a sorceress who would become the White Witch

Treacherin—City of the Forest of Endoria; also called the City of Thieves

Treesant—Tree-dwelling, chameleon-like people who dwell in the treetops of certain regions of the Great Forest

Troyolin—Father of Leonolis and high king

Valley of the Abyss—Valley in the Mountains of Endoria where Abysstine is located

Warrior's Canyon—Assembly ground for amassing Brenolin's troops before battle; a natural amphitheater rising up from the banks of Runland and rising to the foundations of Castle Aerie

Werewolves—A wolf race different from the Wolfen; evil in creation and bloodthirsty for human flesh; they follow Lucian

White Witch—Toralan; Tormentia; mother of Lucian

Wolfen—Wolf people of the Forest of Endoria; fierce warriors of good magic

ADDITIONAL BOOKS BY DENNIS JERNIGAN & INNOVO PUBLISHING

CHRONICLES OF BREN SERIES

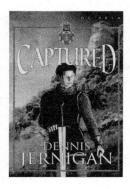

Captured (Book 1): What if your dreams became your reality? Young teen, Lee Jennings, bullied constantly by local boys, suddenly finds himself transported into a world of fantasy and adventure . . . and plunged into a whole new identity as the son of a king! How he traverses this new world and endures captivity at the hands of the realm's resident evil lord is also the journey of self-discovery that will one day serve Lee in his adult life. Full of fantastic beings and magical creatures from this new dimension and wrought with many twists and turns, Captured is just the beginning for Lee Jennings.

Sacrifice (Book 2): What if you learned about all of the sacrifices made—behind the scenes—that helped catapult you to the top? Lee Jennings, our protagonist from Captured, Book One in the Chronicles of Bren series, is now a teenager working on his family farm. While in the field, a strange tornado sucks him up and transports him into a world of fantasy and adventure, where he is king. Led by a benevolent creature called the Voice, Lee, now King Leonolis, discovers the sacrifices that so many have made so he could rule. It is a story of triumph and heartache as he realizes the costs that have been paid to allow him to rule.

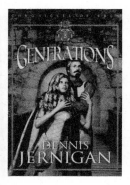

Generations (Book 3): Generations, Book Three in the Chronicles of Bren series, carries on the traditions of King Leonolis and Queen Abila as experienced through the lives of their nine children. If you enjoyed the wild adventures found in Captured and Sacrifice, you will thoroughly find your fill of adventure in Generations. Just as Leonolis did before them, his children grow up discovering their special gifts and talents while living out their very own wild adventures in the process. From magical spiders to Brumbycrocs, from alien beings to glass dragons, the saga of the children of Leonolis is the saga of nine very unique adventures found within the bounds of a single volume!

OTHER TITLES

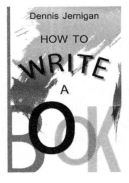

How to Write a Book: Dennis Jernigan is a prolific writer with over two thousand songs, children's stories, fantasy novels, self-help books, and autobiographical works to his credit. In How To Write a Book, Dennis distills decades of writing and publishing experiences into ten simple steps for writing a book. This practical "how to" guide contains ten easy-to-read chapters and a treasure trove of creative, motivational, effective and easy-to-implement tips that Jernigan uses to guide the emerging and seasoned writer. How To Write a Book is a must read for every aspiring author as well as those who wish to become more creative and effective in their writing careers.

The Christmas Dream: The Christmas Dream is the story of a little boy who loves Christmas. He loves the festivities. He loves the decorations. He loves the wonder of Christmas. He loves everything about it. One night, he falls asleep and is transported into a realm where he meets God, and God teaches him about the true meaning of Christmas. Told as an adventure, Dennis Jernigan designed The Christmas Dream as a means of teaching his own son about the meaning of Christmas. This story can serve as a valuable tool in leading your child or grandchild to a saving faith in Jesus Christ. It also serves to remind the adult reader to not stray too far from the wonder of Christmas.

BA/33/P

9 781613 143100